EVERYTHING
in Between

EVERYTHING
in Between

Sarah Anderson

TATE PUBLISHING
AND ENTERPRISES, LLC

Published by Tate Publishing & Enterprises, LLC
127 E. Trade Center Terrace | Mustang, Oklahoma 73064 USA
1.888.361.9473 | www.tatepublishing.com

Tate Publishing is committed to excellence in the publishing industry. The company reflects the philosophy established by the founders, based on Psalm 68:11,
"The Lord gave the word and great was the company of those who published it."

Book design copyright © 2015 by Tate Publishing, LLC. All rights reserved.
Cover design by Eileen Cueno
Interior design by Jomar Ouano
Illustrations by Coleen Anderson

Published in the United States of America

ISBN: 978-1-63449-089-4
1. Fiction / Christian / Fantasy
2. Fiction / Fantasy / Epic
15.09.30

I dedicate this book to my family.

Acknowledgments

I would like to acknowledge my mother and faithful editor, Coleen Anderson, for helping me immensely with this project, as well as my father, Chris Anderson, and my brothers and sister, Jonathan, Samuel, and Elizabeth.

I would also like to thank my best friend, Jimmy, for all his help and support.

I would like to thank all of the friends who were willing to dress up in funny costumes to pose for pictures to be the little people in my book. They helped to bring the story to life.

1

Luna

Luna walked slowly toward the cupboard where Nio's clothes were kept, small case in hand. She disliked packing for these festivals. It always reminded her of the fact that she would be left by herself for a week.

"We're almost ready to go, Luna!" called her Uncle Matthias. "You done with the packing?"

"Yes," she answered, although she didn't expect him to hear her because her voice was so quiet.

She picked out her favorite clothes for Nio and fondly folded them into the small carrying case. A lot of the time, it really wasn't so bad living in hiding, but now—and always when her uncle left for these yearly festivals—she wished that everything could be different. She didn't miss friends because she never really had any. Her role in life was to survive and stay hidden because of the differences that could tear her odd family apart. She had never known her parents; in fact, no one seemed to have known them. She vaguely remembered a dark night and wind blowing her cold. She remembered soft fur beneath her and strong arms around her. Then they had left her, cold and alone, on the step, wrapped in a thin blanket.

Uncle Matthias had told her that she appeared on his doorstep when she was about three years old. Tired, hungry, crying, and cold—he said that she had not been afraid but accepted them readily with open arms. As they fed her and put her to bed, they noticed the truth about her: the golden curls, the violet eyes, the creamy white skin—and that was when she began her life in hiding, almost afraid of the unknown outside.

Mr. Matthias and his wife, Raquel, loved the little girl and named her Luna because of the full moon on the night of her arrival. They lived happily and made a beautiful family for seven years until a baby was due to be born to them. They had been so happy anticipating the addition to their family that they had not noticed the toll it had taken on Raquel. The birth was extremely hard and left her weak and depleted. Six months later, the unthinkable happened. Raquel passed on, leaving baby Nio and ten-year-old Luna to Matthias. The fact that he was left with the two children did not bother him at all, but the loss of Raquel was devastating. Luna often thought of how hard it must have been for Uncle Matthias to bear losing his beloved wife. Even though Luna had been young, she remembered Raquel lovingly and guarded the sparse memories of her deep in her mind and heart.

For the past seven years, Luna had acted as Nio's sister and mother and felt responsible for him. Now Luna walked outside with the tiny case in her hands. Reluctantly, she handed it to her uncle and looked at the ground, studying the dust underfoot.

"Luna," he said in a low voice, reaching out and taking her chin in his large rough hand. "We will come back like always, and everything will be fine."

"I guess it just seems…so lonely, like I'll never see you again." She half-smiled up at him, willing her chin not to tremble.

"Luna, it's okay. The Lord of the Book will take care of you. Don't worry." He paused a moment, the two of them enjoying the stillness. "Now don't be idle while I'm away," he said, a little more cheerily this time. "You can work on your routines or study the medical books I got for you."

"I guess I could do that," she said hesitantly, wanting to say more but not able to express herself.

Uncle Matthias stooped down slightly, giving her a hug good-bye and a kiss on the hair. "I'll miss you."

She swallowed softly and returned the hug. Nio smiled at her from the cart and waved with enthusiasm. She lifted her hand and tried to return the smile as the cart started forward. Her eyes blurred as she watched sadly from the gate of the small yard, and soon they disappeared over the horizon. Luna walked slowly, almost dragging her feet, back to the house. Closing the door behind her, she ambled to her room and sat on her bed.

Suddenly, she noticed the smothering heat in the now empty house, so she stood again to open the window. As she pulled back the curtain, what she saw made her heart falter. There, in the evening shadow of the neighbor's house, stood an older youth watching her yard, a curious look on his tan face. Quickly, she pulled the curtain closed. What if he had seen the event that had just unfolded? What if he had seen her? Luna's mind whirled as she thought on these terrible possibilities. She curled up in the corner of her bed, reflecting on these thoughts and soon fell asleep.

Kyle

Kyle surveyed the area around him and thought about where to start his day. He had been assigned the checklist duty, as they called it in Sandar, and was discouraged at the endlessness of it. He carried the large baskets of pins and stacked them near the mouse cart he had been given to use. They were made of a bit of metal bent in a crown shape with a protruding edge to be attached to a person's clothing. Every person in the kingdom of Sandar was required to wear them on their way to the festival. And Kyle's job was to go from sector to sector visiting every house, making sure its inhabitants were going to the festival. There were fifteen sectors in Sandar, but thankfully, he only had to do five of them. Still he needed to deliver pins to about a thousand people, which could take a while, even if most of them were kids and families. Finally, after loading the baskets of pins and securing the mouse in its harness, Kyle decided he would start with sector one and work his way around the circle.

The festival this year was one of the biggest yet. It was the fiftieth anniversary of finding the Great Book. No one could imagine where it had come from. It was bigger than a house and lay open in the middle of a grassy field near the edge of the great chasm. The edges of the pages were gilded gold and shone brightly in the sun. "If there really were people big enough to make such a giant book…" Kyle just could not imagine how tall they would have to be! He shook his head as if to brush away the ridiculous imagination.

The wind had torn away the first few pages, so no one knew the title of this masterpiece. The cover was black, and it appeared that once there had been words printed there. But time lying on the grass had damaged the cover, and now only part of a large B was visible. It had stories that inspired the reader and that spoke of a God who could do miracles and save people from their evil deeds and thoughts.

In the second part of the book, there were four separate accounts of the same story written by four men. They claimed that the Creator of everything had sent His only Son to live as a real man—God as flesh—and that in the end, he suffered greatly and died to make it possible for all his followers to live with Him in his city of pure goodness in the heavens, if only they would believe in Him and turn from their evil deeds and seek His ways and commandments.

Some believed it was just a story, but others believed that it really was true. Several learned individuals from Sandar and Icelair had devoted their life to copying this book and publishing it in smaller form so that regular folks could read it for themselves.

The good King Jedan of Icelair paid them for their work and had a shelter built to protect the book from the elements. Once a year, a festival was held to celebrate the great find and to allow the common folk to come and look upon the great pages.

Only the "mixlings" were not permitted to view this marvel. A king from a previous reign had declared them imperfect and therefore unworthy. People who were neither purely of the land of Icelair nor of the land of Sandar were considered mixlings. One man began to spread terrible rumors that mixlings were of lower intelligence and were troublemakers. In fact, there were some mixlings that formed a group known as the rebels, and they indeed were troublemakers. But there were others who dedicated their lives to serving the Lord of the Book, and unfortunately, they fell under the same condemnation as the rebels because of their heritage. The king made a law that people from their respective lands were no longer allowed to associate with one another. But some did not obey, and their mixed heritage was often given away by their appearance.

Every year, there were a few who tried to sneak by the guards disguised as being from Icelair or Sandar, but if they were captured, they were arrested and put in the castle dungeon for months. Still there were a few who would risk it, and always, there were a few discovered. Kyle did not understand why the good King Jedan continued to allow this discrimination. The king of Icelair himself had married a woman with mixlings in her ancestry and had borne a son who had the eyes of a mixling. Perhaps he felt that he would lose support if he tried to change such a deeply ingrained way of life. Most mixlings lived out their lives in hiding. Some escaped the two cities and joined the resistance, and some lived in Talenia, a town formed by escaped mixlings far from Icelair and Sandar.

Kyle had gone to several of the festivals, but this time, it was not to be. Kevin, one of his friends, had a younger sister who worked in the castle of Icelair, and he hadn't seen her for the whole year. His duty orders were to stay at the castle during the festivities. Being an understanding friend, Kyle volunteered to trade places with his comrade in order for Kevin to have the week visiting his sister. *I really don't have a real reason to go anyway*, he figured. The only thing he did regret was the fact he would miss out on the trip to see the big book.

Kaylee tugged at his shirt, bringing him out of his rambling thoughts. "Fader says you gonna take me with to count the people," she stated happily.

Kaylee was the cook's six-year-old daughter. The couple who worked as cooks enjoyed their job, especially since they could work together, but a lot of the time, Kaylee was sent with Kyle on his many errands to keep her from getting underfoot. Kyle didn't really mind her; in fact, most of the time he thought of her as a little sister and gladly toted her around with him on his simpler jobs around the palace.

"Hop up," he said, distracted with the anxious mouse, which wanted to be on its way.

Kaylee chatted incessantly as they went from house to house in sectors two and three. While Kyle went up and down streets in sector four, she stayed at a house where one of her friends lived. Soon Kyle had completed his rounds in four out of five sections, handing out the little badges and reminding people that attendance would be taken at this festival. As he neared the house to retrieve Kaylee, she greeted him happily, pleading for permission to stay longer,

"Atsu wants to know if you'll le'me stay and play. Her mom isn't done packing, and they will be here even when you're done with the next section!" she exclaimed excitedly, making her point.

Kyle studied her happy face and thought about leaving her there to play with Atsu. He could pick her up later, and it would be easier than having her walk all that way with him.

"Okay, but when I come back, you had better be ready to go," Kyle told the little girl, who burst into radiant thank-yous and hugs.

After disengaging himself from the grateful little girl, Kyle resumed his walk toward sector five. At the end of the rounds, he looked toward Mr. Matthias's house. Since Mr. Matthias worked as a mouse trainer in the castle, his badge had been given to him that morning at work. He turned to leave, and then stopped. A young girl wearing a blue hooded cape came out from the house, a carrying case in hand. He saw her hand it to Mr. Matthias and then study the ground. *Funny,* he thought to himself, *I don't remember Mr. Matthias having house help.*

He stood there and watched with curiosity as the older man took the girl's chin in his hand and said something, then bent down to hug her good-bye. And as she turned back to her house, a gust of wind revealed hair that flashed golden in the late morning sun. How could she have gotten there? And why did Matthias treat her as if she was his own daughter? Everyone knew that he only had one child, and that was Nio. And golden hair was only seen in Icelair. Bewilderment clouded his face as he watched the empty spot where the carriage had disappeared over the horizon. As he stood in the shadow of the house, he did not notice the watching eyes of the girl in the window.

2

Stephen

In the cabin, Stephen found it hard to understand the reason for the meeting being called. "Since when does the board need to meet over a girl?" he asked himself disgustedly. He opened the meeting-cabin door with a jerk and looked a bit embarrassed as all heads turned in his direction. "Sorry, I'm late," he mumbled and took the only empty seat.

"Agghm, as I was saying," the leader, Carl, continued, "there is a new girl coming to join the resistance, as some of you may know. I want everyone to treat her with respect"—here he paused, holding up a hand to stop the objections, which seemed to be imminent—"even if she doesn't deserve it. Now you are all wondering why."

Carl continued his speech. Stephen felt anxious and inwardly willed Carl to talk faster.

"You all know about the deal with Mr. Matthias and the very important things he helps us with. This girl is his niece," said Carl, with a slight glance toward Stephen. "Now you never know what she will be like. For all we know, she is a housekept girl, but her uncle knows that mixlings can't be kept hidden forever." Again he glanced toward Stephen. "Therefore, he made a deal with me twelve years ago, when he started helping us, that when his niece came of age, she was to be allowed to join the resistance and participate as a full member. She is from a trusted family, so we won't have to worry about her loyalty."

Here was where Stephen spoke up: "What if she can't do anything?" he asked honestly.

Carl looked pointedly at Stephen. "It doesn't matter if all she can do is stir a soup pot. She needs to be accepted as if she is the best, and she needs to believe that we need her. If she doesn't feel like she's valued, her uncle may not back us anymore, and we need his help. He is an inside castle man in Sandar and brings us important information. He also is a healer, and I believe he has taught his niece some of his skills. Does everyone understand?"

There were murmurs around the room, but then nods came from the members, indicating that they understood the situation. "Good! Now with that taken care of, we have other matters to discuss."

Stephen's thoughts began to wander as Carl moved on to other things. *Some people sure have it easy*, he thought. He remembered two years ago when he had tried out for the resistance. He had had to start from scratch. There had been two missions to complete after a rigorous trial. The trial had gone hard for him; he had never seen a bow or arrow before and hardly got within two rings of the target. In both of his preliminary missions, he was sent to retrieve a piece of information from another resistance member who was instructed to evaluate his methods. Both missions had gone well enough. He had to live with another participant of the resistance for six months to be assessed for his honesty and trustworthiness. During this time, none of the important missions were disclosed to him; he had felt like an outsider. From there, he had gone through all the training courses and slowly improved until he was one of the top members. He had worked his way to the top. And now they were granting favors to girls. He shook his head in disgust.

There were around 160 people in the resistance. Most were mixlings, although there were a few who were just sympathizers to the cause. They all objected to the way mixlings were treated. The fact that mixlings weren't even allowed to see the Great Book especially angered them. After all, the differences between Icelairians and Sandarians were minor. The mixlings of the resistance had dedicated themselves to protect and guide other mixlings to a new land called Talenia, a land discovered and settled by outlawed mixlings. It was now a new kingdom in the making—a new frontier. But the journey to Talenia was long and dangerous. Rebels were always looking for a chance to interfere with their activities. New members of the resistance were somewhat limited and were always put through a thorough background check because of the danger of enemies infiltrating the resistance as spies. They had to be careful, or their whole operation could be shut down.

"Stephen?"

His name brought him back to the meeting at hand, and he looked up from the wooden table beneath his elbows.

"The girl is about a year younger than you. You will go pick her up this afternoon from her house in Sandar," Carl stated, looking at Stephen as if daring him to refuse.

"Yes, sir," Stephen responded, though with all his heart, he wanted to object.

He and his friend Daniel had been planning a hunting trip that afternoon, and now he saw his plans crumble into dust. No one refused the leader when given a specific request. It just wasn't respect. There were only a few other girls in the resistance. Janet and Cara were the newest. They had only been on one assignment with him, taking care of children that he was transporting to Talenia. Janet had also gotten in through a valuable relative but was only a caretaker of children and sometimes a messenger. He had not been impressed with her work on the trip. She was self-centered and didn't contribute to anything without being told specifically what to do.

"We will be waiting here for you to bring her back," continued Carl, again breaking him from his train of thought.

"Yes, sir," Stephen again responded, the loudness of his own voice startling him.

As the meeting was dismissed, he noticed the long faces and realized he wasn't the only one who didn't really welcome this newcomer.

Kyle

After a leisurely lunch in the shade with Kaylee, he packed up the cloth and remaining food and called to Kaylee, who was studying a colorful butterfly at the edge of a large puddle. She ran to him, and he lifted her into the cart.

"Can we go see the river?" she pleaded with Kyle.

The sun was hot on his back, and he thought of how good the cool water would feel on such a hot day. He thought for a minute. He wasn't really expected back until evening, and he had finished early. What could it hurt?

"Sure," he answered, smiling at the energetic, happy child.

He turned the cart and started down the hill toward the creek. It was a half-hour ride to the creek, but it was peaceful, and he was glad to get away for a while. They spent the afternoon wading in the river and playing hide-and-seek. Kyle finally admitted that it was time to return, although he was enjoying the day as much as Kaylee.

Kyle shivered as he began the long trek back to the castle. The day had gone fast, and it was already getting cooler. Kyle hardly noticed Kaylee chattering about her visit with Atsu. His mind was on the girl at Mr. Matthias's house. He took the outside road, which was bordered by thick trees and bushes. The road ahead of him took no attention since he knew it like the back of his hand. Suddenly, dust surrounded his cart, and the mouse reared.

"Whoa!" he shouted, pulling on the lines desperately. It was of no use; the mouse pulled incessantly and frantically, breaking the braided grass harness and flipping the cart as it scuttled away into the bushes. He winced at his scraped knees as he got up from the dust cautiously. Three angry-looking faces stared at him menacingly from atop sleek-black mice.

"Search him," growled one.

Another dismounted and hurriedly rifled through his clothes. "He doesn't have anything!" he yelled angrily to the first. "We've wasted our time with this lout." He shoved Kyle to the ground and leaped atop his mouse. They turned their mounts and rode back into the woods.

Bandits! Petty thieves who preyed on people as they passed the thick-wooded lane. Kyle put his head in his hands and sat for a moment to gather his wits about him. He turned back to the flipped cart, and then he remembered—Kaylee!

Rushing to the cart, he called her name, hoping against hope that she was okay. "Kaylee! Answer me!"

A faint whimper answered his frantic call. Hurrying to the back of the wagon, he saw the top of her body moving slightly. "Stop, Kaylee! Don't move!" he said, trying to remain calm. She whimpered softly and then was silent. He frantically surveyed the abandoned houses around him. It was now late afternoon, and the streets were deserted. The only healer in town had already gone, and he was sure the castle healers weren't there either. Why did this have to happen now? If he tried to move the cart off by himself, he might only hurt the girl worse. He grasped the edges of the cart and tried but wasn't able to lift it by himself. They were about half an hour's distance from the palace. He knew it would be too late if he went there for help. In desperation, he stood there alone, not knowing what to do. He bent over Kaylee, trying to comfort her as panic slowly edged its way into his consciousness. There was no one to turn to except the Lord of the Book.

―∘∘∘❊∘∘∘―

Stephen

Stephen made his way slowly on the wooded trail toward Sandar. He had been given nonspecific directions to get to the girl's house, and he wasn't quite sure which house it was. He would have to look for the symbol that was put on the back of the houses of resistance members. A small candle inside a circle was usually located near one of the back windows. As he broke through the outskirts of woods, he stopped beneath large stalks of grass that draped the edges of the trail. He surveyed the area in front of him and was startled by a commotion up ahead. His first instinct was to turn around and seek cover in the weeds; mixlings were not allowed this close to Sandar. He edged behind a clump of grass and waited, his curiosity holding him there, as he observed the scene play out in front of him.

A young man, not much older than Stephen himself, stood at the center of the trail surrounded by three rebels. The rebels were unconcerned with the trouble they had caused for the youth, and now they were searching him. When they realized that he had nothing of value, they pushed him down and rode back into the woods. The young man seemed relieved at first but then began frantically calling for someone. As Stephen watched him pull at the overturned cart, he realized that there was someone trapped underneath it. His training told Stephen to turn and leave the youth to his predicament, but he still paused and watched, hoping someone else would come and help the desperate young man. After looking up to the sky as if asking for help from someone unseen, he knelt down in despair by the back of the wagon, apparently comforting someone.

Stephen didn't realize what he was doing until he was almost to the cart. Uncertainly, he cleared his throat to get the boy's attention. The youth turned quickly, and as he moved out of the way, Stephen saw a young girl under the seat: her eyes closed and lips barely moving. She was making a small crying sound. Sorrow tugged at his heart as he realized the likelihood of the child surviving was near to nothing. He slid off his mouse and dropped the reins.

"Get on the other side," he said in a commanding tone.

The two boys worked together without a word, both deep in thought. Even with two people, the cart was heavy; but with effort, they were able to shift it off the child. They both moved up to the little girl sprawled in the dirt. Her leg was twisted strangely to one side, and blood stained the front of her dress.

"Poor thing!" Stephen said with deep feeling. "Let's get her on my mouse." Stephen grunted as he stood up and pulled the mouse around closer. He mounted and motioned for the youth to get on behind him. With the injured child already in his arms, Kyle slid on behind Stephen and asked him to head toward the castle.

Kyle held one arm firmly around Kaylee, and with the other, he grabbed hold of the young man in front of him. He wasn't sure where this stranger had come from, but he was very thankful. It was as if his prayer had been answered moments after it had left his lips. It was now that he noticed the odd color of the youth's skin and eyes. He had ice-blue eyes and was tall like someone from Icelair but had a light tan and black hair like those of Sandar, clearly a mixling. The people in Icelair had milk-white skin, blond hair, and striking blue eyes. They were also taller than the shorter, stockier Sandarians. Here in Sandar, most people had tan skin, black hair, and green eyes. Anyone who varied from these two classifications was a mixling. And twenty years ago, mixlings had been outlawed. He had never really thought about it much since he had never known a mixling personally. He had heard stories that they were troublemakers, but the youth in front of him seemed to be a regular sort of person. And he had been very kind in helping him.

Sooner than either of them realized, they had reached the castle. The stranger addressed Kyle in a sympathetic tone. "This is as far as I can take you."

"Wait, can you watch her here so I can bring help? The gate is hard to open, and I'm not sure I can do it while holding her."

Seeing the worry in the boy's face, the stranger relented. "Put her there in the shade. I'll watch her till you come back," he said and led his mouse into the cover of the grasses.

Kyle did not wait to hear more but took off running toward the castle, and his feet did not seem to move fast enough. "Shaari! Ilden!" he called for Kaylee's parents, but no answer came to his waiting ears.

In his haste, he nearly ran into the guard standing in the hall. The guard looked at him impassively and stated, "The cooks were needed at the festival. You are in charge of the child while they're gone." The guard finished as if bored by the subject.

"Everyone's gone?" Kyle's voice rang with fear.

"That's right, just us guards…and you remain," the bearer of bad news stated.

"Are all of the healers gone too?" Kyle asked, not believing the news.

"'Fraid so. Someone sick?" the other guard drawled.

Kyle turned away. He would find neither help nor sympathy here. He ran back outside to where he had left Kaylee. Picking her up, he looked around for the youth who had helped him, but he was nowhere to be seen. He felt the panic begin to rise again, and then Stephen stepped out of the deep grass. Kyle explained his predicament, struggling to keep back the tears that threatened to come.

"What do you want to do now?" asked the youth.

"Can you take me one more place?" Kyle asked.

Glancing at the sky, he motioned for him to get on behind him again.

"By the way, my name is Kyle."

After that, they rode on in silence as Kyle directed his host toward Mr. Matthias's house.

3

Stephen

As Stephen urged his mouse on faster through the tunnel of overhanging grass, he thought about excuses he would use that evening to explain this unexpected delay. He still didn't even know exactly where the girl was whom he had been sent to fetch. Even though he couldn't return the favor of relating his name, he did appreciate the fact Kyle had told him his. Stephen could feel the little girl's body pressed against his back with every leap the mouse beneath them made. He felt terrible for Kyle, whom he assumed was her older brother. And he felt worse for the girl. She looked like she was hurt pretty bad.

At the age of eleven, Stephen had been orphaned when his home had burned down. Left alone with only memories of his family, he had dedicated himself to the resistance. His thoughts now turned to his youngest sister who had been five at the time. Roseanna had been his little shadow, and they had enjoyed countless days together playing any sort of game that she fancied.

As they left the grass and turned onto a deserted street, Kyle directed him down a road with houses on both sides. He followed Kyle's directions to one of the nicer houses near the end of the row. Glancing at the sign a few feet away, he saw it was sector five, the same section where he was to find the girl. After he dropped Kyle off at his destination, he would go in search of her and hopefully get back to the cabin in good time.

He and Kyle dismounted, and Stephen accepted the little girl into his arms. Kyle walked over to the house and knocked. After several minutes, he was still knocking, and Stephen began to wonder when he would accept the fact no one was there.

"Please! I know you're in there!" his voice called through the evening air.

Finally, Stephen walked over to join him. He laid his hand on Kyle's arm with sympathy. "There's no one here."

"Yes. There is! I know there is!" Kyle countered.

"Why are you so sure?"

"I saw her! She was here, and she didn't go to the festival!" Desperation began to creep into his voice again. "I think she may be able to help Kaylee. Mr. Matthias is a healer. He works at the castle."

Stephen's eyes widened in surprise when he heard the name. All of a sudden, everything seemed to fall into place: the girl he was so sure about and the fact that she wouldn't open the door. Mr. Matthias? Gently returning the little child to Kyle's arms, he walked around to the back of the house and parted the tall grass along the wall. Sure enough, under a tangle of spiderwebs, there was the symbol under the western windowsill. A mixling lived here. The one thing that bothered him was, how did Kyle know about her?

Luna

Luna had just finished a lonely supper and cleaned up when she heard voices outside. Her uncle had taught her what to do if guards ever came to search for her, but this sounded different. The conversation that happened outside the door floated in to her in her hiding place, and she wondered who Kaylee was and how she might be able to help her. It was true that her uncle had taught her from a young age what he knew about medicine, and she did have a few supplies, but it could be extremely dangerous to show herself to anyone.

"Please!"

"A little girl was trapped under a cart and is hurt!"

"She's only six years old! Everyone else is gone! Please! Can you help her?"

The pleas were accompanied by loud pounding.

Luna knew it was dangerous, but she imagined herself in the same situation with little Nio, only a year older than the injured girl. She finally lifted the door in the closet floor and crawled out into the room, replacing the rug carefully over the hidden trapdoor. Shaking, and with uncertain hands, she pinned her hair up and reached for her cloak hanging by the door. She glanced briefly into the mirror in the hall, making sure her hair was concealed beneath her hood. With some hesitation, she peeked through the window and then opened the door. There was the young man that she had seen earlier through the window, holding a little girl who looked severely injured. *What if I'm risking myself, and I can't even save her?* she thought desperately, sending prayers heavenward.

Luna stepped into her room and brought a blanket from the closet then spread it on the recently cleared table. Its cheerful colors seemed to mock the situation as the boy laid the child onto it. Luna worked quickly, pulling up the dress that was soaked in blood from the wound across her stomach. Luna was perfectly intent on cleaning the wound and did not notice the entrance of a second person who stood near, watching her work.

She first cleaned the cut and then turned to go to her uncle's room to retrieve some medicines. She nearly ran into Stephen, who stood in the doorway. She flinched but was careful to look down in an attempt to keep her face concealed. Luna couldn't help but feel a bit frightened. *What consequences would opening the door have?*

But she soon went back to work on the little girl and forgot about herself. After about an hour and a half, she had splinted the broken leg, sutured the cut, and applied one of her uncle's homemade medicines to the cleansed wound.

"It will help it heal in half the time," she said quietly to the youth as she replaced the medicine to its case.

"Thank you," the boy said with obvious relief. "My name is Kyle…in case I can ever help you with anything. I work at the castle…where Mr. Matthias works."

"You can take the blanket to keep her warm on the way back," Luna instructed Kyle as she went into her room, as if her job was done, and it was time for him to leave.

He picked up the now sleeping Kaylee, wrapped her in the blanket, and retreated outside, saying thank you once again as he left.

"Take the mouse we rode here and tie him on the edge of the wood near the castle. I'll pick him up in an hour," Stephen said to Kyle.

"Thanks again for all of your help," Kyle said sincerely. "She would have died…" His voice trailed off, and he looked at the ground self-consciously.

"Don't worry about it," replied Stephen. "I'm glad we could be of help."

Kyle nodded and nudged the mouse into a trot.

"You know him?" the voice alarmed Luna, who had been staring out the window following the retreating figure.

"No," she whispered, looking at the floor.

"And you opened the door for him?"

"I couldn't help myself…she was hurt…and so little."

"You're a mixling, aren't you?"

At this remark, she removed the hood of her cloak, revealing her golden hair, and looked at him directly. He had seen her light-colored hands when she had been working on her unexpected patient. Her eyes were a strange, piercing violet color.

She stared at him curiously. "So are you." She wasn't really sure what she had been expecting, but she hadn't really been expecting to see another mixling.

"We need to go," he told her.

"Go where?" Surprise rang in her voice as she looked him up and down, not quite believing that tonight she had talked to two different people outside of her family.

"I'm from the resistance, and they have decided to consider you as a member now that you are of age. Your uncle knew that we would come. Pack quickly. I was supposed to be here hours ago, except I ran across them after they were attacked by bandits," he said, a bit too gruffly.

Luna remembered her uncle telling her all about the resistance, and that if they ever came for her, she was to go with them. She shivered with a mixture of fear and excitement. Her life had been so closed in until now; she couldn't help but wonder what adventures lay ahead of her.

Nodding, she went to her clothing chest and began packing her few clothes and shoes. She put on her mouse-leather boots and a riding jumper, which she used when training her mouse, and then donned her blue cloak. In a small leather bag, which she carried over her shoulder and across her front, she placed the medicines and some bandages her uncle had provided her with. She took a picture from her drawer of Nio and Uncle Matthias and tucked it into a small special book, which she then wrapped in a blue-velvet cloth and tucked it in with the medicines. Folding a colorful blanket from her bed, she added it to her clothing.

In less than ten minutes, most of her belongings were packed, and she went back into the main room. Setting her case down, she went to the door to retrieve her bow and arrows then gathered everything and went outside. He waited as she locked the door behind her and went into the small shed on the side of the house. She slipped the harness over her mouse's nose and mounted quickly. Luna held out her hand uncertainly to Stephen and pulled him up behind her. Sadly, she paused and looked back at her uncle's house, wondering when she would see it again. Luna turned and looked once more as they the rode off into the night.

———∞o○❋○o∞———

Stephen

As hard as it was, he had restrained himself from thoroughly bawling the girl out. How crazy was she? Opening a door like that was just not heard of for a mixling. She had endangered herself and also Mr. Matthias. She had handled the child's injuries very skillfully, but other than that, she had acted foolishly, and he regarded her as an assignment. It took almost forty minutes to reach the place by the castle where his mouse was waiting. Kyle had tied the mouse in the tall grass where Stephen had hidden earlier.

"I must be as crazy as she is," he scolded himself. He had also shown himself to a stranger. He shook his head, trying to clear his mind. He mounted his mouse and took the lead on the dark hidden path into the woods.

Now that they were riding separate mice, traveling time went faster. Stephen couldn't help noticing the ease with which the girl handled her mouse. *She must have had some riding experience,* he thought. *And she does have a bow and arrows, so maybe she has had some training.*

When they finally reached the cabin in the woods, he pointed out the shed where she could take care of her mouse. He dismounted and tied the reigns neatly around the post then went up to the door. Suddenly he hesitated. How was he going to explain the reason he had been so late? Any story he made up would be a lie, and besides, he was sure the girl would probably not go along with it. He hated being late.

He put his hands in his pockets and tried to be patient. She seemed to be taking forever.

"Are we going to go in?"

The question came from behind him and made him jump.

"Yeah, sure, just waiting for you," he mumbled.

He saw the humor in her eyes. Yes, she had noticed. As they walked in, all heads turned in their direction.

"Wasn't that a little long to escort someone?" Carl's slightly irritated but relieved voice made him wince.

He opened his mouth, trying to think of what to say. Before he could respond, Luna's voice made him turn in surprise.

"It was my fault, really. Someone from my town needed help and, ummm, he was waiting quite some time for me," she stated confidently.

Carl stood now and extended his hand to the girl, introducing himself. "So you must be Luna. I'm Carl, leader of the resistance. We're all here to consider you as a member on the recommendation of your uncle." He scrutinized her face, and she blushed involuntarily.

"Thank you, and I'm really sorry to have kept you waiting," she answered courteously.

"It's fine, we're always patient with new-member considerations."

Stephen had the urge to laugh at this because usually someone who kept the board waiting was removed from consideration completely.

"We want to ask you if you will join our resistance. Your uncle thinks it would be very beneficial to you as well as to us."

Stephen glanced at Luna and saw that she looked a bit undecided, but her response seemed to please Carl. "If it's what my uncle wants, I will try my best."

"Good, good, tomorrow two other young ladies in the group will come and help you prepare for the trial that will be given to you in five days. After that, according to our decision, Stephen will take you to some of the training posts, or you will be given a mission. How does that sound?"

"Fine," she responded.

Carl led her to a small room in the back of the cabin. "This will be your room for now until we find a more permanent home for you."

"When will I see my uncle again?"

This question seemed to take Carl by surprise, but with a strained smile on his face, he assured her it would be soon. Stephen noticed that the girl seemed worried about this, but she accepted the quarters shown to her and went in, closing the door behind her.

Carl continued speaking to the remaining members. "Thank you, everyone, I'll see you day after tomorrow to discuss the trial terms for our guest."

He stood and pushed his chair under the table. Stephen noticed how tired he looked. All these deals with parents looking for good opportunities for their sons or daughters or nieces were hard on him. Missions were often dangerous. The resistance needed the young and strong, but qualities of cleverness, dedication, and a willingness to accept sacrifice were also important. He noticed that the others seemed uneasy. Carl pulled him aside before he could leave.

"Stephen, I want you and Daniel to go get the other two girls tomorrow morning and explain to them about our new member and tell them about their duty to prepare her for trials. Then during the next few days, I want you to supervise them from afar and make sure everything goes well. I really want this to go well…and I want her to feel welcome. You understand?"

"Yes, sir," he answered and watched Carl walk away. Funny, Carl didn't usually worry so much over a new member. Stephen had a feeling he wasn't going to enjoy the next few days very much, and the thought followed him all the way to his bed.

Janet

Janet felt herself being reeled out of her small comfort zone, and she didn't like it. Why did her schedule need to be interrupted? And who was this new girl who was so important? She and Cara were asked to go out that very morning and help her get ready for the trials to judge her skills. It was still dark outside, but they had been getting ready for twenty minutes, and neither one of them were happy about this assignment. It wasn't like the board anyway to provide personal trainers for a newcomer. Usually, a newcomer was tested as they were when they came. Janet was however a bit excited to see Stephen again. She had heard a lot about him and admired the stories she had heard. Soon she heard voices outside, and she and Cara hurried out the door into the dawn.

"Hi, remember me? I'm Janet." She hurried to introduce herself to Stephen. The young man didn't seem to notice her.

"We need to get going. Luna will be waiting," he said, nodding toward their white mice tied to the mouse post as he remounted his mouse and started toward the trail.

Janet turned quickly, a bit embarrassed and motioned for Cara to mount. They followed Stephen and Daniel's lead, even though they already knew the way.

During the time they rode, Stephen told them they were to treat Luna like she was an honored member—orders from Carl. Janet definitely didn't like this news but didn't argue. Daniel said nothing during the ride. When they arrived, Janet hurried to tie her mouse to the post, trying to be ready for anything. Cloak over her arm and bow and arrows fastened to her back, she wondered where Luna was.

"Luna?" Stephen called, knocking on the door.

Janet watched as he tried the door handle and went in. A few seconds later, he came out. "She's not here," he said. "You girls wait inside, and I'll go look for her. Daniel will stay here with you."

"We could help you," Janet quickly volunteered.

"No, thank you, I'll be faster by myself."

Before Janet could argue, he was gone.

Stephen

Irritation now filled Stephen as he began searching for the girl. Why did she have to pick now to run off? Where had she gone? Did she try to do something dumb like go look for her uncle?

"Yes!"

He heard a faint cheer come from his right. Following the direction of the sound, he came to a training circle where members often practiced their archery skills. Luna had set up a target on one end. She didn't hear his approach and seemed to be enjoying herself. Every time she let the arrow fly, it hit the center of the target, and she retrieved it, stepping back five more steps than before. When she had backed to the other side of the clearing, she walked to the target, removed the arrow that held it to the huge tree, and rolled it up.

Stephen looked up the high tree standing next to him; it seemed to go up and up, and its trunk was so enormous, it would take at least a hundred people to go around it holding hands. The sun glinted through the leaves, causing him to look back down. Diverting his eyes back to Luna, he saw her stroking her mouse. Then kissing its nose, she mounted and rode in a circle around the small field with a joyful smile on her face. He knew she had definitely not seen him yet. He felt himself almost smiling, seeing how happy she was with her accomplishment; but checking himself, he remembered she had been totally irresponsible by leaving when she was expecting visitors.

Stephen almost laughed at the face she made when she saw him; he had definitely startled her!

"I...um...was...just..." She pointed behind her, mouth opening and closing as if she didn't know how to explain, and then she just turned red and looked down, smiling shyly. "Sorry."

"The girls are waiting," he stated and turned toward the cabin. He felt a little bad for ruining her mood. Maybe he should just let the matter lie, but if she did it in the future, it could cause her trouble. As they rode toward the cabin, he contemplated what he would tell her.

Janet

Janet sat down at the table in irritation. How dare Stephen say she would slow him down? *Then again, he probably meant Cara,* she reasoned. She wished she would have met him in different circumstances. Somehow, she decided, she would impress him.

When she had joined the resistance two years ago, she was fourteen. Her mother had died birthing her younger brother who was stillborn, and her father had been preoccupied with his work and other responsibilities. He had arranged for her to join the resistance so that she might learn to be more responsible. Janet was from Icelair, pure in every way, although her skin was a bit darker than usual from being in the sun—but she did not count as a mixling. She was extremely proud of her blond hair and perfect heritage that no one else in the resistance could claim. Her parents had never disciplined her much, so she was unpredictable at times, with selfish interests for the most part. She did, however, enjoy having Cara as a faithful friend, who did whatever she did and looked to her for an example. She suspected that her father paid the leaders to accept her. *They are being compensated for any trouble I cause,* she reasoned.

As she sat there feeling very irritated with this new girl for wasting her time and for the girl's existence in the first place, she thought about the few days ahead of her. Although Stephen had given her strict instructions about how she was supposed to treat this new girl, she had other plans. Janet was not prepared to make her duo into a trio! *Whatever I have to do, Luna is not making the trials*, she assured herself and began to make plans on how to "train" her.

4

Luna

Luna scolded herself as she and Stephen rode back to the cabin. At home, she always woke up and started with some routines to strengthen herself and hone her skills. Her uncle had assured her that when she got the chance someday to be with the resistance, she could put those skills to good use. She had been so happy and enthralled with this new experience that she had forgotten the time, and now she could see that Stephen was obviously bothered. She remembered how she would be trained for the next few days, so this might be her only chance to apologize for her overexuberance.

Mustering her courage, she spoke quietly, then a little louder since Stephen didn't seem to hear her. "I'm really sorry for keeping you waiting. I guess I was excited to be outside, and the time went faster than I thought."

She wasn't sure if he had actually heard her and was about to try again when she saw a slight nod of his head. "He sure is talkative," she mumbled down to her mouse, scratching behind its spotted ear."

Mitzie had been given to her six months ago. Her uncle had found her on a hunting trip in the woods, caught under a fallen branch. Originally, she had named her Mifia, but Nio had always called her Mitzie, so in the end, she changed the name. When she lived in hiding, she would take Mitzie into the house and talk to her softly, gaining her trust with special treats. But now, thankfully, she could ride her out in the open instead of around the living room and in the middle of the night.

"It was good of you to apologize." The loud voice brought her back from her deep thoughts.

"I shouldn't have left without telling anyone," she said a bit shyly.

They rode the rest of the way in silence, both staring straight ahead and lost in thought.

Upon reaching the cabin, Luna went straight to the small shed at the side to take care of Mitzie. She never left her out or unattended if possible; in fact, she thought of Mitzie more as a pet than a mount.

When she came out of the shed, she saw two girls waiting for her. Her first impression was that the girl standing in front was really pretty, her blond hair braided around one side, accented with blue eyes and a very pale tan. A slight smile played on her perfect face, but it had a forced quality, which Luna immediately noticed. The other girl stood slightly behind, looking at the ground and holding one arm with her other hand. She also had blond hair, but her skin was much darker than the first girl. When she looked up, her shy green eyes looked at Luna curiously.

"My name is Janet, and this is Cara," the first girl said. "We are really glad to have you here with us."

Her kind words were overly sweet and accompanied by a fake smile. Luna made an effort to show no sign that she recognized the insincere attitude of the slim figure in front of her.

Stephen

Something in Luna's face told him that she had not missed the insincere attitude that Janet displayed. Stephen observed the conversation with rising concern.

"They've told us lots of things about you," Janet said smirking.

"All good, I hope?"

"Oh, yes, yes. They also told us we were supposed to get you ready for the trials."

"Oh yes, of course, I am sure I have a lot to learn."

Stephen noticed a puzzled look on her face but also the hint of a smile.

"Do you like archery?"

When Luna hesitated to answer, Stephen noticed the two girls smiled knowingly at each other.

"We'll have to get you a bow and arrow."

"That would be nice," Luna replied. "Do you know where they make them?"

"Don't worry, I have an extra one." Janet was quick to volunteer. Stephen watched as Janet hurried back into the cabin and brought out a small bow with a sheath of five arrows.

Luna examined them, and he noticed she was smiling, running her fingers down each arrow. She said, "These are very nice. Are you sure I can use them?"

At this, Stephen almost laughed. Anyone who knew how to shoot as well as she did could surely tell these arrows were pathetic! Janet wore a pleased smile. Stephen wondered to himself why Luna was acting like she didn't know anything about archery.

"Are you girls going to give me a lesson now?" Luna asked Janet.

Janet and Cara nodded their heads and exchanged glances as they climbed on their mice and waited for Luna to retrieve her mouse from the shed.

Stephen sighed and decided it would be best to supervise the first lesson, but he waited until the three girls rode off out of sight. He followed at a distance and tied his mouse to a tree, walking quietly to the edge of the clearing where their practice was to take place.

"Okay, so do you know how to hold the bow?" Cara asked sweetly.

"Yes, I do know that part," Luna replied.

Stephen wondered when she would stop playing along and show them that she knew how to shoot.

"Which part am I supposed to hit?" she asked, nodding toward the target they had set up.

Janet looked over at Cara then said clearly, "We always aim at the outer ring."

Here, Stephen almost interrupted. That was ridiculous! Everyone that the center was the target.

"Okay," Luna responded cheerily and pulled back her arm. The arrow flew through the air and hit about a finger length away from the outer ring...

"That's great for a beginner!" the other two exclaimed.

After this, Stephen watched in disgust as the two girls told Luna every wrong rule for archery and watched her perform them while they watched with glee on their faces. He retreated to the woods and sat at the base of a small tree. After nearly the whole afternoon had passed and he had taken an enjoyable nap, he reentered the clearing, and all three girls turned toward him.

"Would you like to see what I've learned in archery today?" Luna asked him, smiling.

"Wait!" Janet interrupted. "Save it as a surprise for the trials!"

Stephen recognized this clever cover-up but said nothing. He wondered why Luna was playing along with their plans. He hoped sincerely she wasn't taking to heart their mean intentions.

"I should take you two home," he said pointedly toward Janet and Cara.

"Why don't I come with?" Luna surprisingly volunteered.

"If you'd like," he said.

To him, it was a surprise to hear a girl volunteer to do anything. In fact, remembering the experiences he had with Janet and Cara— he did his part and some of theirs, and they did the minimum. He was actually happy Luna wanted to come; it could be interesting to hear other conversations between the now comical trio.

———◦◦◦◖◗◦◦◦———

Luna

Janet did not seem overly sincere in her welcoming, so Luna decided to play along and learn her true intentions. One time when she was fourteen, her uncle had brought one of his cousins to their house for a few days. He had told her that his cousin, Neidy, was going to teach Luna how to make a wonderful pie. Neidy was jealous and had absolutely no intention of teaching her anything correctly, and Luna had not been prepared for this. She had trusted Neidy completely and followed her instructions to the letter. What she hadn't noticed was that Neidy was showing her one thing and doing another. That night, everyone enjoyed the pie and complimented Neidy, which she enjoyed immensely, with looks to Luna. She even said, "I couldn't have done it without Luna." Luna remembered being so happy with that compliment.

The next time Neidy came over, Luna wanted to surprise her, so she tried to prepare the same dessert, but it did not come out the same. Everyone ate in silence, and a humiliated Luna noticed the pieces in the trash later. After the incident and a talk with her uncle, Neidy never came to visit again. And Luna, learning from the experience, promised herself to never trust someone who appeared insincere again. Surprisingly, even though she wasn't around many people during her life, she did know how to read people rather well. It was a skill she had focused on during her long hours watching Nio.

She smiled to herself as she thought about how she had played a perfect show of learning their way. She was saving it for the trial all right! She wondered what they planned to teach her tomorrow. The good thing was, it was only for one more day.

"What will you girls be teaching me tomorrow?" she asked, looking at Janet.

"I think we will do boating," Janet replied thoughtfully.

At this, Luna wanted to laugh. How could they teach her boating wrong?

The time went slowly, and she couldn't think of anything to inspire conversation. Everyone's smile seemed to be forced, and Stephen didn't even bother with one. He seemed distant and gruff. Luna frowned. She hoped he wasn't disappointed in her.

At their house, Janet turned back with an extremely sweet smile on her face. "And tomorrow, I hope we'll all be on time?"

Luna matched her smile with "certainly." She cringed inside and hoped they would not be permanent companions.

Stephen

Luna certainly had handled Janet's accusation nicely. He glanced at Luna, who was still smiling.

"What is in the plan for the rest of the day?" she asked him.

"Nothing in particular." He thought for a moment. "We could race."

"Where to?"

"The clearing?"

"Okay...Go!" shouted Luna as she leaned forward and squeezed her knees.

They were off!

Stephen felt the wind blowing in his face as he urged his mouse on faster. The spotted one, however, was a good runner, probably younger than his. Luna crouched low over its neck and seemed to be singing to it, urging it on. Shrubs and grass towered above their heads as they ran shoulder to shoulder, each encouraging their speed with every second. They dodged acorns in their path and ducked under low hanging daisies. The mice seemed to enjoy the energy of the moment as much as their riders and thrust themselves into the effort completely. They arrived in the training circle out of breath and exhilarated. Stephen found himself smiling. Luna was already there, laughing out loud.

"I'm going to stay here and practice some more," she said. "I want to be ready for those trials."

"You're going to practice what they taught you?" He hoped it sounded like he didn't care much. "Don't anyway," he told himself.

"Maybe. Does it matter?" she responded.

He nodded and quickly pulled himself up onto his mouse. Oh well, if she wanted to play their game, why should he interfere? He wanted to warn her about the two girls' wrong directions. But maybe he should just stay out of it.

Tonight, he and Daniel were going hunting, and he wasn't going to worry about some girl's problems. He liked hunting. Today, there was an order for ten beetles from the trainer. Her name was Eneva. She was raised in a bookly home in Icelair, a mixling hidden away for seventeen years. When soldiers were tipped off by a neighbor, they searched the house. After staying hidden for hours and then slipping out of the city by night, she had lived for several months by herself before joining the resistance. She spent her time in hiding, training beetles her father brought her. When her skills were demonstrated to the board, they were more than happy to accept her. That had been five years ago, and now she spent time with all the members, instructing them in the care and training of beetles.

Daniel and Stephen were dedicated to supplying her with new beetles to train. The beetles had to be tracked down and captured without injuring them. This need provided an occasional invigorating search and a nice activity for the nighttimes when there weren't any missions. Some of the beetles were dangerous and put up a vigorous fight, but with training, most would bend to the will of their trainer.

Stephen told himself over and over again that he didn't care in the least how Luna did at the trials. But his concerns kept coming back to mind, and he found he couldn't concentrate on the task at hand. He did hope she was only playing along with Janet's teaching.

"Stephen! There you are!" Daniel's cheerful voice came to him from the other side of the path. His big smile always reminded

Stephen of a row of white stones. His dark tan made his white teeth and blue eyes stand out. In fact, the only difference between him and Daniel was that Daniel was a bit chunkier. And that he was more muscular—or that was what he told himself.

They laughed and joked as they found the beetle tracks. By the middle of the night, they had a beautiful line of beetles, young and ready to be trained, just waiting to be taken to the trainer. One of them had put up a glorious fight. It was older than the others and had a large horn, which they had finally roped to a tree to subdue the beast.

"You'll have to take them to Eneva tomorrow. I have a training class to supervise," Stephen announced.

Daniel raised his eyebrows in surprise. "I thought the new mixlings were being transported by Ernest."

"Yeah, but the new girl that Carl brought in from Mr. Matthias is very important, and he wants her trained for her trials."

"You're training her?" Daniel asked, surprised.

Stephen explained to him the predicament with Janet and how they had taught her how to shoot a bow and arrow. He didn't, however, tell him how he had seen her shoot beforehand. Daniel thought this was extremely funny. *Just like a girl with popularity problems! Wonder who will win?*

Stephen laughed as well, not because he thought it was funny, but because he felt compelled to do so. In fact, he suddenly felt wrong laughing at her. Secretly, he hoped Luna would win. She seemed to have a bookly spirit about her and had shown herself to be responsible and caring toward others. She tried to do what was expected of her with honest effort. In his experience, that was an unusual quality to find in a girl. Uncomfortably, he changed the subject, and the topic of the girls ended there.

As he went to sleep that night, he contemplated again if he should talk to Luna about the girls' false motives but decided it might only cause problems. She seemed to know what she was doing. She didn't need to know it was because of her uncle and not her own talents that she was here. If she gained status and respect with her skill and helpfulness, people's motives within the resistance would change, and no one would be the worse for it. Content with this reasoning, he fell into a peaceful sleep and waited for morning.

The Resistance Cabin

The gathering was in session. The high people of the resistance sat around the table. A knock sounded at the door. When one of the headmen opened it, a cloaked figure entered. "The good king of Icelair is dead."

Everyone gasped, and their faces went white as they absorbed his words.

"And the heir?" a frightened voice dared to voice the question they all shared.

"It was told he went with his mother to Sandar for the last week of the festival, but all search parties have been exhausted."

"What are you saying?" Carl now demanded with urgency.

"Icelair's king is dead, and the rightful heir has been removed."

Who would reign? No one said this, but even the messenger felt it in the still air, which seemed to suffocate them. The answer was one they all knew, and one they all dreaded: "Elsiper!"

5

Luna

As Luna walked arm in arm with Janet toward the river, she couldn't help but worry. It had been three days since she left her house in Sandar, and her uncle would be back soon. When would she see him? Would he know what had happened to her? Had he known that they were coming for her? The questions distracted her as they walked on.

That morning, when Janet and Cara had come to pick Luna up, Janet reminded her that they would be studying boating today. Luna was skeptical, but it would be fine if she got dirty since she always wore a work-type dress when training or practicing. She had never really liked water, but she could swim.

One night, years ago, her aunt and uncle had taken her swimming at one of the rivers near Sandar. It had been a good learning experience, but nothing she would ever do for fun. Although her uncle assured her that she was very good at swimming, she had never grown to like it, perhaps because she always felt that someone would find them there swimming, and they would take her away. Or maybe it was the fear that a fish or frog might suddenly view her as a quick snack.

Of course, she voiced none of this to Janet but kept a smile on her face and went on with a positive attitude toward the day ahead of her. When they reached the river, she spotted a small green boat docked by the side. It was made of Curnos, the huge green pods that grew on the trees. The stems were tied tightly with a vine rope, and the seams down the middle were glued with one of the boat glues from Icelair. Waiting for Janet to give her instructions, she stood quietly watching the boat sway gently in the sparkling water.

"Do you know how to use a boat?" Janet's voice was sickly sweet. The way she drew out the words irritated Luna, but she tried to ignore it.

"Of course."

"Well, not everyone does, you know."

She bent over slightly and lowered her voice when saying this, as if she were telling her some sort of a secret. Janet continued, "Oh yes, you have to ride alone. Some of the trials require you to take a boat alone somewhere, so if they ask you to demonstrate… well, it's best if you practice it by yourself."

Luna forced a smile and grasped the long strands of grass as she eased herself toward the shimmering water.

Luna laid her cloak down carefully on a log and stepped toward the boat, picking up the light reed oars. Gingerly stepping inside, she steeled herself not to make a face. She pushed the craft away from the shore after situating herself in the middle. As she floated out into the middle of the lake, she felt the boat rock pleasantly beneath her. And in that moment when she began to relax, it happened.

As she dipped the oars into the peaceful water, the beautiful scene was shattered. The boat was yanked from under her, flipping in a complete turnaround. She went down sputtering as the cold water went over her head, and she was slightly aware of her carrying bag floating in front of her. Pushing it down, she easily rose to the surface. She held back tears as she swam toward shore.

She told herself over and over she would not let them know how much it had scared her, especially the fact that at first she thought it might have been a water creature. A boat did not flip itself when you touch the oars to the water, this she knew very well. When she raised her arm in an effort to grab a branch, her fingers brushed against a small, taut fiber in the water. A scream pushed itself up in her throat, but she restrained it as she realized it was attached to the boat. Her "accident" had been no accident.

Stephen

By the time he had realized what the girls were doing, it had been too late. He had rushed to the side of the stream, ready to help in case she couldn't swim. As soon as he saw her swimming toward shore, he immediately turned to the two girls standing by with smirks on their faces.

"What are you two thinking? How could you be sure she knew how to swim? What do you think Carl will have to say about this? I mean, I can't believe you two!" he sputtered angrily.

Behind him, Luna emerged from the water dripping wet. "I'm fine! I mean, I should have been waiting for it to tip! You never can be really sure about getting into boats."

Here, Luna stopped as if not sure what else to say. Stephen stared at her wide-eyed. She seriously did not just say that! Someone could be tipped in a boat and walk away, but take the blame when it was obviously a trick? That was just ridiculous!

"How about I...um...go clean myself up?" She paused. "And we can continue training later?" She added, still shaking from the cold.

"I don't think so," Stephen interrupted. "They've given you enough lessons, and by the time you are dry, it will probably be too late anyway. I'll be taking them home now. You can practice by yourself tomorrow morning and take the trials with what you have already learned."

He was relieved when she nodded in agreement, picked up her cloak, and walked into the woods.

With a last stern look toward Janet and Cara, he went back to where he had left his mouse. He angrily mounted and waited for them. They did not try to disguise their pleasure in what they had done. He should have noticed sooner when they picked up that rope. Also, hardly anyone was tested for water skills, and never had a girl been tested for it. Usually, most girls were deals, like Janet and Cara. Cara's parents were in the resistance too. They just worked in a different part and left Cara here so she could train with another girl. As much as Luna had insisted that she was fine, she had looked strained and had also seemed very relieved that she wouldn't have to train with the girls any longer. There was something in her eyes that told him she was not as okay as she let on. He gruffly led the two troublemakers away, contemplating what action he would have to take.

Luna

Luna had held herself together well until she was out of sight, but the tears came when she removed her now wet book. It was a special handwritten copy of the Great Book that Raquel had given her right before she died. It had the teachings of everything bookly and held great importance and value, sentimental as well as material. Sopping wet as it was, she wasn't sure if it was salvageable. As she carefully opened it and laid it to drip dry beside her, she looked at the soggy pictures of Nio and Uncle Matthias and was overwhelmed by a wave of homesickness. She removed the medicines, thankful that they were stored in stone jars with tight stoppers. They appeared to be undamaged. She laid the bandages on top of a rock to dry in the sun.

"Pulled the rope on ya, I see!"

A gruff voice made her turn smartly around, and she almost shrieked in fright. There behind her stood a stooped elderly man. His hair was white and looked as if it hadn't been cut since he was born. His half-smile revealed a row of crooked yellow teeth somewhere in the tangle of his overgrown beard, and his blue eyes sparkled in amusement. Anyone else probably would have told him to find some other person to bother, but Luna enjoyed meeting new people, even if it was someone who looked like he had lived in the mountains for one hundred years!

"Yeah." She sighed sadly. She really didn't know what else to say but continued looking curiously at him.

"Mean girls…those are mean girls," he stated this as a matter of fact, nodding his head as if it was something the whole world knew. "Not many like to take that…not many."

Luna smiled at the nonchalant way he drew out his words and repeated part of what he said, emphasizing it.

"Should show them who's boss, that you should."

At this, Luna shook her head. "No, I couldn't do that. It wouldn't be bookly."

"Bookly? Ha! What's that?" he barked as he raised his head in an odd fashion, wild hair blowing back off his weathered face.

"We follow the Great Book," Luna informed him. Luna nodded toward the small wet book beside her.

"Humph! And it tells you to act like that? Even when there's them that don't deserve it?" He looked at her skeptically, his intriguing blue eyes twinkling. "I've heard it all before, that I have…" He paused and added, "Well, I'll say, I'm not so bookly sometimes, no siree!"

Luna laughed out loud at this and at many other odd things the man said as they carried on a conversation over the next half hour.

"Got me job to do, that I do, mmmmm!" With this, the old man ended the conversation and turned, leaving Luna feeling much better, still seated on the old log in the clearing.

She watched curiously as he made his way through a tangle of grasses and disappeared from sight. She wouldn't have believed he had been there moments before had she not been there to witness it. An almost sad smile spread across her face as she contemplated the wild hair around his wrinkled face once more. Tomorrow, she knew it would take a lot of courage to be bookly and not disclose Janet to the council. She needed to pray tonight for guidance, as well as for pure thoughts because the thought of dousing Janet with a bucket of water certainly wasn't a pure one!

6

Stephen

Stephen guessed Luna wouldn't be at the cabin but probably in the circle practicing, since it was only half an hour after daylight. As he reached the clearing, he saw her there with a small sand cloth, rubbing it up and down her arrows. He watched as she inspected each tiny palva and every thorn tip. The palvas used for arrows were found on the flowers that bowed down above their heads. They balanced the arrow in its flight toward its target. He noticed she had already oiled the bow and put a new vine thread on it. At least she was prepared.

"Hello," he called, not exactly sure how to announce himself without startling her. Seeing she hadn't heard, he tried again a little louder. "Hello!"

This time, she turned around to see who was there. "Oh, hey! Just getting ready for the trials…I…um…had my bow and arrows in the cabin, and I decided they looked a little straighter than the others."

At this, she smiled and looked happily down at them. Stephen felt genuinely glad she was happy. Then he scolded himself. *She's only an assignment, and you don't like working with girls!* Despite the fact that he told himself this over and over, he couldn't help but feel it wouldn't be that bad being this girl's friend. Blowing it off, he broke the stillness. "Trials are in an hour, and it will take us that long to get there."

"Will we be picking up Janet and Cara?"

"No, someone else will be taking them."

She smiled and looked relieved.

They mounted their mice and headed down a different trail than the one she had traveled before. As they scampered through the tall grass, Luna spoke.

"Do the judges usually test people on 'water' skills'?" she asked, fingering her reins nervously.

"There is one part of the trials that has water, but it's not too difficult if you know how to handle a rope and arrows. You like swimming?"

At this, she smiled slightly and replied with almost a grimace. "It's not my favorite thing to do."

Stephen contemplated this as they rode on in silence. He hoped the judges didn't test her for water skills. She already had enough water testing the day before.

Luna

As they neared the place for the trials, Luna's heart seemed to pound faster. What if she did horrible, and they sent her back to Sandar? Personally, that wouldn't be so bad, but then again, going back to being cooped up in the house for who knew how many more years. A passage from her book popped into her mind, and she mumbled it in rhythm with her mouse's padding feet. "And whatever you do, do it heartily, as to the Lord and not to men."

Today she would do her best no matter what! Smiling with this thought, she rode with her head high into the big clearing in front of the table of judges, who stared down at her sternly. She looked around to see who had come to spectate: there were Janet and Cara, not encouraging but expected. The judges sat at a high table with a shade positioned above them. In all, there were seven of them. On a bench to the right of the judges' table sat another fifteen or so people watching, one of whom was a young lady with a small beetle atop her lap. Janet and Cara sat to the right of the table on the mossy ground along with other three young men, one of whom she assumed was Daniel. She returned a small smile to Janet's honey-sweet grin. She noticed the area around the judges' table was a jumble of things: stumps, small lakes, short shrubs, ramps, and of course, targets.

Carl stood up and began to speak. "Welcome, Luna! The course in front of you is to test several skills. Janet tells me you enjoy water activities, so in your case, we have included the water course. There are two lakes placed strategically within the course. You may fashion a raft, swim, or find another way of crossing these. But you must remain with the trail limits at all times. These are marked with yellow ribbons. The course will be timed. Some of the judges will follow you or be watching from various vantage points while others will watch from the second flat tree."

"Will there be others competing on the course with me?" she asked. Luna already guessed the answer would be no, but she would be prepared in any case.

Carl looked at her tentatively. "As a matter of fact, there is a provision that if you wish to call a challenge, any who wish to answer that challenge may do so." He stood silently, waiting for her reply.

"Then yes, I do call a challenge," she responded.

Finally, after several minutes of suspense, he called out in a loud voice, "Today we are here to evaluate the skills of Luna Matthias. A challenge has been called. Now who will answer that challenge and run the course with Luna to better evaluate her skills and to better their own?"

Two of the young men near Janet got to their feet, and glancing behind her, she saw that Stephen too had accepted the challenge.

Again, Carl spoke loudly, "No other girls are brave enough to join the course?"

All eyes turned to Janet. They all knew Carl was referring to her. Her mouth opened and closed like a fish, and a frantic look came over her face. "I—uhm." Seeing that there was no excuse, she stood and took her place with the other "volunteers."

They were all given a length of rope, their bows and arrows, a small knife, medicine for injuries, a bottle of water, and their belts, which held a small thorn. The boys all wore generally grubby pants and lightweight boots; their vestlike overshirts were made of mouse leather. She noticed that their clothes were of the same style her uncle had used for Nio and her in Sandar. She and Janet wore jumper-like dresses that reached down to their knees. The undergarment that reached halfway down their arms and down to their boots was made of a strong but light material. She glanced down at her boots as they walked toward the starting line; her uncle had given them to her on her seventeenth birthday. They were soft-brown leather made from mouse hide. Sometimes people made fur boots from mouse hide.

Trying to focus, she adjusted her belt a bit more securely around her waist. It contained a small bone knife and a thorn with a carved handle. It also held two pouches of medicine for an emergency. All five of them had left their cloaks lying in a row on the moss. As Carl counted down the numbers to go, the five contestants bent down with one hand on the ground and a foot out in front ready for takeoff. Adrenaline pumped through Luna as she firmly held her bow and set her eyes ahead. She smiled as she anticipated the great race that was about to take place.

THE TRIAL

The contestants ducked their heads down waiting for the final word—"go!"

They were off, running with full force. The spectators tried to decide who to cheer for: Luna, Stephen, Daniel, Janet, or Eric. Who would win? No one knew about the new girl because this was her first trial. Stephen was one of the best. Eric had more time to practice, although no one expected him to win because lately he had dedicated himself more to strategy engineering than training. Janet was known to be a soft girl. Daniel was the strong, quiet type. The competition, they thought, would be between the new girl, Stephen, and Daniel.

All five participants cleared the first wide ramp nicely but came to a sliding stop at the tip of the second. There below was a lake with a marker of twelve rods. A small island was just out of reach. Stephen took the rope from his belt and made a lasso then threw the rope up to a near branch on an overhanging tree; he missed. Luna, seeing his idea, decided to try something similar. Daniel dove into the water below, soon followed by Eric. Luna tied her rope to an arrow and aimed for the strong branch above. She smiled as the arrow hit its mark. The judges paused as they saw her plan. Riding slowly by the course, they followed the contestants' progress.

Luna

The look on Janet's face was totally enough to distract Luna from her trial, but she reminded herself to laugh about it later. As she swung out to the island, she glanced at Stephen who had just managed to catch the branch with his rope. He jumped two seconds after her, and they both landed on the island neatly. The arrow gave way just as she landed, and she breathed a sigh of relief after the near miss. She began to run toward the rope bridge ahead. Luna looked back at Stephen who was still trying to free his rope. The two youths who had dived into the water were almost to the island. Then she looked back at the ramp. There stood Janet looking forlorn and no longer haughty. Luna felt a pang of sympathy. Obviously, Janet didn't know what to do.

As she stared, Stephen's voice distracted her. "The course is that way," Stephen said softly, pointing in the other direction.

"Then what are you waiting for?" She smiled.

That was when she decided. Drawing an arrow, she attached it to the end of her rope and aimed for the top of the opposite ramp. Letting it fly, she smiled as she saw it stick with a thud. Janet looked at her as if she couldn't believe what she was seeing. Then Luna noticed Janet's hesitance. Luna couldn't wait long to retrieve her rope, or she would soon be far behind the others. She tied the other end to a small tree. Stephen had continued on the race as soon as he saw what she was doing. Luna paused for an instant and then continued on, leaving the rope behind. She thought about her rope as she crossed the swinging bridge. The bridge swayed wildly with every step, causing a moment of panic halfway across. She hoped she wouldn't need the rope to finish the race. It seemed to take forever to complete the stretch, but finally her feet were again on solid ground.

Running down the ramp, she saw that the next obstacle was a series of strong stumps set in the ground with fine sand underneath. She read the notice, "Ground is quicksand." She doubted that it really was, but what it did mean was that if you fell in, you might be disqualified. There was still some uncertainty in her mind as she came to the final stump. She crawled under a low bush and through a tunnel of thick grass. As she came into the next clearing, she noticed a zigzag pattern of stumps laid out with targets at varying distances from each stump.

Each stump was at a different height. This tested agility and skill with the targets. In all, there were one dozen targets, and Stephen was already on number five. She took all this in before her jump to the first stump. Thankfully, her archery skills were well practiced, and she let the arrows sing through the air with very little difficulty. The last six jumps were a little more laborious but still manageable. When she was on target four,

Stephen had already reached ten. She quickened her pace but tried to concentrate. For a minute, she thought about leaving a few arrows to save time, but she had already lost two and only had ten left. Something could come up later. She passed target nine as Stephen jumped from the last stump. She was filled with despair as she thought of how long it would take to retrieve her arrows and then reach Stephen. She ran back and gathered her arrows and sprinted ahead to make up for lost time.

As she came to the end of the clearing, she could see that their mice were waiting, tied in the grass. Ahead was a pile of jumps, logs, mud puddles, and grass barriers, nothing you could get through on foot easily. Luna ran to the tall grass and searched for Mitzie. Not seeing her, she whistled. Seconds later, the missing mouse emerged from the bushes. Quickly, Luna examined her, more concerned about her health than the race at the moment. She found nothing wrong, but the reins had been cut. If Mitzie hadn't come when called, it could have ruined the course for her. The thought troubled her. She tried to push the idea out of her mind that someone might want just that.

Stephen

As Stephen untied his mouse, Cara stepped from the tall grass and asked him where Janet was. He replied that he really didn't know. He hadn't seen her since he crossed to the island. He had been waiting for Luna, but then when she stopped to give her rope to Janet, he had left her behind. Anyway, it wouldn't be a competition if everyone waited for one another. A flash of color behind him caught his attention. Glancing back, he saw Luna clear a mud puddle neatly without so much as hesitating. He spurred his mouse forward as she came running up the trail. He thought of making conversation but then saw there would be no time as they surged ahead—their mice neck in neck, each pushing to clear the next obstacle first. As his midnight-black mouse stumbled at a sharp turn, she flew passed him around the next corner. The foliage was thick in this part, and the judges couldn't see every part of the track. He hoped, however, that they had seen her perfect jump. Smiling, he urged his mouse faster, trying to catch up to the bobbing spot of blue in front of him.

----○○○)◉(○○○----

Janet

What was Luna thinking? Just showing off by throwing me her rope! Janet fumed silently to herself as she gingerly jumped from target stump to target stump. She had misplaced two of the last arrows into the white part of the wood and hoped the judges were too distracted by Miss Show-Off to notice. Of course, she had used the rope to cross. It would have been just dumb not to, but if Luna hadn't thrown it, she would have found another way.

"Of course, I would have," she halfheartedly assured herself.

She couldn't really understand why Luna would do such a thing. What if she needed her rope later in the trials? Glancing up, she saw that Eric and Daniel were already on the eighth target. She had suggested a lot of the things in the course to Carl. She had told him that during their training, Luna had particularly liked water and archery. Of course, she hadn't known she herself would be included in this contest. He had also put in a riding course and a racetrack. Although Janet had told Cara to "help Luna out," she was still worried that Luna could come out ahead in the end. Well, at least she won't have a mouse for the riding course.

Janet smiled. Toward the end of the course, the contestants would be given a strange mouse to ride, and judging on how they handled it, the judges would learn what they needed to know. *There will be a mouse for all of us,* she thought grudgingly. But Luna's ride would be pretty interesting! At this thought, she laughed and let an arrow fly into the target in front of her. "Bull's-eye!" she whispered.

Luna

As Luna turned the last curve of the obstacle course, she noticed Stephen was right by her side, pushing as hard as she was. In front of them was a smooth dirt track, and two of the judges greeted them, two mice in hand. They dismounted, and Luna patted Mitzie fondly as she relinquished her to the judge and accepted the cream-colored mouse in return. A soft leather blanket was strapped around its middle and reins adorned its head. Usually, she didn't ride with the "seat" as it was called, but since it was already strapped on, she climbed atop. She smoothed the fur behind the skittery mouse's ears and eased up to the line that marked the beginning of the track.

"Go!"

The resounding call started them off. As she tightened her knees and urged the new mouse on, she felt its body go rigid beneath her, and it shrieked in pain. She anticipated the throw before it happened, but it was too late. As the mouse shook its head and threw up its hindquarters, Luna felt herself being hurled onto the dirt track. She landed hard on her stomach and felt the air go out of her. Pulling herself up on her knees, she sustained herself with one arm on the ground; and with the other, she held her stomach in pain. Her right arm burned, and as she leaned all her weight into it, she realized it had been twisted in her fall.

Vaguely, she noticed Stephen there with his hand on her back, asking if she was all right, but she couldn't answer. As she struggled for breath, tears gathered in her eyes and fell to the dirt below, the shiny mud spots staring back up at her. It took a few minutes of breathing hard before she was able to stand. As she looked up, she realized Carl was walking over. His face was pale and full of concern as he helped her to her feet.

"Are you okay?" he asked.

She checked herself for further injury and then stated with determination, "I am going to finish this course." Looking over at Stephen, she said, "You'd better catch your mouse because when I catch mine, I'm not gonna wait long."

As Carl saw her intentions to recapture the cream mouse, he turned back to the spectators, shaking his head but smiling.

The mouse shied from her, but she advanced carefully, talking softly. As soon as she came within reach of it, her hand went out slowly and clasped the reins. Its whiskers twitched nervously, and it stood on its hind feet in alarm. She gently stroked its sides, and after a minute of her soothing voice, it calmed down and surrendered to her touch. The first thing she did was to reach down and unbuckle the seat. As it fell off, she saw the cause of her catastrophe. There was a sandbur; it looked like a prickly ball. If you applied any pressure, it could cause extreme pain. Removing it and smoothing down his beautiful fur, she reassured him and finally mounted and went back to the starting line where Stephen was waiting. He smiled at her in encouragement, and she smiled back, glad that she wasn't running the course by herself.

<hr />

Stephen

Stephen hadn't actually seen her depart from her mouse, but he had seen her hit the ground, and it hadn't looked good. She had fallen on her right arm, which twisted miserably as she did a complete circle and landed a second time on her stomach, knocking the air out of her. Not knowing what to do, he tried to see if she was okay, but she hadn't been able to answer. He couldn't believe the moment when she had told him to catch his mouse!

Anger pulled at his heart as he watched her remove the bramble from the mouse's fur. Someone had done that intentionally, and whoever it was should be extremely ashamed of themselves. He thought of Janet. She had probably done it, but then a teaching from the Great Book came to mind: "You shall not bear false witness against your neighbor." If he wasn't sure about it, it wasn't bookly to even accuse Janet in his thoughts.

As Luna drew up beside him on the cream-colored mouse, he was surprised that she planned to ride without the seat on a strange mouse. *She must be pretty sure about herself*, he thought.

"Go!"

Luna took off ahead of him. Even though she was leaning up unto the neck of the mouse, he noticed she favored her right arm. At first he thought to let her win but then decided she would be angry if he did that. He pushed his mouse forward; it was a gray one with white markings on its face and left side. He hoped it was as fast as it was pretty. Soon he reached Luna, and they ran together, the mice in competition as much as their riders. As they reached the end of the stretch, he gave a final push to his mouse. He burst ahead right across the finish line, beating Luna by seconds.

Luna and Stephen dismounted and faced the last stretch of the course. It was a slow moving river with five flat rafts tied to posts near the side. On the far side of the river were ten targets; and on the boat side, most of the spectators stood watching. As he neared the river, he noticed the floating rafts had names on them. Picking his, he stood on it and pushed himself out to the middle. The soft current carried him in a straight line downstream between the channel markers. As he hit the first target, he glanced back at Luna and saw she had also grabbed hold of her raft. First he saw her test it carefully, then climb aboard, and she too hit the first target. This part was easy for him, and he hit the targets one after the other as he drifted downstream.

At the fifth target, he heard a gasp and a splash. Looking back, he realized Luna's raft had been faulty. The vines tying it together had suddenly come apart. Quickly, he took the rope off his belt and threw it out to Luna. Once she saw it, she grasped it gratefully and began pulling herself toward him. When she was in reach, he helped her onto his raft. By the time the raft floated to the next target, she added one of her arrows to the one that was already sticking proudly in the wood. They both hit the middle of the tenth target in unison.

Stephen noticed she took more time to pull back her arrow than she had earlier and realized it was because of her injury. He stepped off the raft and helped her off after him. Daniel and Eric were right behind them, and Janet pulled her raft off the water a few minutes later. They were all greeted by the cheering judges and spectators. Stephen and Luna smiled at each other, content, despite the challenges they had faced. He suddenly realized that he was actually proud of her.

7

Luna

Luna remembered how angry and flustered Janet looked when she arrived last. The order had been put up on a board for all to see—Stephen, first; Luna, second; Daniel, third; Eric, fourth; and Janet, fifth. This did not make Janet happy. Everyone congratulated everyone for participating, and then went their own way. Luna now sat on a log in the original clearing where she had practiced early that morning.

"Almost beat 'em, that you did!"

Luna smiled and turned to greet the old man. Although she knew what he looked like, his wild hair still made her feel like he wasn't real. It seemed to come from nowhere and go nowhere, like a wild big white cloud around his kind face.

"You watched the course?" Luna asked him, surprised.

"Ev'ry bit of it! That's right, ev'ry bit!" he exclaimed. After a moment of contemplation, he puzzled. "Suppose you done justified throwin' that rope back to that little mean girl as bein' bookly? That right?"

Luna smiled back at him. "That's right."

The old man studied the hand that kept a constant rubbing motion over her arm.

"Your arm not better yet?" At this, he frowned slightly and studied her for a second. "Come here."

She turned around to see him go through the tall forest of grass. Standing sorely, she pushed through the grass after him. After a good fifteen minutes of following the stooped figure, her legs felt as if they would give way. She knew how to ride, and ride well, but that didn't mean she rode every day. Sometimes a week or more went between the time she sat atop her Mitzie, and she wasn't quite used to it. Now her body was feeling the stress and strain of the last few days and of the bumps she had received during the trial.

"Here she is! That's right, here she is...." The old man swept one shaking arm in front of him, displaying a tiny campsite, obviously hand-cleared. A small covered cart stood in the middle with a campfire and several cooking pots scattered around it. "I'll get what we came for right away. Just take care to keep quiet. My pet's sleeping. Yes, she is."

Too tired to care, Luna sank onto a small rock near the outskirts of the clearing. The old man returned with a small clear flask in his hand. Passing it to Luna, he said, "My granddaddy's recipe. Very good for aching and twisted joints. Just rub it on and then put something warm over it."

Luna took the sparkling bottle and thanked the man. Then they sat there opposite each other and talked. They talked about family and about the kingdoms and lastly about the Great Book that meant so much to Luna.

Kyle

Kyle sat with his elbow on the windowsill, his chin placed reflectively on the palm of his hand. When Kaylee's parents had come back from the festival, they had wanted to know every detail about Kaylee's accident. In secret, he had relived every accurate detail, but to the public, he could not remember her rescuer's name or that she had been a mixling. If it became known that he had not reported the mixlings, he could meet the same fate as other banished mixlings, or worse. Every day he thought about the girl with blond hair. Where was she? And what happened to her? He had related his story to Mr. Matthias, hoping for some answers. Kyle asked him what had happened to the mysterious girl. All that Mr. Matthias had told him, however, was that she was his niece, and she was gone for good. A shrill horn blast ripped through the still evening air, calling everyone to their shift. Tomorrow would be the day all the Sandarians would return home, and then everything would return to normal as if none of it had ever happened.

Stephen

It had been nearly two weeks since the trials. Everyone was there waiting for the last person to arrive. It was a special meeting with the leaders of the resistance, Luna, Daniel, Stephen, and of course, Janet. Stephen looked around the table at all the tense faces. Were they going to confront Janet about the troubles at the trial?

"Hello, Janet."

Carl's stern voice called his thoughts back to the present. After the offending member took her seat, the meeting commenced. "We are here to discuss who will be sent on the next mission. We have all decided that Stephen should go and one other person. We have considered you, Luna, and wondered if you would like to accept this mission?"

"No, no, no, she can't go!" interrupted Janet, sitting taller in her chair.

As everyone turned to look at her, she blushed slightly. "I mean, Daniel is the obvious choice. He and Stephen have been a good team on other missions and know how to work together well."

"I'll have to agree with Janet."

Stephen was surprised to hear Daniel speak up. He was lately silent at such meetings and was not one to give an opinion. "She doesn't know the area of the mission well. She's new, and if anything happened…"

Even though he didn't say it, they all knew what he meant. If something happened to Luna, then her uncle might be upset.

"Well, maybe the next mission, Luna. For this one, we will send Stephen and Daniel," Carl conceded.

Stephen noticed Luna didn't seem to be overly bothered by their decision. In fact, she seemed relieved. As much as he thought she was capable, he was glad that Daniel was going to be his partner. They had been best friends for the last two years and had done a lot of missions together. In a pinch, he knew how he would react. No surprises. After the council explained the details to Stephen and Daniel, they all filed out, and Stephen looked forward to the next night when their plan would be carried out.

Janet

"Listen to me, Luna, whatever you do, don't accept a mission!" Janet whispered.

She was taking advantage of the moment while Carl covered the plan with Daniel and Stephen.

"Why?"

"Such a question! You would never be able to handle the mission, okay? Don't feel bad. Hardly any girls can! In fact, I'm one of the few who can."

She didn't cover the fact that she had never really been on any mission other than a basic transport. To her, that was not important.

Luna smiled weakly. "I really appreciate your concern, Janet, but I don't think I'll know until I do go on one, so if you please, I would rather make up my own mind on whether or not I can manage a mission."

She felt kind of sorry for Janet, who seemed to be very insecure about her position in the resistance. Why else would she constantly be trying to cut her off?

Janet's face burned with hot anger as she sputtered, "If you knew half of what they—"

Here she was cut off by Carl as he cleared his throat loudly and looked her way. "Do you have something to add, Janet?" he asked with obvious annoyance at the ruckus she was causing.

At that moment, the door opened, and a man came in to speak with Carl, who stood and dismissed the meeting, leaving Janet and Luna to themselves. Carl then went into a room with the stranger, closing the door behind him.

Angrily, Janet stalked outside and pulled herself up onto her waiting mouse. She jerked the reins cruelly and rode away. Somehow she would discredit Luna so she would never get another mission opportunity. She and Cara would remain the only active girl members in the resistance.

8

Luna

Luna didn't know exactly when Daniel and Stephen were planning on fulfilling their mission, and for some reason, she wished she would have been the one going. The light was just beginning to show in the sky, but Luna was already riding toward the circle. Having nothing to do at the cabin, she had decided to throw herself into her practice. As she rode, she was careful not to use her right arm. It was still sore, and she hoped she could still shoot evenly. Arriving at the circle, she slid off her mouse and tied her on a long line. She set up her target and stepped back. As she drew back the first arrow, hot pain shot through her arm. Even with the medicine, the old man had warned it could take as long as three weeks to heal. Usually, an injury like this could take months to recover, so she was grateful it wasn't worse.

She set her bow down, discouraged, realizing that she would have to wait at least a few days. She lay on her side, head resting on her palm, on the mossy ground and began to read her copy of the Great Book. She was intrigued by these stories told by ancient people yet recorded for her generation to read. Two hours later, her tired eyes closed, and she fell asleep. The stress and newness of the last few weeks had taken their toll, and now the warm sunshine combined with the story of the faithful follower took her away from the mossy clearing into a land of dreams.

Janet

Janet lay on her bed, her feet propped up on the footboard, contemplating the day ahead of her. If Carl had wanted Luna to do a mission the night before, he might think of one for her to do today. Janet could not let that happen. She reasoned that if Carl was to lose any respect he had for Luna, she would need to discredit her somehow. Then he might even send her away. A plan slowly formed in her mind. She had heard several people lamenting Luna's mishaps on the trial day. What would happen if everyone thought Luna had planted the disasters for herself? If people thought she had placed the bramble on the mouse and cut the grass braids holding the raft beforehand, and had just done it to get Janet in trouble—if they thought that Luna was the troublemaker, then maybe they would send her back where she had come from. Janet smiled at this. Happily, she jumped from her bed.

"Cara! Hurry and get ready. We are going to visit Carl."

Luna

"Wake up!"

Luna felt the soft shake on her arm, and when she realized she had been sleeping, she opened her eyes in surprise. Looking up, she saw the face of the mountain man.

"Wake up! I has somethin' I need to tell ya. Yes, I do indeed. Somethin' real important!"

At this, she sat up, yawning.

"I've come to help you now."

"What do you mean?" she asked, sleep still in her eyes.

"Looky, I've never been one to help the resistance folks much, no, sirree. But there's a story, young lady. Yes, there is. And I has my reasons. Yes, I do."

As he kneeled on the grass there beside Luna, he began to tell his story. "When I was a young 'un, it was. Them kings of them two kingdoms...well, they started takin' away us mixlings. They said we was dangerous 'cause some of the young folk, they was mad at them kings. Yes, they was. Them kings had different rules for us mixlings than for regular folk. Them rebels started fightin' back. Yes, they did. They started callin' themselves the rebels. They done ruined the name of all the mixlings. People said it was 'cause we was mixlings that there was trouble."

"Now back in them days I was a man with a family. Yes, I was." The old man's voice became soft and sad as he related this fact to Luna. He paused and looked off into the trees. Luna reached out and touched his arm, and he seemed to come back from far away.

"That's right, missy, me an' my family, we ran off, we did. We found a place far away. Yep, far away from everythin'. There was others too that came with us. We called this place Talenia. It's a fair piece from here. Yes, a fair piece. My pa was alive then, and we farmed the land so as we could eat. Ya, it was a time of much hope and much fear, it was. I loved watchin' them plants grow and watchin' the little 'uns grow too..." Again, he faded off into his memory until she got up and sat on a nearby log.

"Fifteen years later, I was married, and two young 'uns was born...two little girls. That's when the Great Book was found. Yes, it was. Them that could read it taught us to forgive them folks who had accused us and runned us off. Them kings, they made that Great Book their book, even though they did them evil things. They did them things in the name of the Lord of the Book. They done built the shelter for it. People came every year to look at it. At first, the mixlings had to pay to see it. Yes, they did. Sometimes mixlings disappeared on the trip...people like my wife and daughters…I never saw them again." He stopped again and looked away.

"I'm so sorry," Luna said softly.

After a few moments, he looked down and continued, "When some of the mixlings joined up and started the resistance, they followed the Great Book's ways too. Even though they seemed to be helpin' people, I was mad. Yes, I was mad at all of 'em! I blamed all of 'em, an' I hated the Book too. A man offered me cash if I'd help him steal the Great Book. Yes, he did. An' I wanted to hurt 'em, that I did…so I tried it. But it was a trap. Oh yes, it was. That there king made a decree that forbade any mixling to ever lay eyes on that book again because of what I done. Them mixlings who believed in the Great Book and the resistance hated me too, and I was sent away from Talenia."

"I didn't know…no, I didn't." Here he stopped, choked up and unable to speak. "So I've made do on my own since then. I done lived here and there…always hidin', not havin' much to do with nobody. I blamed the resistance at first, but now I see you is just like my oldest girl. She done loved that book and followed it. She was a bookly one if there was any! I know you have become friends with that boy who fished you out of the river. I been watching you two ever since you came here, and you remind me of them days long ago when I had somethin' to believe in. You done helped me to realize that it wasn't the book that ruined my life, no, it wasn't. It was my own choices and some bad folks.

"I'm too old to make much of a difference now. But I don't wanna see ya hurt…that lad is in danger. He is heading into a trap. An old friend from long ago paid me a visit last night. Yes, he did. He had information that yer gonna need. They know that yer friend is comin' to Icelair. They'll be waitin' on the other side of that bridge. Ya gotta tell 'em not to go. An' there's someone on the inside. Someone that's tellin' what you all are plannin'. You gotta be careful, missy." At this, he stopped as if out of breath.

Then with a pat on her shoulder, he struggled to his feet, leaned on his walking stick, and hobbled back into the woods.

Luna sat there stunned. It was like she was still waking up, and the last few minutes were a dream. Stephen and Daniel in danger? What had he said about the mission? As far as she knew, the mission had been kept quiet, and only a few people knew the details other than Stephen and Daniel. Could she trust the old man? She didn't really know him that well. But remembering the earnestness in his sharp blue eyes, her heart urged her to follow his instructions. In haste, she gathered her book and tucked it into her carrying bag, then retrieved her bow and mounted Mitzie. Riding at full speed toward the cabin, she noticed how long her shadow was. *I hope it won't be too late*, she thought desperately. Pushing her mount harder and ignoring the pain in her arm, she rode with all her might.

Ten minutes later, Luna ran into the cabin. "Carl? Stephen?"

Why did she think they would be here? Turning and running back the way she had come, she collided uncomfortably with the last person she wanted to see: Janet.

Janet

"Luna! How nice to see you!" Janet greeted Luna smoothly.

"Where's Carl? I have something to discuss with him."

"I don't know, I was looking for him too."

Luna's answer only angered Janet, who feared Luna might be looking for Carl to complain about the trial.

"Sorry, Janet, I don't have much time right now," Luna said as she untied and mounted Mitzie. She spun her mouse around and urged her to run again.

She must be up to something, Janet thought. Quickly, she too climbed atop her mouse and trailed after Luna. After a few minutes, she realized where Luna was going. Carl's tent was near the place that the trial had taken place, almost an hour's ride from there. She felt inclined not to go, but curiosity as to why Luna was so insistent changed her mind. Leaning forward, she determined she would arrive first, turning her mouse down a shortcut that she had discovered several months ago.

Sometimes she asked herself why she cared so much about the resistance. It wasn't its cause certainly; she didn't really care if she never saw another mixling. Maybe it was because she was somewhat important to the leaders, and for the most part, they bent to her wishes, or at least that was the way it was before Luna came along.

Luna

Luna sped into the small clearing where Carl's tent was hidden. Mitzie was breathing hard, and Luna worried lest she harm her mouse by pushing her too hard. She slid off and tied her to a bush. As Luna came around the corner, she was surprised to see that Janet had arrived ahead of her.

She could hear Janet's wining voice. "I'm serious. If you don't believe me, I'll tell my dad to talk to you."

Luna stepped forward, slightly out of breath, and addressed Carl. "I have something important that I need to tell you about," she said softly.

He glanced at her and then back at Janet. "Go ahead."

"Is it possible I speak privately with you?" she asked.

"There are no secrets in the resistance," spoke up Janet.

Carl said nothing, and time was passing.

"Where's Stephen?" Luna asked with an edge of concern in her voice.

"He left with Daniel two hours ago. What was so important that you had to come so far to tell me?" His voice wasn't unkind but did have a ring of no-nonsense responsibility. Seeing her troubled glance toward Janet, he assured her that Janet could hear whatever news she had to tell.

"Stephen and Daniel aren't safe! They are riding into a trap!" she said this with an urgent voice, hoping he would realize the truth and not make her explain it in front of Janet.

"Why do you think that?"

"A friend told me."

"Who?" She swallowed hard and hoped he would believe her. "An old man that I'm friends with."

This answer seemed to settle his question, but his eyebrows rose in surprise. "An old man?" he said, in more of a statement than a question.

"I know who she's talking about," Janet intervened. "He's the crazy hermit that lives in that old cart with his so-called pet." She said this with a perfect smile and an attitude of sureness.

Luna protested, "He isn't crazy. He knew exactly where Daniel and Stephen were going and even why. He has a friend who told him there would be soldiers waiting for them on the other side of the dividing bridge!" An urgent note crept into her voice.

Janet jumped in again. "Look, Luna, just because you didn't get to go on the mission doesn't mean you have to ruin it for the right team. You're just jealous and can't stand the idea someone else will get credit for being the hero."

"That isn't true! They are in danger, and you've got to send someone to stop them!" Her voice raised, and her eyes silently begged Carl to listen.

"Look here, girls, I don't have time to stand around and listen to you two fight about who's right. I know the old man you're talking about, Luna. He has been responsible for mishaps within the resistance in the past, and his stories just aren't trustworthy. Go home and forget about it."

"Listen please!"

Tears gathered in her eyes as she watched Carl's back retreating toward the far side of the camp. Had he been angry with her?

She couldn't tell. She avoided looking toward Janet; she already knew what she would find on her plastic face. Remounting, she rode slowly toward the cabin, not knowing what to do any longer. At this moment, Daniel and Stephen where heading toward the bridge, and she was powerless to stop them—or was she?

9

Luna

A million thoughts ran through Luna's mind as she considered what to do. She remembered the old path she had learned to ride on. Her uncle had created the path for her; how, she had no idea. It had so much foliage on both sides that it was completely protected, and the entrance was well hidden. It went more than halfway to Icelair from Sandar. She now knew what to do. She wrapped her hair and tucked it into the back of her cloak, hoping no one would be curious about who she was. Turning her mouse around, she headed full speed toward Sandar. She would have to ride in the open across two very busy roads. It would be risky.

Ever since she had gotten into the resistance, Stephen had seemed to watch out for her: supervising her training, scolding the two girls for flipping her boat. He had been there to see if she was okay when she fell off the mouse. During the trials, he had helped her onto his raft when he could have left her there to swim. It was her turn to help him, and if it was in her power, she would not let him and Daniel ride across that bridge into a trap.

The regular trail to Icelair took about three hours from Sandar, which meant she had less than an hour to reach the bridge. The sandy plains of Sandar greeted her as she came to the edge of the woods. She could see a line of soldiers guarding the perimeter of the settlement. She remembered Carl telling the resistance members that it appeared that there were changes taking place along the city borders. This trip could be much more dangerous than she thought.

She was almost within view of her old house. If she could just get to the old riding trail! She would first have to cross this open area in front of her. Would she be noticed? The stretch ahead of her was clear, but she knew that as soon as she emerged, she would be visible to all. Before she set out, she sent a prayer to the Maker of the book. Then setting her eyes on her destination, she took off at full speed.

Stephen

The Icelair bridge was right in front of them. He and Stephen had stopped momentarily to survey their surroundings. As Stephen observed the sand/ice bridge, he carefully ran through the rest of the plan in his mind. "Think we should wait till dark?"

"Nah, the sun's already going down anyways. It'll be the same now or later." Daniel sounded sure of himself as he referred to the bridge. Stephen thought it odd that Daniel was so careless about their approach. He had always been the more cautious of the two.

They mounted, riding to the edge of the forest. "Okay, let's race. We'll meet in the woods on the far side of Icelair," Daniel instructed. He crouched low over his mouse. Stephen hesitated.

"Ready, set—"

"stop!"

The call came from behind them, and they both wheeled around in surprise. Luna pulled her mouse to a stop, breathing heavily.

"What are you doing—" Daniel started with a growl then changed his tone after a stern glance from Stephen.

"Luna, you've got to be crazy!" This time, Stephen scolded her.

"Listen, you can't cross the bridge! They know you're coming! It's a trap."

Stephen noticed the concern in her voice and hoped she was wrong.

"Look, Luna, you are new here and couldn't possibly know anything we don't. You're interfering with our mission," Daniel said firmly, staring at her in a strange way.

Luna rode in front of them defiantly. "I'm serious! A friend warned me and said they would be waiting for you on the other end. You can't go across the bridge!"

"Did you talk to Carl?" Stephen asked.

"Yes," Luna replied.

Daniel interrupted, "And let me guess...he didn't believe you!"

"I'm telling the truth!" Luna exclaimed with mounting frustration.

"Look, Luna, it's nice of you to care, but if Carl didn't think it was important, it probably isn't. We have a mission to take care of. Go back home, and we'll forget about it," Stephen spoke kindly. "Anyway, no one knows about the mission except for a few trusted resistance members."

Luna frowned. "My friend also said that someone in the resistance is a spy."

"Oh, come on!" interjected Daniel with impatience. "Now, that is just nonsense! Everyone is thoroughly screened, and there is no way there is a spy! We really don't have time for this!"

"You just won't listen to me," Luna said in disbelief. "If the resistance lost you two, it would be a tragedy, and both of you know too much! I trust the person who told me, and even if you don't believe me, I know it's true."

Taking her carrying bag, bow, and arrows off her back, she handed them to Stephen. "Here, hold these. I will prove that what I said is true."

"What..." Stephen sat holding her things, wondering how she was going to show them.

She suddenly wheeled her mouse in the direction of the bridge, and before Daniel or Stephen could do anything, she was on the bridge, riding fast. Stephen and Daniel watched her ride, openmouthed, uncertain of what was about to occur. Her cloak extended out behind her, flapping in the wind as if waving good-bye. Time seemed to pass slowly, and with rising horror, Stephen realized she wasn't coming back.

10

Stephen

Stephen and Daniel couldn't see the other end of the bridge clearly, but suddenly the evening stillness was broken by shouts and loud voices. They waited uncertainly in the tall grass for over an hour for Luna, but she still had not reappeared. Finally, Daniel, who had been pacing back and forth, suggested that Stephen return to the cabin and inform Carl that the mission was off for now. He said he would wait for another hour to see if Luna would return. Stephen was reluctant to leave but in the end acquiesced to Daniel's repeated urgings. Although Stephen hadn't objected, he personally was worried. If she had been captured, he wondered what they would do with her. Many mixlings had disappeared, but no one knew for sure where they had been taken. Some thought they were kept in the dungeon of the castle, but there were rumors that there was another place. He hadn't planned on feeling so responsible for Luna, but he just couldn't stop thinking about her. He looked down at her belongings, and a pang of guilt washed over him. He should have listened to her warning.

When Stephen had come back from the failed mission and explained what had happened, Carl became furious and then seemed so uncharacteristically worried that Stephen left the cabin feeling confused. They had, in the end, decided to give her until tomorrow. Sometimes he hated having to be an outcast. It was the rebels' fault he told himself, but he knew many people were to blame. Now the people in the main cities couldn't stand the sight of mixlings. Many people had reported their neighbors who had been childhood friends. He now wished he would have believed Luna, turned around, and forgotten the mission. But that was not the choice he had made. Now they had failed their mission and lost Luna too.

Frowning, he walked to the practice circle. He sat down gingerly on the damp moss next to a mushroom. At first, the smell of fungus almost overwhelmed him, and he nearly got up to find a better place to sit. But the moss was thick and comfortable, and after a minute, the smell seemed to fade away. It was dark, and the dew was growing on every blade of grass. The water droplets seemed to glow all around him in the moonlight. Staring at the sky, he wondered why Carl hadn't sent out search parties right away. He seemed so concerned about Luna's safety, but he also always seemed to be angry at her. Stephen sometimes wondered if Carl was concerned about Luna or just worried that her uncle, Mr. Matthias, would be angry if something happened to her.

The top people in the resistance knew Mr. Matthias was one of the best medicine researchers in any of the settlements, although he didn't disclose this fact to everyone. Mr. Matthias could create almost any medicine. The one he most supplied to the resistance was "wound curer." If applied to an open wound, it would heal three times faster than it would without the medicine. There was another for broken bones, which could help heal a bone in half the time that a regular break took to heal. Mr. Matthias also provided them with valuable information from the Sandar castle since he worked there as the top mouse trainer. The resistance could not afford to make Mr. Matthias angry—nor let him down.

As he contemplated all this, he also thought of going to look for Luna himself. But Carl would be angry if he went off on his own without orders. So Stephen sat there, in the dark, and prayed to the Lord of the Book to protect Luna and help everything turn out right. He was sure Luna was on everyone's mind that night. The stars shone brightly above the dark shapes of the trees and grass, and he listened to the night sounds around him. As Stephen sat there praying for Luna's safety, a dark figure rode swiftly through the night forest, ahead, full force, and determined.

The Castle of Icelair

Guards readily opened the huge door to the cloaked figure standing without. Elsiper sat atop his throne, a greedy smile on his face as he observed the man come before him. "We have him?" his voice rang against the glistening ice walls.

"The plan was revealed, and he never rode across the bridge…" The messenger's voice was quiet and trembling slightly.

"Outrageous!" the new king shouted, slamming his fist against his majestic seat. Standing up, he began to pace. "Why? I demand an explanation!" His voice was controlled now, but one could easily hear the anger entwined in each word.

"Tell me why!" Again, he lost control as neither the timid guards nor the brave messenger were forthcoming. His voice echoed eerily throughout the cavernous room. "I hired you to do a job! Now you can do it or you can't! I don't appreciate failures. It took me long enough to get here, and my plans won't be ruined by a daydreamer! Do you hear me?"

The king descended the icy steps and now glared into the face of the messenger. His voice was frosty clear as it reverberated against the echoing walls. His face was flushed with rage, and he dared anyone to cross him with his withering look.

"We captured a girl," the dark figure finally mustered to report.

"A girl?" He snorted. "Ahhh, yes, a girl." He closed his eyes, and his lip curled dangerously. "What will we do with her?

Put her to work in the kitchen?" Sarcasm tinged his voice, but nobody dared laugh. "I am not paying you to catch *dishwashers*! I am hiring you to bring the *resistance* down! And if you can't do the simple assignments I give you, I'm sure I can find another desperate creature to relieve you, as well as remove your dear sister from her miserable existence. ya?"

"Yes, sir..." The messenger slowly retreated back to the cold outside.

Desperation gripped him as he contemplated what to do. The wind whipped his hair into his eyes. If he failed, there was no telling what the king would do. The threat to injure his sister had never been carried out, but what if? He remembered another cold night a long time ago when all of this had begun. He and Diana had been walking through the dark night, trying to reach shelter on the outskirts of the city.

"Are we almost there?"

"No, Diana, it's a bit farther, but it's worth it. You'll like it. It's perfect, and I made it just for you."

"You're the best brother ever." Her small hand had grasped his hand, which had been trembling from a combination of fear and cold.

He shivered and tried to clear those memories, which followed him like ghosts. He hadn't seen her for those seven years. That sweet nine-year-old would now be sixteen. Would she even remember him anymore?

Elsiper was not known for his kindness, especially judging by what he had already done to become the next king. The beautiful queen and her son flashed into his mind. Their fate troubled his sad heart for only a moment. This girl must join them; if she returned to the resistance, she would only cause trouble. And the last thing he needed now was more trouble.

Diana

Diana stared out the foggy window. This evening was like all the ones that had come before it. A tear rolled down her pale cheek. She wiped it away as she tried to think of cheerier things.

"Di, I'm here."

She turned expectantly and greeted Sven. He was always there. A castle guard, he was the one who had kept her going for what was it now? Seven years? She welcomed his company as she did all other nights. His stories and cheer always lifted her spirits.

"Have you been crying again?" She noticed the dismay in his voice.

"No." She looked at her boots in shame.

"I've told you before, no crying. I have news that will make you smile and fill this room with sunshine."

Diana tried to feel brighter. "What is it?"

"You're going to leave this place!"

"I'm…I'm going back to my brother?" she asked hopefully.

"No, but I've found a way to get you to safety. You're going to live with my grandmother, and no one will be the wiser…and someday I will marry you. I will wait for you and for the day when you can be free. But I'm sure your brother will eventually find you again. Maybe soon."

She tried to be grateful to leave the gray room that had been her home for the last seven years, but she couldn't help but feel the burden she carried become heavier. Would she ever see her brother again? What had become of him in the past seven years?

Luna

It had been at least four hours since Luna rode across that bridge. Her arms ached from the uncomfortable position they had tied her in. Luna thought again how the scene on the bridge had played out: racing across the bridge and then being surrounded by soldiers, just as the old man had told her. She had tried to excuse herself by saying she had just been out riding, but the soldiers had refused to believe her story. They had pulled off her hood and easily discovered that she was a mixling. She had been standing here tied to this post ever since. Several times she had attempted to slip her wrists free, but it was useless.

The two guards had long since fallen asleep by the fire.

"Pssst!"

A whisper behind her caught her attention. Try as she might, she could not turn her head around to see who had called out to her. Her wrists were pulled as far up behind her back as possible, and any movement was restricted.

"Hold still, that's right, hold still," whispered a familiar voice.

A small smile of relief spread across her face as she recognized the voice. The old man had come to rescue her! She felt his gruff hands laboriously untying the rope that held her. It loosened but not fast enough. Approaching footsteps and voices announced the arrival of more soldiers.

"Hurry," she whispered, although she knew it would make no difference. Before, she had given up hope of escape, but now that it was so close, excitement pulled her nerves tight as a bow. As the ropes fell loose and the old man retreated into the woods, a man wearing a hooded black cloak and three guards stepped into the dim firelight.

"Wake up!" the cloaked man yelled angrily at the two sleeping guards. They jumped to their feet and quickly looked to Luna, as if frightened she might have gone somewhere in their slumber. Luna held her aching arms steadily behind her as if they were still tied.

"Take her to *the place*," the hooded figure commanded angrily, still bothered by their carelessness.

"T-to the place?" the older soldier questioned in a voice that made Luna pray even harder she could escape.

"Would you like to join her?" the testy voice challenged the questioner.

Luna was observant as they moved toward her post. In the back of her mind stirred a feeling that there was something familiar about the man in the cloak. She couldn't see his face, and she was uncertain what had made her think so. But now was not the time for thought. It was time for action. She took a deep breath and waited for her chance.

As the guard advanced and went around the left side of the post, Luna quickly ducked to the right and began running for the woods. She hoped the old man had retrieved Mitzie. As she dashed headlong into the outskirts of the woods, her foot caught on a vine, sending her sprawling. Pain shot through her shoulder as she felt it hit the ground. She gathered herself, the sounds of yelling voices and running feet behind her. As she placed the offending foot to the ground, it almost buckled beneath her.

"Dear Lord of the Book, please help me!" she prayed desperately as she stumbled and fell through the dark foreboding forest of boulders, undergrowth, and tall grass.

Stephen

Stephen woke with a start. The wet mossy ground had cooled, and he felt chilled as he got to his feet. How long had he slept? It was still dark, but the eastern sky was lighter than the west. It must be nearing dawn. Now Luna was just taking too long. Somehow Stephen knew something wasn't right. He didn't want to go against orders, but he couldn't stand just doing nothing either. He tried telling himself it was his imagination, and she was probably just embarrassed to tell everyone she had been wrong about the old man. She'll probably be back in the morning with some wild story. Even as he reasoned with himself, he was already mounted.

Where would she go? If she was captured, she would probably be in Icelair since that was where she had disappeared. He rode toward Icelair with anxiousness and caution. He noticed the eerie darkness as he got into the thick grasses; the dense forest seemed to close in on him. Even though he assured himself there was nothing to be afraid of, he felt a huge foreboding, like a black cloud above his head. He stopped uncertainly and thought of owls. Owls were large birds that could swoop down without a sound and snatch up a man and his mouse in a second. They often took mice that were left outside in the night. He shook his head, trying to dispel the thought. He was letting his imagination get the best of him.

A rustling sound in the grass ahead made his heart pound in his ears. His mouse's ears twitched nervously, and it shied suddenly, making him almost lose his seat. Suddenly, another mouse with two riders came crashing through the grass. In the early dawn light, he could make out the form of a large man hunched over the mouse's neck, and behind him, he recognized the familiar blue cloak that Luna always wore. It appeared torn and dirty, and he could see that something was wrong.

"Luna!" he called, as the mouse came to a halt.

Luna slid down from the back, and Stephen could see that she stood with effort. "Hey." Her voice trembled slightly. She had a cut on her forehead and many scratches on her hands and arms. Her hair was disheveled and dotted with bits of grass and leaves, and her clothes splattered with mud.

The old man leaned forward heavily on his mouse. "I'd best be off," he said as he turned and rode off into the dark forest. Luna looked on worriedly as he rode away.

Stephen didn't know whether to feel relieved or angry. "What were you thinking back there?" he scolded.

She looked at him and wavered for a moment. "Look, Stephen, you've done a lot for me since I've been a part of the resistance. I knew he was right. I couldn't let you walk into a trap. And he was right. They were waiting."

Part of him was angry. She shouldn't have just gone out on her own. She could have been hurt or worse. She turned and started limping toward the cabin.

"Come on, get up behind me," Stephen offered.

She didn't resist, and he could tell she was in some sort of pain. She made no mention of her mouse. He supposed it had been taken by the guards in Icelair.

Without a word, they headed back toward the cabin. The sun came up, golden and glorious, much too cheerful for the way either of them felt. Stephen thought about the other thing Luna had warned of before she had so brashly taken off across the bridge: "There is a spy in the resistance." Could that really be true? The screening for resistance members was so thorough. Stephen couldn't think of anyone who could be a spy. There were very few new members these days, and those who had been members for years would have no conceivable reason to spy on the group.

When they arrived, she slid off the mouse wordlessly and moved toward the door. She paused a minute, swaying slightly, and straightened her cloak before entering.

"Where have you been?" Carl's voice, louder than usual, greeted them both.

"There were soldiers on the other side of the bridge. I was detained." Luna's voice sounded tired as she walked across the room and waited for a response.

"We'll discuss the assignment in the morning."

Carl dismissed the others. When the room was empty except for the three of them, Carl stood, staring at Luna for nearly a minute before he spoke, "And they let you go?"

"No, I had some help escaping. The old man untied me and carried me most of the way back on his mouse."

"The old man..." Carl paused. "I see. So he was involved in this too." Carl seemed troubled. "And did he say who had given him this information about the mission?"

"No, he just said an old friend had visited him the night before and told him," Luna replied wearily. "And that there was someone on the inside who had informed them about the mission," she added. She swayed and put her hand on a chair to steady herself.

"Well, go get some rest. I'm glad you were able to return in one piece," Carl said with a gruffer than necessary voice.

Luna nodded, and Stephen watched as she retreated into her room and closed the door softly. Carl sighed and sat down heavily on his chair. He looked worried and a little angry.

Stephen left with a worried feeling. Why was Carl acting so agitated with Luna? Weren't they all supposed to be supportive of one another? Even so, he himself was running low on patience. The mission to search for the heir had gone awry. And with all these important things going on, why did they have to have the distraction of a new girl?

———◦∘◦❧◈❧◦∘◦———

Luna sat painfully on her bed after throwing her cloak across a chair. She examined a long scratch down one arm. She was trembling slightly and felt drained of energy. She paused a minute and thought of the events that had happened so quickly. She had been running through the forest when there were two soldiers in front of her; it had been too late to stop when she saw them. She had pulled and struggled but in vain. Then all of a sudden, the old man intervened again. In that moment, she broke free and ran through the maze of grass and rocks, falling several times. She had obtained several scratches and bruises, as well as the cut on her forehead in her flight.

Taking a flask of medicine from her carrying bag, she applied it to her scratches and the cut. She smiled to think that tomorrow, most evidence of her injury would be gone, all except the throbbing in her head and twisted ankle. Luna relaxed back on the soft bed beneath her. *How did the old man know I was in trouble?* she thought reflectively. And why had Stephen come looking for her? He had always seemed aloof and not very happy about her presence, although he had been helpful to her during the trials.

She wondered if the old man was okay. He had seemed weak and almost ill on the ride back to the resistance. She hoped he hadn't been hurt in the struggle with the guards and decided she would have to go and check on him in the morning.

As Luna turned her head toward the wall, she noticed a small picture propped on her bedside table. She had put it there the first night when she had unpacked. How long ago that seemed. "Two weeks and three days," she muttered softly.

Luna wondered if her uncle sang Nio to sleep. She wondered if her uncle remembered to cook Nio's eggs extra long, the way Nio liked them. And lastly, she wondered how Nio would fall asleep without the story she told him every night. It had been a routine ever since he was old enough to walk. She would make a wild tale, weaving it from her imagination and then she would pray with him before he drifted off to sleep. Her uncle had often called her Nio's little mother.

Homesickness overwhelmed her, and she felt tears running down her cheeks. She missed her family so much; and as much as she would miss the outdoors, in her heart, she knew what she really wanted was to be with them. Hugging one of the pillows on her bed, she fell asleep, sadly remembering Nio's face, his smile, and his laughter.

"I don't know why you would even consider her!" the voice screeched.

Luna jumped to a sitting position on her bed. The sun was high in the sky and poured through the window brightly. How had she slept so long? It seemed just a second ago she had been remembering—here she cut herself off. "I won't ruin a perfect day feeling sorry for myself," she commanded her thoughts. She stretched stiffly and cautiously stood. Her legs were sore, but she was feeling much stronger. She hastily changed into a pale blue jumper. She could hear the rise and fall of voices in the meeting room. It sounded like an argument.

Slipping out the open window, she silently tiptoed to the full water barrel along the back of the cabin. "Please, please, please, stay inside!" she whispered to herself, hoping that no one would see her in her current state. With her wet hands, she smoothed down her hair and dipped them again into the clear water, splashing it on her sleep-marked face.

A tap on her shoulder brought her spinning around. An alarmed look greeted the person behind her. "Don't do that!" she exclaimed, a scowl in her voice as well as on her face. The grin that Stephen wore was extremely annoying.

"I think they're waiting in there for you," he said. The fact that he was suppressing laughter was even more annoying to Luna as she tried frantically to arrange her hair in a presentable fashion.

"I'm coming."

"I guess everyone has their bad mornings," Stephen sputtered. This time, the humor in his voice was completely audible.

Luna turned to stare at his retreating back in agitation. "He enjoyed that," she muttered. She had not appreciated his prank.

When she was halfway satisfied with her presentation, she again entered the cabin through the bedroom window. Putting on her worn boots and quickly smoothing the ruffled bed, she went to the door. She could still hear arguing on the other side.

"I don't know what your problem is! She is skilled. In fact, she beat you in the contest despite the problems she had, and she even went back to help you."

"That isn't much to say! She set those things up for herself so you would feel sorry for her."

Luna grimaced as she recognized the whining voice at last. She hated to eavesdrop, especially when it was about her.

Never listen in to other people's conversations. It will only cause misunderstandings, which will hurt everyone in the end. Her uncle's voice seemed to sound in her head with one of his most known sayings. She let her thoughts flicker to that unpleasant event for one second. The conversation she had overheard was her uncle and his brother talking. They had been talking about a "she" who was extremely annoying to keep and how they couldn't stand it any longer. Of course, Luna had taken it the wrong way. Being only ten at the time, no other reasonable explanation came to mind other than that they were talking about her. After two months of buried hurt feelings, she had finally confronted her uncle about it. He had explained with laughter that it had been an exotic beetle they were talking about. A small smile touched her lips as she mentally gathered the courage to enter the turmoil in the room beyond the door. Breathing in deeply then letting it out, she turned the handle.

Stephen

Stephen watched in silence from the doorway. He had to bite his lower lip to keep from smiling as he remembered Luna's face when she had turned from the water barrel. He had seen her there with bare feet and the window open and had plainly guessed she had overslept. After last night, that wasn't a surprise. Whether others believed it or not, he did have a sense of humor, just not many opportunities to put it to practice. Startling Luna had been one of those rare opportunities!

"Stephen!"

A rough voice pushed these amusing thoughts to the back of his mind. He tried to focus on the person addressing him.

"What do you think?" he repeated.

Stephen hardly knew what they were talking about; it was something about Luna. "Um...well...maybe everyone else should summarize their ideas in a more orderly fashion so I can decide." He noticed, with a little disdain, that Luna, who had just made her entrance, concealed a smile.

The smile was soon gone, however, when she heard Janet's comment: "You never know how someone who would set up false problems for herself on a trial would handle an assignment like that." Her voice was wheedling and delivered with a smile, but everyone heard the underlying challenge it put forth.

Stephen noticed the entire room looked toward Luna, who wore a disbelieving mask. "Oh yes, I came early and rigged the mouse seat, unwound my raft, and cut my mouse loose from the tree, where she wasn't even tied until minutes before we got there." Her voice was calm, but everyone could read the suggested anger.

"Oh, did I mention someone who makes up silly stories because she wanted a certain mission?" retorted Janet.

Stephen saw the anger flicker across Luna's face, although she quickly covered it.

"And what about yesterday?" Luna said as she turned and looked directly at her attacker.

To this, Janet paused and thought a minute. "How are we supposed to know there really were soldiers? You know it's not fun being proven wrong," wheedled Janet.

At this, Luna's anger was slightly more noticeable. "No, it isn't fun, and I wonder how you would know?"

Janet turned red at this and turned to Carl and almost yelled, "See, and now she's calling me a liar!"

Luna looked slightly embarrassed. "Look," Luna's clear and controlled voice interrupted the rising murmurs that were growing around the room. "I don't know what this assignment is, and I don't understand what the problem is here, but I really have some training to catch up on. If it's okay with Carl, I would like to excuse myself and let you all decide what you will."

At Carl's slight nod, she walked stiffly across the room, picked up her bow, arrows, and cloak, then brushed past all of them out the door.

After watching her leave the cabin and walk into the woods, Stephen turned his attention back to the stress-packed room.

Daniel was saying, "I don't agree with Janet. In fact, I think Luna should train him."

As Stephen looked with surprise toward Daniel, he realized, by the grin on Daniel's face, that he was enjoying the argument. Daniel had, from the beginning, scoffed at everything Luna had done. Why was he now being so supportive? Something niggled at the edges of Stephen's mind, but he put it aside and tried to focus on the conversation as it shifted from one to another.

They were talking about Key. His father had joined the Talenian Arrangement Board years before and recently enrolled his fourteen-year-old son into the resistance. Key's cousin was the chief strategy engineer's son, Johan. At sixteen, Johan had extraordinary talent with bows and arrows, as well as fixing things. "He takes after his father," many had said, meaning the strategy engineer's many invention skills. Again, he realized his thoughts had strayed from the matter at hand.

Stephen decided that if someone were to train Key, why shouldn't it be Luna? At least, it would keep her busy. Stephen broke into the arguing. "I think Luna would be a good choice, considering the circumstances."

The room was suddenly quiet. Carl looked at him surprised. "Your reason?"

After thinking a minute, he continued, "Her skills at the trial, despite the complications, are proof she knows her stuff. Besides, it would keep her busy."

"But she—" interrupted Janet petulantly.

Stephen overrode her comment. "No, we don't know that she created those mishaps for herself, that just doesn't make sense." He looked hard at Janet. She was really beginning to get to him.

Janet was red with anger but held her tongue.

"Go find her, Stephen, and tell her our decision," Carl commanded. For some reason, it made Stephen happy that Luna would be training Key.

———∘oo⦗◈⦘ooo———

Luna

Luna couldn't help but feel upset. Why was Janet trying to turn everyone against her? Some of the things that she had said had gone deep. She never made up stories! And why did it seem the others believed Janet? And why wouldn't they listen to her warnings from the old man? She had been captured. It seemed as if they didn't believe that either. Sometimes everything seemed too complicated to figure out. She didn't really know where she was going. She was just going anywhere, away from the cabin.

She stopped suddenly, and looking around, she saw that without realizing it, she had come to the little clearing where the old man lived. Or had she realized it? "I hate how things have become so muddled!" she muttered, kicking a small stone out of her way. She did want to see how he was anyway.

She stood looking at the trees for a second while she sent up a quick prayer for guidance and then entered the clearing. It was like the last time, everything pleasantly disorganized, the mice curled up in the leaves waiting. Luna wondered where the old man was. His walking stick, which she had always seen him with, stood leaning against the covered cart. Suddenly she looked around uneasily. Something wasn't right. She went toward the fire pit, a strange feeling pulling at her heart. She called out to the old man, but there was no answer. It didn't feel safe and special, the way it had when she was here before. She felt cold and alone. A shiver ran down her arms as she surveyed the smoldering fire ring.

Luna gasped. She could see a crumpled form lying on the ground on the other side of the cart. Dropping her things, she ran and knelt beside the old man. A cold wave of fear went through her like a shock. Kneeling beside the old man's form, she reached for his wrinkled hand. "Wake up!" she said softly. No sound greeted her anxious words. "Please! Wake up!" Her voice reduced to a whisper as she finished the plea. Warm and bitter tears pushed at the back of her eyes as she studied the kind face that had cheered her when she had felt alone.

A slight moan made her tense. The old man opened his eyes. "Luna," his voice was so soft, so small, and just barely audible.

"You're going to be okay," her voice cheered him.

"No…no, I'm not," he whispered softly, squeezing her hand. "My time has come."

"Oh, please don't say that." A catch broke her voice as she stared lovingly down at his face. She had only known him shortly; in fact, she had only seen him three times in all, but it seemed she had known him all her life.

"You've got to take care of my pet, teach her to be bookly, like you." Again, his voice was only a whisper.

"Sure, I promise." Luna laid a shaking hand on his old shoulder.

"I've lived a long time. So proud…meet you." His voice began breaking up, and he breathed with more effort. "Take…care…bookly…" he mumbled, and she knew he was repeating his previous request.

"Promise," she whispered through her tears.

"Don't worry…me. Found Lord in…book. Coming…for…me."

She smiled down at his faded blue eyes and touched his weathered cheek.

"Elsip…glass…city…every mixling…prisoner…careful…"

She watched helpless as he took one last breath. Then his head fell to the side, a peaceful smile on his face. "No, please!" she begged him softly, but she knew it was too late. Crying, she sat there and realized she would never be able to talk to him again.

At the Border of the Woods

The guards were everywhere. In supervision, a man in a black cloak pointed them to their stations. Although he had chosen this life, being bound to the king in exchange for the safety of his sister, second thoughts were hard to quiet. Something was being done that had never been done before. The border was now peppered with soldiers. As the shrouded figure surveyed the scene, he put on an air of confidence. These men must respect him, and if they didn't, all would be lost.

"Everyone is so unsuspecting," he heard a voice at his side declare with a satisfied smile.

"Be quiet and get back to work!" the troubled leader silenced his follower.

Would he ever be able to silence the guilt in his own mind? The trusting looks of those in the resistance? Those deep sad eyes of the children he sent to a place of certain hardship? He shook his head trying to clear his mind. Concentration and focus— that's what would keep him going. The command had been passed this morning:

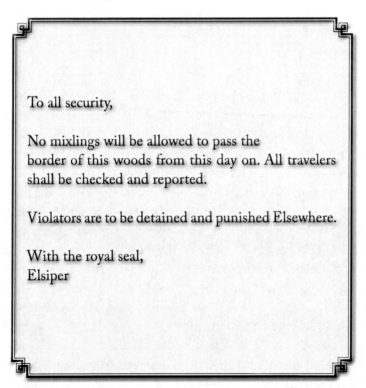

To all security,

No mixlings will be allowed to pass the border of this woods from this day on. All travelers shall be checked and reported.

Violators are to be detained and punished Elsewhere.

With the royal seal,
Elsiper

Elsewhere was another word for—no, he wouldn't think of that. He must learn to control his thoughts.

"The resistance will receive no more members from this side of the island," his second-in-command informed him as he pushed past, heading back toward the castle.

That should make the king happy, he thought ruefully as he watched him leave. *When will he stop hurting people?* He shook his head sadly as he heard the voice of his conscience. He thought again of his sister and the words she said at their parting: "I won't be scared 'cause I know you'll be coming back for me. I love you." The troubled man ducked his head with sadness and watched as the rest of the guards took their positions. Would he ever get back to those trusting green eyes?

Luna

Luna stumbled blindly toward the cabin. Everything had happened so fast. Stephen had been there, telling her that the old man was gone. She had already known this, but it had been hard hearing it out loud. *Why* kept pounding through her head. "And we know that all things work together for good to them that love God, to them who are the called according to his purpose." The verse popped uncalled into her mind. How many times had her uncle said that to her? It was a verse from the Great Book. That was what everyone seemed to believe, but where was the good? She could see no good in any way from the things that had just taken place.

A hand on her shoulder stopped her blundering steps. She knew without being told that Stephen was stopping her so she could get a hold of herself. In a way, Luna almost thought that it was strange to be so sad over the old man. She had only met him three times. But he had been her best friend since she joined the resistance, the only one she felt she could trust and didn't need to impress. She stared down into the water barrel in front of her. She washed her face quickly, fixed her messy hair, and then adjusted her cloak.

"I'm ready," she mumbled.

As they walked toward the cabin, she told herself she would think about the old man later. Right now she needed to concentrate on being strong.

Stephen

After Luna had washed up, Stephen noticed he could hardly tell she had been crying a few minutes before. He gave her a nod when she paused at the cabin door. She sat there at the table, staring at nothing while he explained things to Carl.

"We will bury the body." Carl turned to Luna. "You can take care of whatever is in the wagon since you seem to have been his only friend."

I wonder why he died? And right after the incident of Luna's capture, Stephen thought to himself. Luna didn't seem to have been taking it very well. She must have known him before the time that he came to warn her about the soldiers at the bridge.

But now Stephen felt bad for her. In the beginning, he had hated the idea of another charity case for the resistance. After a few weeks had passed, he had to admit he had come to respect Luna and how she handled herself. Generally, he wanted to be unattached to anyone. Though Daniel was his best friend, he really had few attachments. He contemplated these thoughts as he walked toward the chief strategy engineer's house. He had to tell him about the old man and make arrangements for burying the body. Johan would probably help. Between Johan, Daniel, and himself, they could probably get it done. Thinking on this, he kept walking.

Luna

Luna jerked her head up when she heard the familiar voice.

"Uncle!" she squealed excitedly and threw herself into his arms.

"Whoa, slow down there! You'll knock me off my feet!" He was supposed to be scolding, but laughter brightened the room through his jolly voice.

"I'm so glad to see you!" Luna said this with all of her heart. Turning from her uncle, she hugged Nio, filling his outstretched arms.

Maybe they've come to take me home! The idea made her already big smile grow. "Am I—" She paused for a second as if wondering about the words she was about to say. "Am I going home with you?"

When her uncle heard the question, his happy face turned sad and pained. Immediately, Luna recognized something was wrong. "What's the matter?"

He looked at her and hesitated. "I came here to talk to you. They said it wasn't a good idea that I come at all—"

Here he stopped and looked away as if the next part was too much to say. "It is no longer safe to keep mixlings hidden in the cities. Searches happen every day at random houses. Someone doesn't even have to report anything."

He swallowed and forced himself to look back at her pleading face. "The resistance is having a very hard time getting the people out of the cities any longer. Elsiper has closed the borders of the city, passed new laws. People are disappearing. There are a lot more mixlings than you would have ever thought. They have found at least ten mixlings in the last two days. We have tried to get them out but…most of them never arrived at the resistance. I don't want to worry you, but I can't…just can't let that happen to you. You are much safer here. And you can be an asset to the resistance."

He reached out a hand and stroked her cheek. "I came to say good-bye."

"You came to say g-good-bye?" Her voice broke slightly, and she struggled to keep her chin from trembling.

Everything that had just been said, had it been real? Could this really be happening to her? "Why can't you move out here?" The question seemed selfish and silly as soon as it was out of her mouth.

"If I disappeared from my castle job...it could be very bad for the rest of our family. And I am able to keep track of what is happening from there. Maybe someday things will be different, but for now, I won't be able to see you. The danger is too great. I could be followed and then everything would be compromised."

After this, they talked about many things, both of them holding back tears. Every detail of the visit seemed to scream at them, *Last time! Last time! Last time!* At the end of an hour, and after many reminders about household matters from Luna, came the worst part of the visit. As Luna hugged her uncle good-bye, she told herself not to cry.

"I love you and will always miss you," he whispered softly into her ear.

"Me too." She hardly recognized her own voice.

Before Uncle Matthias opened the door, he brightened and said, "I did bring someone that I think you will be glad to see."

As they walked out together, Luna couldn't believe her eyes. There, tied to the post, was Mitzie. "How did you?"

"She came home this morning with no harness, no bridle. I figured she had gotten away and returned home. Carl filled me in on what happened in Icelair. Now you listen to Carl. He's a good man. I'm so glad you are safe."

"Oh thank you, Uncle Matthias!" Luna hugged him again. She gave Nio one last hug and kiss as they mounted the mouse and turned to go.

As Uncle Matthias and Nio rode off into the distance, she turned to Mitzie with agony in her heart. She was thankful to have her mouse back but so sad at the finality of saying good-bye.

She buried her face in Mitzie's soft fur and tried to absorb what had just transpired. "Why is this all happening?" She tried to smother the depressed thoughts that threatened to fill her mind. She felt as if all good things were very far away.

11

Luna

The sweet smell of the large flowers above Luna tickled her nose. She had found the smallest ones in the whole forest. She knew that the old man would no longer be there with his sparkling blue eyes and wild white hair to greet her. They would have taken care of him by now, but still she wanted to pay some sort of respect. She smiled a little as she thought of the last minutes she had with him, and he had managed to tell her he had found the Lord of the Book. Suddenly, a puzzled thought edged its way into her already busy brain. How would someone teach a pet to be bookly? And what pet? She had only seen two mice in the clearing. She pondered this as she entered the clearing. Everything was exactly as she had left it except that the body of the old man was gone. Going to the place where he had been, she laid the flowers softly on the ground.

As Luna stood, she tripped on her cloak, which was hanging over her arm. Falling against the cart, she jarred it. As she turned to leave, she heard a soft crying kind of sound. With a slightly shaking hand, she drew back the woven cloth from the doorway of the cart. A bundle on the far bed in the back of the wagon was moving slightly and making the noise. The clutter was considerable, and Luna almost didn't feel right walking through the now deserted living area, but she couldn't help her curiosity. After all, she had promised the old man to take care of his pet. Surely the bundle must contain it.

As she neared the wriggling bundle, she could see it was pinned closed. Reaching out, she carefully removed the pin. As the blanket unfolded, her sharp intake of breath broke the stillness. Staring up at her from the slightly soiled blankets was the prettiest little girl she had ever seen. Bright blue eyes set in an extremely light-tanned face smiled in curiosity at her. She studied the baby's small face who responded by extending her pudgy arms out to Luna. No one, not the strongest person on earth, could have resisted that adorable face. Reaching down, Luna scooped the tiny body up; beautiful pale-golden curls fell down the baby's shoulders. Cradling her in front, Luna addressed a question, "What's your name, baby?"

"Oooee." It was more of a giggle than a name.

"How old are you?" It pleased Luna when three tiny fingers responded. "At least I know how old you are!" She laughed softly, and she realized with surprise that she actually felt happy for a moment.

Setting the child on the bed, she searched in the small wooden barrels sitting nearby and soon discovered that one held food and the other clothing for her new charge. A whimper turned her attention back to the little girl on the bed. Going back, she scooped her up.

"You need some cleaning up," she said through her smile.

She held her while she looked around and stuffed several outfits into her carrying bag. She found a pale-blue dress and some small shoes and laid them out on the bed. She found a cloth and a pot of water and a small sliver of soap. She cleaned the child and changed her clothing then wrapped her in a small clean blanket.

Then slipping on her cloak, she checked herself in the large piece of glass sitting against one side of the bed. Luna noticed that if she held the little girl against her middle, the bulge was hardly noticeable. Smiling, she returned to her mouse and made her way back to the cabin. She would take care of the girl just for a bit and then ask to send her to a nice family in Talenia.

When Luna returned to the cabin, she was surprised to see Carl and some other resistance representatives standing in the meeting room waiting for her. She had tied her mouse quickly at the post outside for the first time ever in her hurry to get to her room. She greeted the faces with what she hoped was more than a grimace. Carefully, she sidestepped past the men. Turning suddenly and attempting to enter her room, she almost ran into Stephen. He gave her an odd look and let her pass.

Once in the room, she laid the little girl on her bed with strict whispered instructions. "Stay right here and don't make a sound, okay?" To her annoyance, all she got for a response was one of the little girl's giggles, although she did have to smile at the adorable face staring up at her. Closing the door, she greeted the people waiting with what she hoped was a normal face. "Hi. Sorry, I had to do something."

Carl nodded. "Luna, this is Eneva. You will be moving in with Eneva so Key can live here." Carl indicated the lady she had seen at her trials with the beetle.

"Move in?"

Move in, move in, move in—the words pounded through her head. How was she going to move in with the little girl? How was she going to keep her promise to the old man?

"When do I need to be ready?" Her voice sounded too loud.

"As soon as possible, preferably by this afternoon, within a couple of hours," responded Carl.

"Two hours! All right, I'll be ready."

Turning quickly, she went back to her room, not without hearing Stephen's whispered comment, "Eat a little much today?"

Aggravation gripped her as she worried that if Stephen had noticed the bulge under her cloak, who else might have?

Kyle

Kyle sat heavily down on the log by the castle gate and enjoyed Kaylee's happy chatter that accompanied him. He remembered that day almost three weeks ago when things had looked so grim. The memory of that night made him shudder despite the warm sunshine shining through the leafy shade structures.

"Kyle!" a rough voice called him. "There's a message that needs to be delivered to Icelair."

The guard extended a white parchment, which was rolled tightly and sealed with the king's seal. Responding with prolonged conversation was not necessary. The guards liked to be obeyed, and if you made any fuss, they would make trouble for you. Kyle had always dreamed of being a real soldier, not that he didn't have sufficient responsibility. But still it would be nice to have another rank than just the random whatever-needs-to-be-done person.

Taking the message, he went to the mouse barn. It was one of his favorite places, and on a day when he had time, he might stay and brush the glossy animals. Absorbed in his thoughts, he ran straight into Mr. Matthias, the mouse trainer.

"Going somewhere?"

For some reason, Kyle had a feeling it wasn't just out of curiosity he was asking.

"To Icelair, with a message."

His abrupt response was, again, only the necessary. The supervisors did not like inefficient talk and insisted on complete order with only the shortest and most essential conversations.

Mr. Matthias looked around to see if anyone was listening and stood for a moment, searching into Kyle's eyes, as if trying to decide whether he could be trusted. "I have something for you to do." His somber voice made Kyle wait with anxiousness. "On your way to Icelair, deliver this to a hole at the bottom of the *big wood* by the bridge. And be quick. Don't be seen doing it."

The big wood was a very large tree, probably the largest in the whole forest. Mr. Matthias handed him a small package wrapped neatly in parchment and another white scroll similar to the one he had obtained previously. He was uncertain of how to respond. He wasn't used to being involved in secret doings, but since the accident with Kaylee, he noticed that some in the castle looked at him differently.

He nodded to Mr. Matthias. As he turned to go, Mr. Matthias put his hand on Kyle's arm and said with deep concern in his voice, "May the Lord of the Book be with you as you travel…and when you arrive at your destination."

There was something in Mr. Matthias's kind eyes that caused Kyle some apprehension. Kyle thanked him quietly and, with trepidation, prepared his mouse for the trip.

As he rode toward the edge of Sandar, he wondered again what the package was all about. And he thought about other odd goings-on in town. He thought of the book lesson he had attended the other day. Something had seemed different about it, but he couldn't quite place what it was. He didn't have his own copy of the Great Book, or he would have looked up some of the things that had been read. Some things had just seemed different.

He had voiced his concerns to Kevin, his best friend. "Not to get me wrong, but it just seemed strange." He continued riding past low hanging leaves and weed stems without speaking. "More like he used to be my best friend," he mumbled to himself.

Lately he and Kevin seemed to have a lot of disagreements. Before the festival, they did everything together; but ever since Kevin had gone to the festival to visit his sister, he had been different somehow. Sometimes he had completely avoided Kyle.

And he wouldn't say anything about his visit to Icelair. In times past, they used to sit and fantasize about working in Icelair or tell each other all their experiences. The Great Book had been one of their favorite topics, but now when he even mentioned it, Kevin seemed to get nervous and avoided the topic completely.

He grimaced to think how hot it would be coming back. Now seven in the morning, it would take him about two hours to get to Icelair. The trail wound through thick grasses and over some rough terrain. He was thankful for the shade the grass provided. The sun seemed so intense, he could imagine being cooked if he sat in one place too long.

As he left the outer perimeter of Sandar, he noticed that there were guards on the border of the woods. What were they doing there? They had never had any problem with the mixlings coming into town. As Kyle drew near to the big wood, he felt his breath come short as he considered the danger he could be in. What did this message contain? And what about the package? The worries pounded through his head as he thought of the frightening possibilities. Why were there so many soldiers? Were they looking for someone?

By the time he had dismounted and reached the big wood tree, his hands were shaking badly. He slipped the package and the mysterious message into a crevice at the bottom of this huge tree. Frantically covering it with moss and debris, he hoped that no one except the intended receiver would find it. Remounting his mouse, he rode on with growing urgency. Little did he know that the greatest danger still lay ahead of him.

———∞◦⊱◈⊰◦∞———

Luna

"His house is right over that hill. If you could deliver these pastries to Eric for me, I would be very grateful."

Eneva's instructions fell on a distracted mind as Luna received the pail offered her. Yesterday had been no breeze, hiding the little girl during the move. Having saved part of her breakfast that morning, Luna had fed the very hungry child then left her with a strict command to stay put and remain quiet. She had to admit, living in a closet wasn't going to work forever, but after having spent the night with her, Luna was hoping more and more that she wouldn't have to send her to Talenia.

Eneva was nice enough. In fact, she reminded Luna of what she imagined a big sister would be like. Hadn't she always wanted one? Despite this fact, her move could not have come at a worse time. For the moment, Luna had called the girl baby or sweetheart, but she tried to think of different names as she rode to accomplish the errand Eneva had given her. *Ooeee* was what the little girl had said was her name. It just didn't seem like a proper little girl's name.

Eneva claimed Eric had ordered the pail containing baked goods, which Luna now carried. But whenever Eneva had said his name, she blushed and looked down. Luna smiled as she recalled the blushing look Eneva gave her as she gave instructions of how to deliver the goods. Luna had heard nothing about Eneva running a bakery or collecting pay for the goodies. Eric was the same young man who had run the trial with her. Suddenly she wondered why he had disappeared so soon afterward. In fact, he had seemed rather embarrassed as he had said good-bye with haste to his companions and the judges. She laughed as she thought of the stories she had heard from the others.

Soon Luna had crossed the hill that had been pointed out to her. Looking down, she saw a large black foreboding fence. Two official-looking people greeted her.

"What do you want?" asked one, not very kindly.

"I've brought some baked goods that Eric ordered," she answered with a hint of curiosity in her voice.

The guards looked into the pail, even picking up one of the pastries and breaking it in half. Nodding with a satisfied grunt, the first one motioned to the second, and they drew apart the huge gate.

Were they thinking I brought a file to break him out with? she mused to herself. She suppressed the giggle that threatened to bubble forth.

Stepping inside, she felt somewhat self-conscious, gazing around the vast area of green moss surrounding the odd house inside the tall fence. She imagined an unseen watcher from the upstairs window. She had heard rumors of a mystical creature that was keeping him prisoner. Maybe it was there watching her. She smothered another unbidden giggle.

"I'm fine! Seriously!"

Luna recognized Eric's bothered voice from outside the tall building in front of her. The house was made of wood, and round a like a big cylinder. As she stared up at it, the bang of the door being swung open startled her. Luna noticed Eric seemed distraught about something but happy to see her.

"Umm let me see…Luna! That's right, Luna. The amazing girl from the trials!"

Luna smiled in amusement at his excitement.

"Eneva finished your baked goods order," she offered, holding out the pail in her hand. He looked around behind Luna as if expecting someone to be there. She saw a flicker of disappointment in his eyes but then he replaced it with his energetic smile.

"Where are my manners?" He ignored the outstretched bucket and continued as if he hadn't heard her. "Come in! Come in!"

Luna followed him in, and he led her to a room off the main part of the house. There were several comfortable-looking seats and cushions.

"Sit down!" he offered, extending his hand around the room as if happy to finally have someone to occupy it. She walked carefully over to one of the chairs and sat on the edge of the large cushion.

Eric talked and talked, telling her how much he appreciated Eneva's pastries. Luna couldn't help but notice that was where the conversation kept going. Toward the end of her visit, he told her that he had a silkworm farm. "Would you like to see it?"

"Sure, but now Eneva will be waiting now. How about another day?"

To this, he seemed a bit disappointed. He told her to come again any day and encouraged her to bring Eneva as well next time.

"You could come and visit her at her house," Luna offered.

He looked around behind him as if someone were listening and lowered his voice. "Oh, I would like that very much!" he whispered. "But it's very hard for me to get away…" He trailed off again, looking around behind him nervously. He twisted a string in his hands anxiously, and Luna felt that she should go before the mysterious whatever-it-was came out of the shadows and chased her away.

As they walked back to the door, Luna took in every detail of the large house. How intriguing it was! There was a large parlor room and a staircase that wound around to the second level. Long deep-green vines covered the walls and hung from the upstairs to the first floor. There was a large round glass panel in the roof that let the sunlight pour in onto the water fountain in the center of the room. On the second floor, there were rounded doors leading off into various rooms behind the bannister, which was draped in thick vines. The sunlight and plants gave the whole house a feeling that it was part of the forest.

As she went out the door, she turned once more. "Your pastries?" She held out the pastries again, and this time, he took them quickly, looking down and blushing. He thanked her for coming and reminded her of his previous invitation. She assured him that she would come again. He stood in the doorway watching her go. On her way back to Eneva's, she contemplated everything she had seen. Why did it seem that Eric was locked up in his own house?

Stephen

That afternoon, with much effort, Stephen had retrieved the small package and message from the big wood tree that Kyle had delivered early in the day. He had waited several hours for a chance to get the message without being seen by the guards. Carl had received word that it would be there, but how it had gotten there—they were all baffled. He had just come from delivering it to the strategy engineer's house.

As he absentmindedly headed in the direction of Eneva's house, he thought about what he was going there for. That was when he saw the familiar sight of Luna's spotted mouse ahead of him. Pushing his mouse forward, he soon caught up with her.

"Hey, what brings you this way?" she asked him cheerfully.

Well, at least she's in a better mood today than the day by the water barrel, he thought. Then again, that had sort of been his fault. A smirk came to his face just thinking about it. "Just checking in on Carl's favorite recruit."

Luna laughed. "Yup, I'm sure I'm number one on his favorite list." She delivered it with a sour look.

They had slowed their mice down and were now at a walk.

"What really brings you this way?" she asked again.

"I really was passing by to check up on you, make sure the move was successful, and tell you that you are going to help transport about a dozen youngsters to Talenia in two days. You will be working on training Key after we return, but you already knew that."

"I see," she answered as she digested his words. She looked almost worried about it. "That is, unless…you want Janet to do it instead," he teased.

She laughed. "Very funny."

He smiled at her good mood.

"You know Light here could use a good run." He looked at her, wondering if she wanted to race. Secretly he had been running Light, so if he ever got another chance, he might beat Luna, unlike the last time they had raced.

"A race?" she stated.

He could tell she was considering the idea.

"Well..."

Then suddenly she shot off through the brush. Neither one of them knew exactly where they were going. She had gotten a head start, but now Stephen had almost caught up to her. Now side by side, their mice pushed hard against each other's speed. They went on and on, each trying to get ahead of the other, following a sort of trail, one that looked as if it hadn't been used for a long time.

As they burst through a barrier of leaves and vines, they both drew up their mice in awe. Stephen looked around him breathlessly. "What is this place?"

The clearing was so immense and mysterious, it sent chills up his arms. Vines grew unbidden across large stone pillars. The trees here were towering and bigger around than any he had ever seen. There was a wall of thick shrubbery around the whole place, like a living fence. They had only happened on it because some of the bushes had died, leaving a break in the fence. As he walked through the maze of ruins, he felt that Luna was as enchanted as he was.

It was the building in the center of the secret place that seemed to call them forward. It loomed above Stephen's head, and he gazed at it in wonder. It was made of a crystalline substance, transparent and white at the same time. The sun glinted sharply off its shining walls and caused him to squint his eyes.

"Let's go in!" Luna's voice seemed too loud, even though she spoke in almost a whisper.

Neither of them felt like speaking above a whisper, and they looked at each other in shared excitement.

"In there?" But even as he asked for reassurance, he was walking up the smooth white steps entangled with wild plants. The large wooden door opened easily, and they entered cautiously.

The main room was beautiful. It was like stepping into a fairytale. A soft green rug, lush in every way, extended itself throughout the entire room. From the outside, the building had appeared grand, but on the inside, it looked even more spacious and incredible than either could believe. The semitransparent walls reflected sunlight onto everything. Ornate furniture perched on the plush carpeting as if ready to receive kings and princes. Paintings adorned the ceiling, and the glass windows were entwined with jeweled flowers. A spiraling staircase led up on either side of the round room to a second floor above. Large cushioned seats took their places along the walls, and the prettiest cloth adorned the windows as curtains.

Looking up, Stephen noticed that there was also a curtain separating the upper balcony from view. As the two stared in wonder, little did they know the terrible story the enthralling place held.

Kyle

As Kyle was led into the ice castle, cold chills engulfed him. He had never imagined this castle would be so cold! Although he had offered the scroll to the cloaked servant who had greeted him, he had only motioned him to enter the great hall. As he approached the beautiful throne on which sat the much-feared King Elsiper, he couldn't help but let his imagination fly. Why had the mysterious cloaked man kept his head down as if his features were a secret? Why did he seem so sinister? Why did the king look at him like a cat waiting for a mouse to run? As he held out the scroll to the king, his fright grew. The foreboding figure on the throne was indeed intimidating. The king accepted the message silently and laid it aside as if it wasn't important.

Finally, when Kyle felt he was nearly at a breaking point, the king spoke. "Do you know why you're here?" The hoarse cold voice neatly fitted the king's demeanor.

"T-to deliver a message to you, O king?"

The statement was more of a question.

"No…" He reached his hand out impulsively and threw the scroll back at Kyle. He caught it perfectly. "Open it," the king commanded in a gloating manner.

For some reason, Kyle's hands shook as he opened the now threatening scroll. As he unrolled it, the sharp intake of his breath made the king laugh. Not one word appeared on the scroll. "You have been temporarily relieved of your duties in Sandar and have been brought here to answer some questions."

The curled smile and the way he said *questions* made Kyle quake. He had a feeling that these wouldn't be ordinary questions. With a panicked feeling creeping through him, he looked down once again at the paper in his now trembling hands. Its blank face stared at him and mocked him with its silence.

12

Luna

All that morning, Luna had been jittery with excitement. The day before, she and Stephen had agreed to meet back at the enchanting place they had found. Mysteries that might be held within that place made Luna wish she was there already. She had decided that since she would be gone for a long while, she would take the little girl with her and hide her somewhere while they explored.

That morning, she had taken care of the many assignments Eneva had given her. The beetles were very interesting to Luna. She had listened attentively while Eneva told her their names. Her favorites were Zip and Nappy. They came up to her knees and had a glossy beautiful green shell with occasional black splotches. A delicate horn completed their features. They were curious creatures. Their hard exterior and unmoving eyes could make a person forget how intelligent they really were. And they were quite trainable. They made excellent guards, especially in large groups. The really large beetles with the huge curved horn on their heads were less intelligent, but they could be trained to work, to push logs and to move things too heavy for a man to move. They were very frightening when angered.

"I'm going meet Stephen for some training," she told Eneva, struggling to keep the excitement from her voice.

Eneva didn't seem to notice, Still bent over her baking, she mumbled, "Don't forget your cloak. It could get chilly later."

Hurrying to the counter, Luna scooped up some leftovers from the day before and almost ran to her room. She was happy that Eneva was baking her flaky pastries. They were better than the best! The day before, when Luna had returned from her escapade, she had told Eneva how much Eric liked her cooking and that he had invited them to come see his silkworm farm. Eneva had smiled, blushed, and hung on every word. Luna giggled just thinking about it. They had speculated more on why he seemed to be trapped in his own house, but neither of them had any concrete answers.

Now she went to the closet and opened it up. The little girl was not inside. She had put her there an hour ago.

"Where'd you go?" she whispered softly, hoping that Eneva was still lost in fantasizing thoughts. "Come out now!"

She hoped this whisper sounded threatening. Sighing deeply, she began a search of the room. As she bent to look underneath the bed, a sound startled her. Turning around, she was relieved to see it was the child.

"I've got to name you something," she mumbled to herself as she scooped up the now laughing bundle and tickled her under the chin. She noticed that the clothing her joyful charge was wearing was now dirty. She couldn't imagine how she had gotten so soiled since she had been in the closet the entire time.

"I'm gonna have to wash some clothes," she said as she hunted for another set of clothing. Luna found a clean jumper and a long-sleeved shirt for her and helped her dress herself. Tucking the child's wriggling feet into her tiny boots, Luna had second thoughts about going exploring. "It will be fine," she tried to reassure herself. Then picking the little girl up, she tucked her carefully under her cloak and went out the front door.

As she left, she noticed Eneva staring dreamily out the window. After mounting her mouse, she rode toward the mysterious place they had discovered, balancing the child in front of her while driving with her right hand and grasping her bow in the other.

Upon nearing the palace they had discovered the day before, she found a smaller house in a fenced area. It was there she left the little one with a variety of things to keep a little girl busy. She had been amazed at how well the girl followed instructions to keep quiet and stay put when she had to be left. She seemed fearless, and Luna imagined the old man had trained her to be so, since at times, he had left her as well. Still, Luna was uncomfortable with the situation. She wished there was someone she could leave her with. There was always danger, and always that fear that came from being so small.

———❖———

Stephen

Stephen had strangely enjoyed Luna's reaction that day by the cabin when she'd overslept and wished to repeat the experience. They had promised not to explore at all without the other the day before when they parted company. So to keep his side of the promise, he must wait. About ten minutes earlier, he had carefully concealed his mouse behind some brush and then concealed himself right by the entrance to the garden. Soon he heard her coming. *Is she talking to herself?* he thought with a smirk. He watched as she dismounted and called his name a few times. Then carefully, she looked around the entrance. He waited, not wanting to come out at the wrong time. He was also curious if she wouldn't indeed explore without him.

Puzzled, he watched as she walked back to her mouse and then he stared in surprise. Closing his eyes tight and shaking his head, he looked again. It was unmistakable. She was walking toward one of the small houses with a little girl clinging to her hand, a small bundle underneath the opposite arm. Cautiously, she went inside the fenced yard and opened the door of the house, leading the little girl inside. A few minutes later, she emerged and almost ran back to her mouse.

As she passed where he was hidden, he jumped out from his cover and watched her reaction with satisfaction. After about three seconds, he doubled over laughing. "Your face," he managed.

"That isn't nice!" she mustered angrily through her shock.

He smiled as she turned red in embarrassment. "You know, you really shouldn't scare people, although it seems to be your hobby!"

He smiled and struggled to keep another fit of laughter from erupting. He could tell she was worried if he had seen the scene that had just taken place and realized he would have to put her fears at ease if they were to have any fun.

"I just heard you walking up, so I jumped out. If I could have seen you coming…then it would have been even better."

This seemed to dispel her fears. She gave him an annoyed smile and retorted, "For you."

They tied the mice to a large pinecone just inside the break in the hedge.

"Where are we going to start?" She changed the subject.

"Why not the huge house?" he asked.

There were lots of smaller, more regular houses nearby. There was one small house behind the one they had entered the day before, but none of them had quite the appeal of the crystal palace at the center.

"Race you!" she called, running toward their destination.

He took off after her, and they reached the double doors breathing heavily and laughing. Leaning against the door beam, he struggled to catch his breath. "Ladies first," he exclaimed, gesturing ceremoniously to the door in front of them.

"Age before beauty!" her smug reply came, asking for a better saying.

"Since I have my share of the beauty, I guess we'll both have to go in at the same time!" He laughed.

Seeing that she was stumped, he swung open the second door. It was wide enough for twenty people to enter, and as they stepped inside, their playful mood seemed to be dampened. It certainly took their breath away. Stephen looked around and drank in the glowing reflections of the warm room. The sun seemed to be coming from everywhere at once, and little rainbows danced along the crystal walls. Seeing that Luna had made no move toward leading the exploration, he headed to a door at the far side. Opening it, he again gestured for her to enter first.

This time, it seemed curiosity got the better of her because she stepped through readily. What greeted them was a long hallway. It was wider than any hallway Stephen had seen, and he gaped in open awe at the beautiful paintings on the arched walls. On either side of them were doors made from extremely rare whitewood with a different jeweled flower at the top of each.

He noticed Luna reaching for the handle of one. "Wait, you're just going to open that?" he asked her.

"Sure, why not?"

"What if someone's in there?"

She looked at him incredulously. "If someone is in here. we shouldn't have come in the first place," she admonished.

Shrugging his shoulders, he gave her the okay.

The door opened into a small room, which was not to be outdone by the main room. A deep-blue-shaded carpet and fancy furniture complimented its pale pink walls. Stephen watched as Luna walked to a bookshelf on the right wall. She ran her finger across the spines of the books while looking curiously around the room. He soon joined her by a crib at the other side of the room. They stared down at the unmade sleeping place and wondered why the owner hadn't made the bed. As they explored other parts of the house, other small details jumped out at them, details that seemed out of place. A drawer of ladies' clothes pulled out, a bed untended, a few dishes on the counter—they even found some old dried food still in its pot! They said nothing, but the mold on the leftout food told its story. Whoever had left hadn't left with the intention of doing so. They had been in a hurry, and the evidence of a rapid departure scared Stephen.

At least two hours had passed before Stephen and Luna had finished going over every inch of the beautiful house. It fully seemed to be a palace, but what would a palace be doing out here, and why had he never seen it before or even heard of it? Now they were walking down the smooth path leading back to the exit of the palace grounds.

"You have to promise not to explore the rest of the houses without me," Luna was saying as she kicked small pebbles with her booted foot.

"Of course not!" The smile and tone of voice he used made her look at him, as if pleading.

"Seriously," she pressed.

"Yes, seriously." He tried to keep a straight face and listened in amusement as she told him everything that would happen if he didn't wait for her. Though in the beginning he had planned to pretend that he didn't know about the child she had brought with her, he decided it would be inevitably necessary to tell her, so why not enjoy the process just a bit?

Upon leaving the entrance to enchanted place, he interrupted her midsentence. "Aren't you forgetting the little girl in that house?" he asked with a completely serious voice and face.

Her face turned a bit pale, and she stopped and stared at him as if she did not know what to say. "What?" she asked.

"The little girl you took over there." Again, he pointed toward the house where she had left the girl. He started walking toward it and soon heard her behind him. Apparently, she had resigned herself to the fact that he knew. Luna opened the small gate to the fenced area and went inside. She opened the door to the house, and the little girl ran up to Luna and hugged her around the knees.

"You're not planning on telling anyone, right?" The question was supposed to be a statement, but Stephen noticed she was uncertain.

"Where'd she come from? And what's her name?" he asked, ignoring her question.

"The old man left her in my care," she answered him, staring down lovingly at the little girl.

"Zoeeee!"

"What?"

"Zoeeee!" repeated the smiling little girl.

Luna looked at him and laughed. "zo-ee" she stated. "I guess I didn't understand her before when I asked her name."

Stephen watched her carefully pick up the little girl and wrap her up in the blanket she had left with her.

"Come on, Zoe, we're going home," she said, and as she passed, she smiled at him.

Stephen wondered how Luna planned to keep Zoe hidden, but he didn't ask. Instead, he lamented that with the little girl riding with Luna, they wouldn't be able to race on the way home.

Luna

Luna slipped carefully out of her room. Not sure if Eneva was awake yet, she didn't want to disturb her. A small heap of golden pastries crowned the counter, and Luna had to deliberately look the other way to avoid snatching one. Zoe had not fallen asleep until late in the night, so hopefully she wouldn't wake up for another few hours. Five in the morning wasn't her favorite time to get up, but it did feel good sometimes to be the first one stirring. Yesterday, she had felt so scared when Stephen had revealed that he knew about Zoe. Sure, he had been friendly, and she had enjoyed exploring the wonderful buildings with him, but that didn't mean she could trust him. Smiling, she couldn't wait to get to the cabin. The mission of transporting the children still made her giddy with excitement. She had decided to get there early, and then on their way back, pick up Zoe.

After grabbing a quick breakfast of half a wild grape, she ran out to prepare Mitzie. Her soft wet muzzle greeted her happily as usual. She loved mice because they were so big. Luna was just barely able to look over Mitzie's back. Her feet barely reached Mitzie's middle when she was riding. Although many people had heard of a smaller breed of mice, they enjoyed the big ones common in these parts. They were strong and fast and were useful for a wide variety of tasks.

Hoisting herself atop Mitzie's tall back, she led her out of the shed; then they took off toward the cabin. The ride was short, even with the slow pace Luna held Mitzie to. As she arrived, she heard children's voices. Opening the door, she was greeted with a dozen smiling faces. They were all folding blankets and packing small cases of their belongings. For a second, a stab of pain hit her heart as she remembered that day, seemingly so far away now, when she had sadly packed Nio's clothes for him to go to the festival.

"Good morning!" she called out cheerfully and hung her cloak on the familiar peg by the door.

"Good morning!" The chorus of little voices warmed her heart, and she smiled sincerely at them.

The eldest of the group was in the corner and seemed to be about her age. Walking over, Luna extended her hand. "Hi, I'm Luna."

The girl gave her a relieved smile and accepted the extended hand. "I'm Madai." She smiled shyly.

Relief flooded Luna as she stared at the timid girl in front of her. "Thank goodness not another Janet!"

"You're going to be transporting us to Talenia?" Madai's voice was like laughing water and fit her kind, thoughtful face perfectly.

"Yes, I think someone else will be leading us," Luna responded. She was happy at last to have found a girl who was truly happy to have her around. Madai was also a mixling and for this reason was being transported to Talenia. Her skin was of a darker shade, but her oval face and bright blue eyes were Icelairian features. Brown tousled hair was pulled back with two braids fastened at the back of her head. They chatted for several minutes, and Madai introduced her to the little children who kept up a constant giggling while preparing for departure.

Soon a knock sounded at the wooden door, and Luna navigated her way between small arms and legs to reach it.

There stood Stephen. "Ready to go?"

"Yes, though we have to stop by Eneva's to pick something up."

He nodded knowingly, but not without a slightly annoyed expression. Luna smiled and turned back to Madai. She was happy it would be Stephen and not Daniel leading the transport of children. Daniel did not like her. He was positively cold toward her. And she was also happy Stephen knew about Zoe. Now she didn't have to worry nearly as much. She rushed the little children out to the cart, which was waiting for them. They ranged in age from about two to sixteen.

The ride in the cart was much slower and clumsier than riding on mouseback. Four stout black mice pulled the cart. Luna tied Mitzie to the back of the cart next to Stephen's mouse, Lightning, and Madai's brown mouse. They would tag along for the trip back. They would be leaving the team of mice and the wagon in Talenia.

Luna and Madai chatted incessantly together and found they both liked a lot of the same things. There was one thing they did not find in common, and that was that Madai didn't particularly like dangerous excitement. She was more cautious and afraid of things that were unknown. Luna didn't exactly love the word *dangerous*, but she did enjoy a good, exiting adventure!

They soon arrived at Eneva's house, and Luna slipped inside unnoticed by her still-sleeping living partner. She retrieved the bag she had packed for Zoe the night before. She carried the sleeping child back to the cart and slipped inside. Madai looked at her strangely but said nothing about the sleeping little girl in her arms. Soon, most of the children were lulled asleep by the rocking cart, and Luna could feel her own eyelids drooping. Talenia was a good day's ride if you were riding by yourself on a fast mouse, but in a cart, it could take as long as three days. It seemed she only closed her eyes for a moment then was jolted awake. After checking her small sundial, she realized it had been six hours since they started. Stephen must be extremely tired! A pang of guilt passed over her as she thought of her slumber.

Tucking Zoe in next to the rest of the children on the jiggling bottom of the cart, Luna stepped to the front and sat next to Stephen.

"Can I drive for a while?" She knew if she offered to give him a break, he would turn it down immediately. She often wondered why guys were like that, not wanting ever to show they were tired. *Well, I'm the same way, I suppose,* she thought ruefully while waiting for Stephens's response.

"You? Drive?" he asked, seemingly surprised by her question. "You'd probably flip the cart."

"Would not!" she protested with irritation.

He gave up the reins. She was surprised it had been so easy. *He must be more tired than I thought,* she mused. He waited for her to climb up to the front and then clumsily retreated to the back.

The mice were not hard to control, and the path was well marked, but it was still tiring and repetitive. After an hour of driving, she glanced at the rear of the cart and saw that Stephen was leaning on the far corner, sleeping. She half-wanted to wake him up and repent of her offer, but focusing on the road ahead, she began reciting memorized book passages to pass time. Three days! This was going to be a long time! But determined not to be the one to complain, she concentrated on her passages and kept the mice in line.

Stephen

Stephen woke with a jerk. Surprisingly, Luna was a pretty good driver, and he had fallen asleep quickly, but now a bump in the road brought him back to consciousness. When she had offered to drive, he had not wanted to give in too quickly, but he had been rather tired. That morning, he had started his day at four in the morning since there were several things to take care of before leaving. Then six hours of the slow driving had taken its toll. He noticed the shadows were much longer as he looked out the back of the cart. He must have slept a few hours. The cart was a large one, and it could be difficult to control at times. It was necessary to use a large cart to transport the thirteen children to Talenia, plus himself and Luna. He wondered how long he had slept. Pulling a small sundial out of his pocket, he saw it was already five in the afternoon. "That means she's been driving for four hours," he mumbled to himself.

At the sound of Stephen's yawn, Luna glanced back his way. "Finally up, sleepyhead!" she exclaimed with a tired smile.

"Yup," he replied and reluctantly crawled toward the front to take his position.

"Finally! Your turn." She sighed and willingly scooted over while handing him the reins.

"You're the one who wanted to drive," he reminded her with a daring smile, wondering if she would admit the fact it had just been to let him rest.

"Oh no, I enjoyed it," she quickly claimed as she looked away across the top of the hill they had just climbed.

He watched as she reached back and picked up Zoe, who was now awake. Everyone else had woken up and were readily accepting the food offered them by the other girl, whom he had heard Luna call Madai. Luna set Zoe in the middle of the seat board and was feeding her some bread. Stephen thought about how differently this trip was going than the other ones he had been on. Last time, he remembered, Janet had been on the transporting mission. She had stayed in the back of the cart and barely remembered to feed the five children they had been transporting. When they had set up camp, he had made the sleeping shelter and had to take care of getting water and firewood. He remembered with disdain how little effort Janet had made on that trip. He assumed with Luna it would be different, more of a team effort, considering how she had already taken on some of the driving responsibility without even being asked.

He tuned back in to the conversation around him. Apparently, one of the youngsters had asked for a story. Luna had started a tale about some animals that were having a sharing issue. Though he told himself he was much too old for stories, it still helped to pass the time, and he had to admit it was pretty good. Three hours later, all of the younger charges had fallen asleep again, and they finally reached the place where they would spend the night.

As he pulled up to the clearing, he knew it would take some time to set up the shelter. Luna jumped carefully down from the cart, followed by Madai.

"What do you want us to do?" Madai asked uncertainly.

Though he had expected them to help somewhat, he wasn't sure what to tell them to do.

"Are we supposed to cut branches, or are there some around here?" Luna asked, walking toward the edge of the clearing.

"Uhmm, there should be some near the woods' edge," he said, pointing toward the woods. He watched as Luna took her cloak off and laid it by the stump of a tree. She turned to Madai, nodding toward a pile of stones.

"There are some stones over there you could make a fireplace with," she encouraged.

These hidden clearings were placed regularly along the path to Talenia, but whenever someone used them, it was customary to conceal the parts used for the fireplaces and shelters. The materials were left for later passing groups to use. He glanced back to see Madai arranging the stones carefully in a circle at the base of a giant boulder and went to help Luna with the logs.

The logs were about as big around as his leg and twice as tall as he was. They were concealed by leaves and vines. They were quite heavy, but he could handle one laboriously by himself. He soon realized that if he insisted on doing it by himself, he would be more than exhausted by the time he finished building the shelter. He looked at what Luna was doing. She had taken a small length of vine and tied three of the logs tightly together on both ends. She now stood at one end and seemed to be waiting for him to take the other. It was a good idea. After an hour, they had hauled all the logs and vines they would need to build the shelter. As they set to work tying the logs together with vines, he realized how much better it was having help.

Luna

Luna kept up a tired smile as she and Stephen hauled the last of the logs into the clearing. Her legs ached like crazy, but she wouldn't admit it for anything. She was determined to keep up with Stephen as long as she could. As he began fashioning the first wall for the shelter, she offered to go find water.

At his slight nod, she took two wooden buckets from the back of the cart and headed downhill. After about five minutes of walking, she arrived at a clear river, which seemed as wide as it was deep. She carefully looked for a place where she could approach the water without risking falling in and filled the two buckets full. The return journey seemed twice as steep, and halfway up, the buckets seemed to turn to lead. A few seconds before entering the clearing, she stopped and rested for a second until her strength returned. "I can't look worn-out when I get there," she mumbled to herself, catching her breath. Finally ready, she picked up her cargo and emerged into the clearing.

The shelter was nearly finished; just the canvas to cover the top was missing. There was a long roll of canvas in the cart to put over the walls to make the roof. As she reached the cart, she saw most of the children were waking up for the second time. She retrieved the rolled-up canvas and deposited it near where Stephen was working. It took them until it was almost dark to complete the task of finishing the shelter. It was simple to construct. There were three sets of trees that were fairly close to one another and had a small clearing behind the trees. The trees were very large. The shelter was tied together with vines, and the walls were supported by the trees. The front of the shelter opened into the clearing. The cart was parked with the back facing the clearing next to the shelter. The fireplace was in between the openings of the wagon and the shelter to provide maximum heat for the sleeping occupants. Inside the shelter, poles that were flat on one side were laid together to keep the sleeping children off the ground. There was a hedge of thick bushes and grass between the shelter and the trail, so it was not visible to passing travelers.

While Stephen finished the shelter, Luna took a shovel and some canvas to fashion a crude bathroom for the group to use below the camp. While they worked on these things, Madai cooked a hot stew to feed the weary travelers.

After they were done, Luna was exhausted, and she noticed Stephen's step was slower than when they had arrived. She realized then that even if they were really tired, someone needed to be keeping watch the entire night. Luna walked over to the cart and helped Madai distribute bread and the stew to the children then took a trek to the little bathroom in the woods, leading the wide-eyed children with fears of the dark. When they returned, she tucked the five little boys into the wagon beds and told them a story while Madai tucked the eight little girls into their beds in the larger shelter. After a few requests for drinks and more reassurance, their charges were finally asleep. Stephen rolled out his bed in the wagon next to the boys. Madai and Luna laid out their beds in the shelter with the girls.

Luna had talked with Madai, and they had both agreed they should share the duty shift with Stephen. They decided that since Stephen would drive first in the morning, he should take the first shift. Madai agreed to take a turn staying with the little boys in the wagon while Stephen kept watch. Since there was no way to accurately tell time at night, they would go as long as possible then wake the next person. Madai had warned them both that she wasn't very good at staying awake, so they impressed upon her that she must wake the next person before she fell asleep, even if it wasn't very long. Luna stumbled in with the little girls and checked on them one last time before falling exhausted onto her hard bed.

Stephen

Stephen had argued plenty with the girls when they presented their plan for the journey, but he did have to admit it made sense. When he had been on that trip with Janet, he had almost fallen asleep several times when they were driving. Since then, he had gone on several transport missions, sometimes by himself, leading a small group of adults and occasionally with two or three children. But the council liked to send a girl or a lady with the young children so they could take care of their many needs. He did agree with this wholeheartedly because by the time he was done with driving, making shelters, finding water and starting a fire, he was exhausted.

He added some sticks to the fire in front of him. He realized he wasn't as tired this time around and accredited it to the two girls' helpfulness. Not wanting to get bored and sleepy, he replayed the reason for having to keep watch all night in his mind. The reason, he thought ruefully, was because of rebels. They were often hired by the opposing kingdoms to take the resistance down. Till now they had not succeeded, though they tried very hard. If the resistance transporting teams would leave their shelters and fireplaces up, then upon returning, they would find everything in ruins. The shelters would be burned, the stones for the fire disbursed, and the whole place would be turned to rubble. Also, during transporting missions, a band of rebels could attack and destroy the camp. There had been stories about them even arresting the mixlings being transported or leaving the people beaten nearly to death. It was for this reason that there was always someone on guard, and adults who came with them needed to know basic bow-and-arrow skills. The better at it they were, the safer. He thought on this and several other things through the next few hours.

When he felt he absolutely had to go to sleep, he stumbled to the wagon and knocked loudly on the wood. After a long while of making a racket and hearing no response, he groaned. "We didn't plan on what to do if Madai is a sound sleeper."

A figure pushed past him and entered the wagon where the little boys were sleeping. Soon, both Luna and Madai emerged from the structure. Madai, rubbing her eyes in sleep, mumbled apologies, "I'm sorry, guys, I told you I wasn't good at staying awake."

He watched, confused, as Luna led Madai straight to the girls' tent. When she walked toward the fire, he called in a whisper, "Isn't it her turn?"

Luna smiled. "I can make it till morning. She wouldn't stay awake more than five minutes!" Luna laughed at his uncertain face. "As soon as I took her inside, she was asleep as if nothing happened," she said.

Too tired to care, he nodded and entered the boys' wagon. It seemed as soon as he laid his head down, he was awakened by birds' songs and the smell of breakfast.

———∘∘○🔷○∘∘———

Luna

Rubbing sleep from her eyes, Luna was relieved to see buildings ahead. The last few nights had been much like the first night. Madai had volunteered to take care of packing up and breakfast since she really wasn't capable of the watch shifts. Though Luna wasn't exactly scared, she still felt somewhat nervous sitting by the fire in the dark by herself and was glad they were finally almost there. As they neared the city, huge gates loomed above them, and at least twenty mixling soldiers greeted them. As soon as they told their identity, and the guards saw the children, they were granted entrance.

Luna was sitting on the front seat with Zoe and another little girl in between her and Stephen. She laughed when he comically extended his arm and introduced the town. "I welcome you to Talenia, the greatest city ever!" he exclaimed.

She laughed again out loud, half from amusement and half from relief. They were finally there. They drove up to a medium-sized, two-story building made completely from wood, like the cabin that was so familiar back at the resistance.

The weary travelers were greeted by a nice, motherly woman, who welcomed them all with open arms. Luna and Madai showed all the little children in to wash their hands before supper, which the lady told them was already waiting. As she and Stephen walked laughing and talking into the dining room, they gasped almost in unison.

"Daniel!" Stephen exclaimed happily. "What are you doing here?"

Luna noticed Daniel seemed to be a bit short and preoccupied. "I was sent two days ago to deliver a message," he informed them.

"So you'll be riding back with us?" Luna asked cautiously. Ever since the bridge incident, Luna had never really trusted Daniel. He had seemed really harsh, and she had even heard him tell Stephen that he had no idea why he was being so friendly with her: didn't he know girls were just problems?

"No, I have to get back tonight, but I'm sure you three will get along fine," he said with disdain.

"Three?"

"Oh yes. The message is that you are to take Madai back with you as Luna's companion so you won't have to take care of her anymore. She has been accepted into the resistance." He nodded slightly in Luna's direction.

"I see," Stephen responded.

As Daniel stood up to leave, Stephen accompanied him out. Luna turned and scooped up Zoe who had been tugging at her dress. "Are you hungry?" she asked cheerfully. At the baby's eager response, she carried her to the table, which was generously laid out with food. She had mixed feelings about Daniel's message. She was happy that she would have Madai as a friend and companion, but what did he mean by saying then Stephen wouldn't have to take care of her anymore?

Two hours later, she was sleeping in a room with Madai and some other older girls. Madai had been very excited to hear she was going back with Luna. They had talked about all they would do together till they were shushed by the others. Earlier, Luna had tucked in Zoe with the other little girls in the room down the hall. She had closed the big glass window and spun a story about a big friendly rabbit to settle them down. She thought again about their sweet smiles and giggles in the moonlight, which was streaming through the window. Smiling at the dark ceiling above her, she closed her eyes and fell into a deep sleep.

———∘○∘-❧◈☙-∘○∘———

Stephen

Stephen jerked awake at the crash of breaking glass. Smoke was heavy in the room, and the heat was unusual since it had been cold when he had gone to sleep. As soon as he realized what it was, through sleep-hazed eyes, he made the urgent cry. "Wake up! Everyone, wake up!"

The two older boys woke up instantly and began waking the younger ones still sleeping.

"Fire! Fire!" The call was now heard throughout the halls.

As he opened his door, he saw the children streaming down the stairs toward the door. Horror engulfed him as he looked at the roof and saw the yellow flames licking at the carefully built structure. It all seemed like a nightmare as he looked through the suffocating smoke. After his room was evacuated, his first instinct was to follow the flow of people, but then he remembered Luna. She was on the second floor, and although there had been several smaller girls coming down the staircase, there was still no sign of Luna.

"Madai!" he called as he recognized her in the fray. "Have you seen Luna?"

"She w-went back upstairs."

"Back?" He gave her no time to respond but turned and dashed up the stairway, which the flames were now threatening. The many children coming down stared at him incredulously, as if he had lost his mind going the opposite way.

"She'll be fine," he tried to reassure himself, but a dark foreboding told him otherwise. The mass of bodies pushing against him gave him unwanted time to think as he tried desperately to reach the top. Children's frightened cries tore at him as he went. Rising panic gripped his heart, and he told himself it was because of what Carl would say, but he knew the real truth: Luna was now his friend. He remembered the fun times they had had: when he had scared her by the barrel, going exploring, and setting up camp a few nights ago. These thoughts gave him motivation.

The top of the stairs was hot, hotter than was bearable. The smoke was thick and choking. An eerie feeling enclosed the ghostly golden hallway, the crackling timbers above dropping hot sparks on his back.

As he raced down to the end, he was relieved to see Luna there in front of him, until she spoke. "She's gone!" she cried, tears streaming down her sooty face.

"Are you sure?" he yelled above the loud crackling. Even without her saying, he knew who she was talking about.

"I checked her room first thing when I realized there was a fire. It was empty, so I thought she was downstairs, but she isn't. I can't find her!" Her frightened cry wrenched at his heart, but he knew they had to move fast. She doubled over coughing.

"Go down now!" he commanded, but even before he did so, he realized she wasn't going to obey.

"I'm not leaving without her!" Desperation rang in her protest.

He raced to the far room and knew he was followed by the stubborn searcher. They searched room after room on their knees below the thickest smoke, but Zoe was nowhere to be found. Finally, choking, he gave her a push toward the stairs, and this time, she went down the smoldering steps. They ran as fast as they could, hoping to get down to the only exit without their clothes catching fire.

When they got outside, Stephen and Luna began frantically searching for Zoe. When every child had been gone over twice, they realized she was not among them, and he watched helpless as Luna stood crying, heartbroken. Though Madai tried to comfort her, he saw her simple reassurances were empty. There was no way that Zoe could be found alive if she remained in that building. This horrible thought froze him despite the scorching heat as he watched the huge golden bonfire tumble to the ground.

13

Stephen

Stephen sat up and dully went over what happened the night before. They had been led to a different house in the vicinity, and he had noticed the slowness of Luna's step. He wondered what had happened to Zoe. Had she wandered into one of the downstairs rooms looking for Luna? He remembered watching Luna walk sadly through the rubble the night before when the fire had burned out, looking, searching for anything that might mean Zoe had been there. It still puzzled him how they had found nothing. The fire had been swift, but he couldn't imagine that there would be nothing remaining of Zoe if she had died in the fire. He was thankful that all of the other children had been safely ushered out of the building in time. Some had minor burns, and all were somewhat traumatized, but they would be all right in time.

He now stood stiffly and proceeded to dress himself. Their bags, which had been left by the door, had been pulled out, undamaged, though they smelled very strongly of smoke and brought only bad memories. Luna and Madai were downstairs. They had their carrying bags with them and were ready to start their return trip to the resistance camp. Stephen noticed Luna had ceased her crying but looked as if she could easily start again at any moment. He motioned tiredly that he was ready and thanked the kind lady of the house for the bag of food she had stuffed in his pack. They mounted their waiting mice and began the long day ahead of them. It was still dark out, and hidden fears lurked in everyone's minds. As they rode past the huge gates, he couldn't help but notice Luna's longing glance backward.

Kyle

Kyle stared at the damp, dripping walls that enclosed him. How had this all happened? A replay thundered through his dejected mind. As he had anticipated, King Elsiper's questions had not been ordinary. He had heard somewhere about the mixling who had helped Kaylee by treating her injuries. Kyle had insisted that all he knew was that there was a mixling who had helped him lift the cart and that he had left shortly after treating her injuries. The king did not believe him. After much yelling and threats of violence, the king had sentenced him to the dungeon until he decided to be more forthcoming. He wanted to know the identity of the mixling and which house he had come from. He insisted that he didn't know who he had been, and he didn't mention the girl at all. He knew that Mr. Matthias was already in danger because of what had happened. He shuddered as he recalled the mean, icy stare the king had fixed on him during the questioning, but there was something that scared him more than that: rats.

He remembered tales that the guards had gleefully told him when he was younger, stories of wild rats with gleaming eyes that roamed the dungeon's dark hallways and attacked and ate prisoners through the bars. When Kaylee's parents had heard some of the horrible tales the men had been telling him, they instantly put a stop to it. Thinking of the whole experience, he shuddered again, crouching further back against the wall. His head pounded in pain from the lack of water. He hadn't had anything to drink for two days, not to mention his grumbling stomach. As he leaned his already dirty head against the cold stone behind him, he wondered how long his misery would last.

Luna

Luna stared blankly ahead of her as they travelled down the path. Everything along the way reminded her of the lost little girl. How could she have been so careless? She should have insisted that Zoe sleep with them in the big room. She fought to blink back tears as the bumpy road and slow pace of the mice jiggled her up and down. Suddenly, as if in a haze, she noticed that Madai was shoved off her mouse. Before she had time to react, rough hands yanked her off her own mount. Stephen swerved sharply to avoid the shove meant for him. Luna noticed him reach for his bow and arrows and then put them back in their proper place slowly. Who were these people and what did they want with them?

Stephen

As they rode their mice slowly on the winding rough trail in the early morning twilight, Stephen felt as if someone was watching them. Twice he heard a sound behind them, and once his mouse darted ahead, nearly bumping into Luna's mouse. He stopped several times, looking behind them into the tall weeds but detected nothing. Finally he decided that it was just nerves from the experience they had just survived. Maybe the smoke smell was making the mice nervous. So he was caught off guard when the girls were suddenly shoved off their mice.

When the men pushed Madai and then Luna from their mice, he grabbed for his bow, but it was apparent that he would just endanger the girls if he tried to fight them off. He decided he would try a more diplomatic approach.

Stephen noticed Luna wince as the young man behind her pulled her arms up harshly around a sapling. He felt angry with himself for not being more watchful. Soon Luna and Madai were tied side by side, watching him, waiting for what would come next. There were only three men, and they appeared to have been expecting them. Stephen suspected earlier that someone had been following them.

The older man, who was evidently in charge, pulled Stephen aside. "I'll tell you what. We were hired to capture all of you, but I'm willing to negotiate."

Stephen stared at him wearily. "I doubt there is anything we have that you would want," he told the rebel in front of him.

The man looked at the ground for a moment. "One of our men has an injury...," he began.

"Thomas is getting worse!" A young boy came bursting into the small clearing where they had been talking.

Frustration registered across the leader's face. "And the little girl?"

"She's fine," the boy supplied the man with the wanted information.

Stephen looked curiously at the lad before them. He had sooty clothes and a few small burns on his arms. He had obviously been at the scene of a fire very recently.

"Where are we going to find a healer?" the boy asked urgently.

The older man turned back to Stephen. "As you can see, we have a dilemma. We were hired to capture you, but our earlier efforts failed, and now that we have captured you, we have need of your help."

"Our help?" retorted Stephen, somewhat angrily.

"Yes...the girl." He nodded toward Luna. "Is she not a healer?"

"Well, yes," Stephen admitted uneasily. "And what would you give us in return?"

"We're not allowed to let prisoners free, especially you, but I'm willing to make an exception if you are. I am not so much in favor of Elsiper as some might believe."

Stephen looked across at Luna, the question in his eyes. She nodded with a resigned look on her face. "All right, but if we help you, you agree to let all of us go."

"I'll let all of you go if she helps Thomas," the leader said as if expecting complete cooperation. "This injury was not in the plan," he muttered. He nodded to the other men. "Untie them."

As Stephen watched, two brawny young men hauled a badly injured man into the clearing on a crude sort of board.

"This is Thomas," the taller one declared as he set the board down.

Stephen could see the concern in the leader's face as he gazed at the injured man. *Must be his son.* Stephen thought.

Luna knelt beside the injured youth and, despite the circumstances, felt a pang of genuine sympathy for him. Like the boy who had burst into the clearing, he was covered in an assortment of burns, but the worst injury was his leg. By its odd angle, she knew it was broken. It was bleeding steadily, and his face was pale and pained.

"Can you help me?" He groaned.

"I'll try," she said gently as she looked for other injuries. "I'll need some clean water and some cloth for bandages," she said to the other men. "And I'll need you to make a fire to keep him warm."

She pulled out the little cloth package that held her medicines and spread it on the ground next to her. Carefully she cleaned and bandaged each burn, putting a few drops of medicine on each wound. The medicine was one of Uncle Matthias's finest. Finally, she enlisted the help of the men watching behind her for the task she was dreading the most. "We will have to pull his leg straight to set the bone," she said gravely, looking into their eyes. "It will be painful."

"Here, bite on this cloth," she added softly to Thomas. "The pain will be bad, but only for a few minutes. Ready?"

He closed his eyes and nodded.

"Now!" she said sharply, and the men pulled. She guided the bone as it crunched back into place. Thomas let out an animallike scream of pain and then drifted mercifully into unconsciousness. The men backed away, pale and shaken. It had taken a toll on all of them. She splinted the leg expertly and bandaged it.

"Keep him still and warm for a few days, and he will recover," she declared. "Keep his wounds clean." She lingered next to the sleeping youth and said a prayer to the Lord of the Book that he might recover and might learn better ways to spend his life.

As she moved to stand, Thomas opened his eyes. His hand grasped hers, and he weakly thanked her. Tears came to her eyes, and she struggled with herself not to cry again. "You're welcome," she replied softly then stood and walked over to where Stephen stood with the others.

Thomas motioned to the older man to come to him. He spoke quietly to the man, who nodded and then motioned to another. This man left the clearing and returned with a bundle, which he handed to Stephen. "Take her, and all of you go quickly," he said.

Stephen gasped when he saw who it was that had been handed to him. He turned to Luna, who burst into tears and scooped up the sleeping Zoe. The little girl was dirty and had several small burns but appeared to be all right.

"How did you—," began Luna, but she was cut off by the gruff voice of the older man.

"Go, I say, before I change my mind! There's a right big reward for whoever can bring the lot of you in, so stay off the main trail!"

Luna, Madai, and Stephen mounted their mice and quickly began making their way back to the trail. They paused there to get their bearings. Luna gratefully looked down at the soft innocent face and smiled. Stephen was relieved that all had ended well, but he continued to be concerned. How had they known where they were staying in Talenia? And had the rebels started the fire? Who was paying the reward for their capture? And if they knew where they were staying, were there others who knew where they were now? They would have to make their own trail through the tall grasses but keep close to the main trail so they wouldn't get lost. Travel would be much harder from here on out. The weight of responsibility weighed heavy on Stephen's shoulders, but he was thankful that they were on their way once again.

Luna

Luna mumbled reassurances into Zoe's ear more for her own benefit than for the scared little girl. When she had seen the injured youth lying there, despite the fact that he was the enemy, she had felt compassion and sympathy toward him. The injuries were indeed major but easy to treat. She had left the rebel leader with strict instructions on how to keep them clean. After she had finished, she had happily taken Zoe into her arms. What a surprise! She wondered if the rebels had started the fire. The hours of travel went quicker now that she had the comfort of having Zoe safe in her arms, and to her, it seemed like no time before they finally reached the familiar path to the cabin.

"We'll pass by the resistance campsite, since it's on our way, to report to Carl," Stephen's voice informed his relieved but tired followers.

They made their way toward the camp, and Luna looked forward to seeing a familiar face. She supported Zoe's sleeping head laboriously on her left arm while clutching her small waist and guiding the mouse. Familiar sights became more and more frequent, and Luna looked up at the darkening sky and hoped that she and Madai would get back to Eneva's house before it was too dark. Concentrating on Zoe's head, which kept falling off the crook of her arm, she almost ran into Stephen's mouse, which had come to a complete stop in front of her.

Looking up, she had to suppress a cry of horror. The once beautiful resistance camp, which had been so busy and productive, was gone. Flattened and charred, the only remnants of their memories were the half-burned carts and decimated tents. Luna looked at the dismal scene, and as reality dawned on her, a dark foreboding took its place in her heart. Where were Carl and the others? Had they escaped? Who had done this? She looked around warily. Was the danger gone, or were there enemies still lurking in the area? Stephen motioned to Luna and Madai to follow, and they left the path for the cover of bushes and grass and slipped quietly into the woods.

Kyle

"Tell me!"

The king had been staring into his face for the last hour and now almost sounded like a whining child pleading for a cookie.

"Look, I really don't know who he was! All I know is that a mixling helped me and then disappeared. I know nothing about the information you're looking for." Kyle felt out of breath as he finished his statement.

"Mikol!" The king yelled angrily out the towering door. His cold voice matched the halls and bounced from one to the other.

A young man came from one of the adjoining tunnels. "What can I do for you?" The man's voice was confident, and Kyle couldn't help but notice his nice clothes.

"Take him back to his cell. Record everything we know about the situation." As the king dismissed him with a wave of his hand, he called over his shoulder, "Tell my sister I'll be over for dinner."

Taking advantage of the moment while he was being escorted back to his prison cell, Kyle tried his best to make conversation. By the time he was secured back into his anything-but-welcoming cell, he had learned that the guard had married the adopted daughter of the king's sister. "He'll probably need marriage counseling before long if his wife is anything like her uncle," he mumbled to himself. "Too bad, he seems like he was a pretty nice man at one time." With this in mind, he tried to concentrate on different things to keep his mind off the dizziness that he felt.

Stephen

Stephen watched his red-and-black target without diverting his eyes, despite distractions that otherwise would have called his attention. "Gottcha!" he exclaimed as he gently placed the ladybug into his woven sack and headed in the direction of Eneva's house. Several days ago, after their return from Talenia, greatly distressed, they had gone to the cabin. Thankfully, Carl, as well as some of the other resistance members, were there. Carl had explained that while they were attending Key's trial, the camp had been guarded by three of their most valued members. Upon returning from the trial, they found the charred remains, and the guards were gone. They had set up temporary establishments with several independent members. Key, Stephen, and Daniel were all to move in with Eric. The news about recent events had been bad, and Stephen's face sobered at these disturbing thoughts.

When he reached Eneva's house, she told him that Luna should be back any minute from her first training session with Key. Apparently, his trial was not overly impressive, and her assistance was indeed required. Fifteen minutes later, Luna appeared and assured Stephen they could leave the house right away. He was surprised and wondered what she had done with Zoe but decided not to ask.

As they rode leisurely down the path, she mentioned it offhandedly, "I left Zoe with Madai and Eneva." She looked over at him as if waiting for him to respond. "You know, in case you were wondering," she finished, looking straight ahead, ignoring his seeming indifference.

"Well, to be honest, I was wondering...I found her...something." He noticed Luna's curious look. Pulling up his mouse, he offered her the still-closed sack.

As Luna withdrew the small bug, she laughed. "I'm sure Zoe will enjoy it!" She handed the sack back to him after replacing the gift. "You can give it to her later." She smiled.

They kept up a friendly chatter until they reached their destination. They both wanted to continue exploring the abandoned village and were glad they finally had the chance.

"Well, I wouldn't be surprised—." Luna cut off in midsentence.

He looked at her strangely. "What's wrong?" he asked with a tinge of concern.

"I heard something." She looked around cautiously.

"Don't be silly, you were talking! How could you hear anything above that?" He noticed her subdued glare and smiled at having succeeded in bothering her with his comment, but he realized she was serious.

"There it was again!" She seemed excited at proving herself and led her mouse toward the huge house in the middle.

Stephen heard it too now, some sort of grumbling, which seemed to grow and fade with the speaker's emotions. Stephen and Luna tied their mice quietly at the post by the bottom of the stairs and walked up the steps, trying to contain their anticipation. They both took their bows and readied an arrow. They pushed the doors open in unison and were as speechless as a tiny stooped man turned to face them.

The man blanched, and his mouth dropped open when he saw them. Stephen looked at the man and noticed he held an almost full sack by his side. Was he stealing? Who was he? Was he a rebel? His clothes were different, almost fancy, and he wore an odd hat that looked as if it would fall off the side of his balding head at any moment. He gaped at them, looking like he might bolt if given the chance.

Luna

"What are you doing here?"

Luna grimaced at Stephens's rough tone. The man began to mumble something about knowing it wouldn't be a good idea, but Luna couldn't completely understand him.

"Are you a rebel? If you are, you're not wanted here!"

The stress with the rebels must be getting to him! Luna thought as she observed the figure in front of her, who was obviously frightened. "Stephen…" She pulled him aside slightly. "You're scaring him. Try a softer approach, maybe?"

Stephen looked at her with mild annoyance and then turned back to the man. "How about you take a seat?" Stephen motioned to a chair, and the man stumbled to it, sitting on its edge in fright. Luna sighed in relief at his softened tone. "Now…what are you doing here?"

"I'm not stealing! I promise! I know the owners." Then he looked around worriedly. "I mean, I met the owners. Well, I saw them once, but I am supposed to be here!"

Luna saw that he was uncomfortable and was not sure what to say. "Well, we could always get the resistance leaders involved…" Here, Stephen trailed off.

"No, no, no! That is not necessary!" The man stood now and began looking frantically around, as if for escape.

"I'm afraid you can't leave…until you tell us what's going on."

The man looked very shaken to Luna, and he seemed defeated. "All right. I'll tell you." He took a deep breath, as if preparing himself for some sort of difficult challenge. "The queen sent me to bring me her things."

"Do you mean Queen Anara?" Luna asked.

He looked at them as if waiting for them to execute him on the spot, but even if they had wanted to, they were both too stunned to do anything right at that moment.

14

Luna

Luna stretched her arms above her head and made sure Zoe, who was sleeping between her and Madai, was all right. She thought over everything that had happened the day before. The man had been more than willing to help them once they had established their good intentions. He had told them that the queen had sent him to retrieve some clothing and belongings for her and for the young prince. Although he had seemed very helpful, he still would reveal nothing about where he was from or where the queen was.

As he left, he had handed Stephen a small book. Luna had been dying of curiosity ever since and hoped Stephen would keep his promise that he wouldn't read it without her. Luna groaned inwardly as she saw the small mountain of dirty clothes, hers as well as Zoe's. Taking her last garment from the cupboard, she slipped it on without particular care to details and hurried out to find Eneva.

Eneva had told her that there would be pastries to deliver in the morning. After she had prepared and left Zoe with instructions to listen to Eneva, she and Madai set out. Countless stories and fantasizing had gone on the night before talking about

Eric's peculiar situation. When the guards at the gate inspected the pastries in the familiar bucket and troubled themselves to even break a few open, the two girls looked at each other and suppressed laughter.

Soon they were at the huge green door and knocked tentatively. The door opened, and they stared into the foreboding face of a very tall woman.

"Hello?" the woman said, and Luna knew she was attempting to ask why they were there without being outwardly rude.

"Hi...uhmm...we're here to deliver pastries to Eric," Luna spoke up bravely, although she really didn't feel very brave under the lady's piercing green eyes.

"I'll take them. It was nice of you to stop by."

The next sight that greeted their eyes was the huge door rushing toward them. "Mom! Meet my friends!" Eric's friendly voice interrupted the rebuff of his mother.

"Ahhh, yes, son, I just met them. Good-bye, girls."

"Mooom!"

"Son, they are very busy. In fact, they were just in a hurry to leave when you came along." Her artificial smile was directed at them, and Luna had to force herself not to giggle. Did she really think they didn't notice that she wanted them to leave?

"Actually, your mom's right. We are in a bit of a hurry," Luna said reluctantly to Eric and tried to ignore his disappointed face.

As his mom turned him in the other direction and began closing the door, Eric quickly turned and called over her arm, "Come back any time—"

The door slamming cut off the rest of his friendly intentions. As soon as they left the outer gate, Luna burst into laughter with her companion. They both knew that the door had not accelerated in its closing for no reason!

"I think we know now what is keeping Eric at home!" Luna said through her laughter.

———∘∘∘❁∘∘∘———

Stephen

"My goodness what have I got myself into?" Stephen paced back and forth; he had been waiting for Luna for over an hour.

"Sorry, I'm late." Her voice sounded truly sorry, but her curiosity was unhidden. They sat themselves down at the small table inside Stephens's tent and opened the old book between them.

The first entry greeted their waiting gaze:

> I was advised by my dear sister to keep a log of the strange happenings that have taken place lately in our lives. And so I shall begin it now.
>
> We have been moved. My lady promised us that this place would be no different from the last, but I must say, she was mistaken. The big house has much of the same grandeur, but it isn't the temperature we are all used to at all. Even so, all of us have decided that we will be loyal no matter what. We all love little Elihu. He turns three tomorrow, and we are all meeting in the ladies' hall. I must attend to my duties. I see no use of this log, but again, upon my sister's insistence...I suppose it could improve my penmanship.
>
> Laraan

Stephen caught Luna's gaze over the table and knew without asking that they both were waiting for the other to turn the page.

> It has been two weeks. I can't express what I feel, but it isn't good. My lady has informed us that beetle trainers will be visiting regularly now. Security has been increased. We aren't allowed out of the village compound. It feels more like we are locked in than that we are keeping someone out, although they assure us that is not the case. Small houses have been built for all of us, and a protecting garden is being placed about the edges as well.

> I tell my sister she should write this, but she says I can use the practice. I must go help my lady with Elihu.

Another entry followed on the next page.

> I can't believe Elihu is already four! It has been a while since I have recorded events here, but there has been nothing worth recording in the last year. We live a simple life, serving my lady and staying within this tiny piece of paradise. The king makes regular visits, three times a week, to be precise. He will be arriving soon, so we are all preparing for his visit. Elihu loves to make things for his father. He is growing so quickly!

Stephen and Luna scanned through many more entries; they were all about Elihu and my lady and about the compound. The more they read, the more they saw the similarities between the abandoned village and the book. "Hey, look at this one," Luna interrupted his thoughts.

> Elihu is six now. His father came yesterday; he doesn't visit us very often anymore. He came to warn us about his brother. He said we could be in danger. There is much tension in the palace. He said something about a perfected city that his brother wants to build. All of the servants are worried, but my lady tells us we will all be fine. I suppose our fears are simply that: fears.

Stephen looked up when he heard someone outside. As he turned to hide the diary, he realized Luna had been faster. A second later, Daniel walked into the tent, and his cheery smile turned into a scowl when he saw Luna.

"Figures." He grunted disgustedly. "I came to ask you if you wanted to help fill another beetle order, but I see you're quite occupied."

Stephen's head spun with stress as he tried to think of an explanation. Lately it seemed he was losing his best friend. Whenever Daniel asked, Stephen always made the point that the only reason he spent time with Luna was because he had to. Of course, it wasn't the truth anymore, and he didn't seem to be a very good liar. Slowly, Luna's friendship had snuck up on him, and he almost thought of her to be as good a friend as Daniel. Though if he ever told him that—Daniel had never hidden his opinion of girls: "Girls can definitely not be a friend! They are last and unhelpful, more trouble than they're worth. I mean they're basically like an untrained beetle you drag around with you. Right?" The comment had been made more than once, and Stephen had never had a reason to argue. After all, Janet pretty much fit that description! These days, Daniel always seemed frustrated, angry, or up in arms about something or other.

Luna's clear voice interrupted his turbulent thoughts. "Well, I guess we have that worked out. I have some things I've got to do at home."

Stephen noticed her slip the diary behind a stack of clothes sitting on a chair as she retrieved her cloak and went outside.

"So what were you working out?" Daniels cynical voice filled the tent immediately after Luna's departure.

"Why do you have to be so mean about it?" Stephen evaded the question.

"You know, you say you just associate with her because of the deal with her uncle and all, but I think it's more than that."

"She wouldn't be that bad of a friend if you just gave her a chance!" The words were out of his mouth before he could think. It was sheer reaction.

"Friend? Friend? So now it's friend!" Stephen winced as Daniel's voice rose in volume.

"I didn't mean that she was my only friend, I just meant if you gave her half a chance, you might find that she is a good person...," he now hotly defended himself.

"Someone's defensive! You know, I always thought you agreed with me as far as girls went!"

Stephen looked at Daniel defiantly. "I did, I mean do, in general," he stated in what he hoped was a reassuring voice as he longed for Daniel to overlook his slip.

"Sure." Daniel's voice had lowered again.

"Can we go hunting and back to the way it used to be?" Stephen dared to ask.

"Hunting, yes, but it will never be the way it used to be as long as Luna is still a part of the resistance."

Stephen did not contemplate the sentence fully but followed his comrade out the tent door and tried to ignore the feeling that something was really wrong.

Luna

Luna stared nervously at the ground in front of her; she and Stephen were standing outside the familiar cabin waiting for the courage to enter. The other evening, they had completed reading the diary. Its last entry reminded Luna of an untold tale with an unfortunate ending, just waiting to be discovered. The chilling words still haunted her thoughts, and she couldn't help but go over them one more time:

> How the years have passed. Elihu is twelve already, a young man...He has been a joy to all of us with his endless questions. He is always ready to help those who need it, an unusually empathetic and loving child. But things here are falling apart, and I fear for him. Why is this happening? Nobody will tell me. I keep hearing the name Pyramidis... It's a city, and they say we must move there.

There was just one more entry, and Luna felt goosebumps on her arms as she read the final words.

This morning, the servants were arguing in the courtyard. They say that Elihu's father is dead, but no one knows for sure. There has been shouting all morning down below, and we are not allowed to leave this room. My fear drives me to write this down. I don't know what to expect, but my suspicion is that something bad is afoot. Soldiers are coming through the gate. I will record what happ

That was where it ended. There was a mark on the paper after the last word as if she struggled at the last to continue her sentence. The page was wrinkled and ripped on the bottom corner, as if the book had been torn from someone's hands.

After a bit of a discussion, she and Stephen had decided that they needed to take it to Carl. Thoughts of the last time she had brought important news to Carl flickered for a second in her mind. Suddenly, she realized Stephen had opened the door and was waiting for her to enter. *Whoever made the rule that girls have to enter first?* she thought in annoyance. Countless times, people (especially men) made a big deal about it when it could just be avoided.

"Agghem, I hope you know you're interrupting a meeting." Carl's stern voice made her quake.

Stephen spoke up and defended their entrance. "It's something very important."

At least he doesn't insist I speak first as well, she thought. She watched as several men filed out after Carl dismissed them. She and Stephen sat down at the rough wood table and laid the diary out in front of Carl. The next half hour was spent relating their discovery.

Janet

Janet grumbled as she rose slowly to answer the door. "It's almost dark and starting to rain. Who would be knocking at this time of night?" she muttered irritably. As she swung open the door, she was very surprised to see Daniel.

"Daniel…what are you doing here?" Being polite had never been one of her strong points.

"I see our feelings are mutual," Daniel responded, observing her blunt, unfriendly question. "I'm here to request your presence at a meeting tomorrow, orders of the high council," Daniel stated evenly, as if offering her a cup of tea.

"Come in out of the rain," she replied grudgingly.

Daniel looked around the room and then stood at the window staring out into the dark, willing the rain to stop so he could be on his way.

"Have you heard the latest?" asked Janet after the silence had stretched uncomfortably to the point of making them both feel terribly awkward. He didn't reply, and after a pause, she continued the one-sided conversation. "Luna and Stephen have been selected to go on a mission."

"A mission?" Daniel replied, turning from the window. He found he was unable to keep the curiosity out of his voice. "Why Luna and not me?" he added irritably.

"Well, she is the new girl," responded Janet. "And apparently, Carl isn't sure where your loyalties lie due to a recent occurrence."

Daniel snorted and turned back to the window. Janet observed him with a smile. "But of course, you wouldn't want to talk about that," she said carefully.

He said nothing in reply, and after a few minutes of tense silence, she tried again to engage him in conversation. "So, do you suppose Luna knows why she was really accepted into the resistance…and that Stephen was assigned to take care of her?" she queried.

Daniel turned and gave her a piercing look. "What are you getting at?" he asked quietly.

"Well, maybe if we were to tell her the real reason she was let into the resistance—"

"She might not really want to continue," he finished the sentence for her. He nodded and turned the idea over in his mind. Maybe she would decide to go back to live in Sandar if she knew about the arrangement that had been contrived by the leaders and Uncle Matthias.

"They will be coming here shortly to tell you that you will be training Key for one session tomorrow. We can tell her when she gets here," Janet added.

He said nothing, but a spark of hope that this interfering girl might go away now glowed in his heart. It would be her own decision if she chose to leave the resistance. They both stood looking out into the night silently, each preoccupied with this new plan.

Stephen

The rain slowed to sprinkles, and soon they heard voices outside. As Stephen and Luna entered Janet's dwelling, Stephen stopped in surprise when he saw that Daniel was there.

"Why are...?" He left the question unfinished and let his puzzled face convey his feelings.

"Oh, we're just working some stuff out." Daniel's voice was angry.

"Stuff?" Stephen asked, bewildered by Daniel's unusual demeanor.

"Oh hey, Luna!" Janet greeted Luna like some long-lost friend.

"Hey?" Luna responded as if afraid to trust the unusual pleasantness.

"You don't have to pretend anymore," Daniel interjected.

Stephen looked at Daniel, surprised at his comment to Janet.

"Pretend what?" Luna said in bewilderment as she looked from Daniel to Janet. Luna's question struck dread into Stephen's heart. Was this Daniel's way of getting even?

"Oh sorry, I heard that they already told you." Daniel's voice held feigned concern.

"Told me what?" Luna looked toward Stephen with a puzzled look.

"What are you talking about?" Stephen exclaimed.

"Oh, come on, Stephen! You know what we're talking about!" Daniel replied. Daniel's response only heightened his anxiety.

"Can someone please tell me what everyone is talking about?" Luna exclaimed.

"Well, if you really want to know the truth…," Janet presented the idea with a smile and a smug look at her fingernails.

"Yes, the truth is…," Luna prompted.

"I don't think—"

But the rest of Stephen's comment was lost in Janet's next comment.

"Well, if you insist. We have all been pretending to be your friends. Really, your uncle and Carl made a special agreement to have you accepted."

Janet observed Luna's shocked face with a self-assured look on her own.

"Well, for you and Daniel, that's not surprising…" Luna's voice trailed off.

Suddenly everything dawned on Stephen as Janet continued, "No, it's not just us! It's everyone, I'm surprised you didn't notice. You were given to Stephen only as an assignment. He was told to pretend to be your friend, but he doesn't even like girls. He told me himself how silly girls are." Janet flopped into a chair like having completed some difficult job.

"Stephen?" Luna's voice sounded strained as she turned toward him, waiting for him to confirm the truth of Janet had said.

"Wait, you didn't think Stephen was really your friend?" Daniel's mocking voice responded to Luna's question before Stephen had time to think.

"Aren't you…?" She still directed the question at Stephen, and this time, he answered it with stammering uncertainty.

"Of course, I am," Stephen defended himself, willing her to believe him.

"Don't lie to her, Stephen! You know you always agreed with me when I said girls don't make good friends." Daniel's voice fell as a reprimand, and Stephen felt despair fill him as he realized that all those times of not speaking up against Daniel's remarks about girls were now going to come back at him in his face.

"Luna, at first you were an assignment, but it's different now."

Luna looked back at him, now sadly. "So you were just pretending?" Her voice was disappointed, and before he had time to sputter an answer, she turned and was out the door riding into the woods, atop her mouse.

"What's wrong with you, Daniel?" Stephen exclaimed angrily.

"Nothing's wrong with me. You are the one who has changed," retorted Daniel. "Since when has a girl become so important to you?"

"It has nothing to do with her being a girl. She is a fellow resistance member. She is a good member, and we have a common goal. Have you forgotten that?" Stephen was pacing back and forth, agitated and angry with what had just happened.

"Yes, I know all about goals. But all I did was tell her the truth. She is a paid-in member, and everyone is just pretending. She might as well know the truth of it," Daniel responded.

"Well, I'm not pretending," exclaimed Stephen with deep feeling. "You hurt her feelings, and I think you are trying to push her out of the resistance. Why?"

Daniel turned away and thought for a moment.

"She's getting in the way of our friendship. We really don't need her," Janet piped up.

"That's right. We don't," Daniel agreed.

Stephen shook his head. "Well, whatever your reasons, treating any member of the resistance like that isn't going to forge a very strong friendship with me. It just isn't following the Great Book or anything else you claim to believe in. What are we doing, fighting for the rights of our people when we can't even treat another member of the resistance with decency? You've been my best friend for a long time. I thought I knew you better than that! You've changed, and I don't think it has anything to do with Luna. It's just wrong, and I am disappointed in both of you!"

With that, Stephen left the house and headed back to the cabin, ignoring Daniels protests for him to wait. They sounded sincere, but it seemed that lately, nothing about Daniel was sincere anymore.

15

Stephen

"I've made up my mind. Daniel or Janet can go with Stephen."

Stephen winced as he recognized Luna's familiar voice.

"You can't leave now. We need you," Carl reprimanded Luna.

Stephen stood in the open doorway in strained silence as he awaited her response. As he suspected, she was very angry, and rightly so.

"Well, you can tell my uncle that I decided I would rather not be 'needed' by people who are dishonest. And I won't be bought and sold like an object."

"Who told you that?" Carl began to question Luna, but she cut him off, which Stephen had never known her to do.

"Actually, it doesn't matter. It's about time I find out who my real friends are. I'm asking your permission to leave. Of course, it's your decision," she finished.

Carl looked down, and he suddenly looked older and sadder than Stephen had ever seen him. "Luna…I'm sorry you were hurt…Not everyone in the resistance is kind…I wish you would change your mind, but if that's how you feel, I won't force you to stay." His eyes were filled with unfallen tears as he said this, and he looked down.

At his affirmative reply, Stephen's heart sank.

"Why did everything have to go so wrong? Where will you go?" asked Carl tiredly."

"I will go to Talenia, if they will have me. Maybe there I will able to forget this happened. I'm sorry I didn't live up to your expectations." Luna stormed out of the door, and her hurt, angry face sent a stab of pain to Stephen's heart.

"Luna, wait," he called after her and ran to catch up. "Look, Luna, I'm really sorry about what happened. Yes, at first I resented being responsible for you, but that was before I got to know you. You really have made friends here, and does it really matter how it started?"

As she continued to ignore him, he reached out and turned her around by her shoulder. Her pent-up anger exploded.

"Yes, it matters how it started! You and I had so much fun exploring and racing and...and everything else. When I needed help finding Zoe, you were ready to do that too. And I thought it was because we were friends. I thought that we were going to look out for each other like friends! But now, I see it was all my imagination. I can't believe you wouldn't tell me! There is nothing you can say to change my mind. The others don't want me here. And Daniel doesn't want me interfering with your friendship."

Her voice broke, and after a moment, she continued, "I'm leaving."

As she mounted her mouse, he called after her, "Luna, wait, we can talk about this!"

Her response was simple. "We just did." And with that, she rode off while Stephen stayed there watching, trying to hold back the angry feelings he had toward the offending members of the resistance.

Luna

The next morning, Luna and Madai set off on their recently groomed mice. The night before when Luna had explained everything to Madai, she had given her complete sympathy and insisted on going with her. They both agreed, however, that it would be best to leave Zoe behind. The trip would be too dangerous to risk the little girl again. Luna and Madai had become quite good friends since Madai had come to be a part of the resistance.

Luna thought back now to the sad history Madai had related. She told her that when she was about twelve, she had come back from school, and her family was gone. The neighbors had told her that there was a terrible fire at their workplace while she was away, and they had been killed. It had clearly been a hard experience for Madai, and Luna felt sad for her. As much as Luna wished she could have known her parents, it was still better not to have known them than to have known them and then have them die. She thought on this, as well as calming texts from her book as they rode along.

Was she making the right decision? Would the Lord of the Book do this, if the same had happened to him? Maybe she had acted in haste. Could Stephen have been speaking the truth? She felt turmoil inside. Thoughts blurred into one another as the monotonous road ahead kept going on and on and on.

"Please watch where you're going!" the man said as he and his mouse bumped into Luna's.

She pulled Mitzie abruptly to the side of the trail. Where had he come from? She had been lost in thought, riding carelessly without thought of her surroundings. As she looked up into his inquiring face, she gasped in recognition. It was the tiny man whom she and Stephen had met in the abandoned village! At the thought of Stephen, a shadow crossed her face, and the man looked at her with concern.

"Are you all right?" he asked.

"Yeah, I'm fine. Umm, I have some questions—"

At the word *questions*, the man disappeared faster than he had appeared.

Luna continued her way, her thoughts scrambling to make sense of the man she had just seen. She and Madai puzzled together over what he had been doing on the lonely trail. Luna felt a sudden wave of thankfulness for Madai. Madai was the one true friend that she had, someone she could confide in. Their friendship was real, and right now, that was what counted.

16

Stephen

Stephen sank half-exhausted against a smooth round acorn in the clearing. He was reminded painfully of Luna for a second. "Why do girls have to be so sensitive and reactive?" He huffed to himself in feigned annoyance. The truth was he missed her.

That morning, since dawn, he had thrown himself into target practice, running, and exercises. Now sweating and resting on the mossy ground, he thought back to all the fun times he had enjoyed, talking and training with Luna. He had discussed the matter with Carl, and so far Carl had decided to completely delay the next mission, if not cancel it. Jumping back to his feet, Stephen tossed his knife expertly into the direct middle of the target with one more grunt of frustration.

Luna

"Keep your elbow even with your wrist," Luna admonished gently to Madai, who was practicing her archery skills.

"Luna, I don't think I'm cut out for this," Madai said, dropping her bow to her side.

"Don't give up so easily." Luna laughed. "You are doing fine. You know how important it is to be able to learn some basics! It just takes a bit of practice."

Luna was surprised to see the mysterious man from the day before standing at the edge of the campsite. He looked embarrassed and cleared his throat nervously, twisting his hands together.

"I...um...thought about what you said yesterday...you know, about the questions. I guess I just panicked."

Luna smiled. "Well, the diary you gave us was very helpful, but I need more information," she ventured cautiously.

"This could take some time." The man sighed anxiously.

Luna directed him to the small campfire near the tent where she and Madai were staying. "Sit down," she invited pleasantly to a log near the fire. As the man took a seat, Luna set a cup of coffee and some sweet pastries before him then took a place across from her visitor.

"So what's the story?" she asked, and the man began to talk.

THE MAN FROM THE VILLAGE

"I-I-I should probably start at the beginning...," the man stuttered and looked around the campsite as if he expected company at any minute. "Fourteen years ago, King Jedan of Icelair was married to a beautiful girl named Anara. She was anyone's dream princess except for one thing. Though she herself had perfect Icelairian features, her ancestors were mixlings. Jedan's parents and his younger brother begged him to reconsider before the wedding, but he would hear none of it. He was enchanted with Anara, and nothing could keep him from her. Their wedding day was celebrated far and wide. Everyone came for the wedding, and again for the baby shower two years later.

"It was a rosy story until the birth of their baby son, Elihu. Elihu had inherited the worst thing he could ever have, the eyes of one of his great-grandparents. His eyes were a striking green, taking from him his royal esteem. His parents and grandparents were horrified, but nevertheless, nothing could keep them from loving the little bundle of joy. He bore the grace of his mother and the charm of his father. In every other way, he appeared Icelairian.

"Elihu's father, who could deny nothing to his perfect wife and beautiful child, built them a castle with every comfort imaginable for a young mother and son, complete with courtiers and servants.

"All of the servants were more like family than servants. They cared so much about their loving mistress, they never even called her your majesty as was custom, but my lady. Anara was kind to everyone, a very caring and gentle woman.

"Elihu grew and became as well-mannered as his mother, but when he turned three, there was a family quarrel with Jedan's younger brother. He insisted that the child was not fit to carry on the royal line because of his mixling eyes. He insisted that he himself would be next in line for the throne. King Jedan was very angry. But he could see that his family was in danger, so he sent them into hiding."

"At the village we found?" asked Luna, her eyes wide with rapt attention.

"Yes, the village. He built a crystal palace deep in the wooded country and planted the living hedge around it. He hired beetle trainers and fenced off the area just inside the compound to be guarded by the beetles. He moved the queen and their son there and hired tutors to teach the prince. He visited them often at first, but as time went on, he feared he would be followed, and so his visits became fewer. We all wondered what was happening. We were there nearly nine years when tragedy struck.

"During the feast at Talenia, King Jedan was killed by a band of unknown raiders—some say his brother, Elsiper, arranged this tragedy to gain control of the throne. Shortly after, the village was compromised by an inside spy, and the queen and prince were taken captive in a raid. I escaped but followed my lady to a mysterious city. On the outside, it was beautiful, more beautiful than anything you could imagine: towers half as high as the trees, plains of beautifully kept moss, and sparkling castles, but those were just appearances. On the inside, it's a prison, filled with captive slaves who are building it, working day and night. Dark dungeons are there for those who do not carry out orders, and work schools are there to train young students. Many children spend several years of their lives there, away from their families. And that's not the worst of it. The slaves are all mixlings!"

Here he stopped and looked at her, his face pale and pained. He passed his hand over his bald head and looked around the campsite again as he had earlier. He lowered his voice and said, "The queen and her young son are in one of those dungeons, and soon every mixling there ever was will be trapped in that city. They will be forced to work, and the Icelairians will control and mistreat them forever. It's only a matter of time before they take your friends at the resistance as well, and even you. I know there is a spy within the ranks of the resistance, although I don't know who. There are guards on all of the borders. King Jedan's brother is none other than the evil king Elsiper. And as I already said, there are suspicions that he is responsible for the death of King Jedan.

"And that's why I've decided to help you, help them." He looked at her expectantly.

Suddenly, she knew what he meant. "No, I can't go back to the resistance. They were all lying to me, and they never wanted me there."

"Look, this isn't about you anymore! This is about all of the mixlings. I don't know what happened between you and them, but there are more important things at stake now. There are lives at stake, and even the future of the young king."

The man made sense, but Luna was resistant to accept it.

"You are pouting," he added, somewhat impatiently.

"I am not pouting!" her voice rose in indignation.

"You need to think about forgiveness. The Lord of the Book would want you to forgive them, even if they did hurt your feelings…Remember, pray for those who mistreat you and use you! That is His way," the man spoke kindly but firmly and handed her a map as he walked to his mouse. "This will take you to the glass city. Don't let us down. And don't get caught…It won't be easy, but you and your friends work well together."

And with that, he looked around once more as if he thought someone might see him, mounted his mouse, and slipped away into the tall grass.

———∘∘∘▸◉◂∘∘∘———

Stephen

Stephen pushed back the window curtain with extreme surprise written across his face. *That couldn't be?* He was out the door in a bound. Luna and Madai were riding toward the cabin, although her head was down, and she looked anything but happy. He himself had never been happier to see Luna and Madai.

"Luna, you're back!" He greeted her without even trying to disguise his excitement. As she dismounted, he gave her braided hair a friendly tug and began his planned apology.

17

Stephen

"So, I'm really sorry, and I really hope you'll forgive me," Stephen finished his I'm-sorry speech, which he had rehearsed in his mind since she left.

"That was planned, wasn't it?" Luna asked him with a faint smile.

"That's not funny," he said, trying to keep a straight face.

"Okay, speaking seriously now, I forgive you and appreciate your apology…I guess"—here, she paused a moment—"I was also wrong and shouldn't have been so easily hurt. I should have considered all the facts a little more." Luna sighed as if finishing a great task. "I guess there are some here who really don't want me around, and I suppose I did really let it get to me. I'll try to grow a tougher skin!"

Then changing the mood, she addressed a more serious topic. "I have more information about the queen."

Stephen looked at her expectantly and then to his annoyance, she ignored his look, tied her mouse, and went into the cabin. "Luna!" he called in irritation. A laughing Madai was right behind him.

Luna apologized to Carl for acting so hastily, and Carl, who said little, seemed quite relieved.

"Can Madai go with us?" Luna asked.

"Well, has she had any training?"

"I have been working with her the past week on her archery skills. She is making progress."

Madai, who was now blushing, looked down and said nothing.

"I don't see why not," Carl said with only one cautious glance toward Madai.

Carl told them that the mission should be carried out the next morning. From what the man had told Luna, the situation was urgent. Johan would be going along. Luna suggested that perhaps it would be best if few people knew where they were going. "The man said that he knew there was a spy in the resistance. The old man had said the same. Perhaps it might be wise to tell as few people as possible of our plans."

Carl thought for a moment. "I suppose you are right. I can't imagine there truly could be a spy among us, but this is a very important mission."

As they walked out the door, Luna asked Madai if she could ride ahead and check on Zoe.

"Why ever did you ask permission for her to go?" Stephen asked her.

"Because she's my friend…and she is a sincere friend," she added firmly.

"This mission is not about friends!" admonished Stephen. "Madai does not look like someone who is ready to fight off a band of rebels."

"And I do?" Her question surprised him, and he realized that she had shown that she could if necessary.

"Fine, but if she gets hurt or captured, it's going to be your fault," Stephen warned her.

The Castle of Icelair

"I'm afraid there was nothing I could do to stop the whole thing. They know, and they are sending out some representatives to find the city."

The hooded figure's voice wavered slightly with the bad news, and his frightened heart trembled at the thought of delivering unwelcome tidings to the temperamental king.

"No way to stop them? See, that's the difference between you and me! I let nothing stop me, but you let a meaningless friendship stop you from doing the most basic of things."

"If I blow my cover, it will all be over!" the man pleaded with his approaching master.

"That's right, it will be over! So you better get this right. We will be ready for these representatives, but now it's time you start your work on Talenia."

He wished he could take back his involvement with the king and his doings. But he knew that now there was absolutely no way out. That night so long ago rushed back to him when he was in the woods with his sister.

"Here it is, Diana!" he had exclaimed, leading her toward a small shelter he had built in the cove of some bushes. A small flickering fire had lit his masterpiece.

"It's beautiful!"

Her simple praise had meant so much to him. What would she think of him now, in light of everything he had done? Would she ever forgive him?

Luna

Luna leaned back against a rough tree in the clearing and stared up at the bright stars. Madai had warned her that it probably wasn't a good idea to go out in the dark by herself, but Luna saw no danger. After all, Stephen's tent and the cabin were within hearing range, and if she screamed, she was pretty sure someone would come. Besides, she had her bow and arrows, which should keep her safe. She was thinking smugly how unnecessary all this paranoia was when suddenly a hand clasped itself over her mouth, and a strong arm pinned her tightly to the tree behind her.

"Let me go!" she attempted to say, although she herself couldn't understand her words. She pushed and struggled but made little headway and was soon stilled with a violent shove, which sent pain shooting everywhere through her back and arms.

"If you scream, I'll show you something to scream about." The voice was very harsh, but something about the way the words were pronounced was almost familiar. Whoever this was could do quite a bit of damage in hand-to-hand combat; he was obviously stronger than her.

"Who are you?" she said, readjusting her arms in pain. Luna couldn't help but notice the full black cloak that seemed to completely envelope him. "Who are you and what do you want?" she asked, forgetting to keep her voice down.

A kick to her lower leg struck fear into her heart.

"What's wrong with you? Are you crazy?" she asked, standing up a little straighter then leaning again back against the tree, her back beginning to ache.

"You don't need to know who I am. In fact, no one does."

Luna turned her head to the side, avoiding the black hood that was now next to her ear.

"My warning is this. Tell Carl to end this mission, or lots of people are going to get hurt!" he whispered menacingly. "If you know what's good for you, you won't go to the city!"

Had she heard his voice break? He gave her wrists one last squeeze and turned to leave. "Don't forget to deliver the message," he called over his shoulder. And with a final shove, he was gone.

With a slight groan, Luna gently massaged her now throbbing leg. Luna thought about everything that had just taken place.

Who was the man who had just confronted her? As ideas spun around and around her frazzled head, she tried not to panic. What was he planning to do if they went on with the mission? How did he even know about the mission?

"Luna!" the soft call made her jump in fright, but she was relieved it was Stephen.

"What are you doing out here?" His question held concern.

"Just out for a nighttime walk," she exclaimed, trying to laugh. She stood shakily, trying to conceal her pain by looking in the other direction.

"What's wrong? Are you okay?" Stephen noticed that something was out of the ordinary.

"I'm fine."

Stephen looked at her strangely. "Why are you limping?" he asked.

"Someone came to give me a warning," she mumbled.

He bent down and looked at her bruised leg. "This doesn't look like a simple warning," he muttered angrily. "What did this person say?"

"He said not to go on this mission, or a lot of people would get hurt."

"Who was it?" he asked next.

"I don't know. He was wearing black cloak and gloves," she said tiredly. "He seemed familiar, but I don't know who…"

Confusion pounded in her hurting head. She felt frightened and distracted as Stephen helped her back to Eneva's cabin. Then she tossed and turned as the cloaked figure haunted her in her dreams.

The Spy

The dark figure's hands trembled slightly as he left the clearing. What had he just done? Or a better question was, what had he become? He had taken his anger out on the girl Luna. He thought of her name with frustration but also with a reluctant respect. She reminded him of Diana.

When he had first started working for the king, he had been given simple assignments: stealing something, telling a lie. The king had conditioned him not to feel his conscience any longer. The king completely trusted his training, but there was one thing he had never been able to remove, and that was his care for his sister. He had always been willing to do anything for her, and that much had not changed.

He rode hard on his mouse toward his tent. The cold wind blew against his troubled face. Before Luna had come, this infiltration had been so easy, lying every time he opened his mouth, but now? Luna was so trusting, so bookly, and she had shown him forgiveness and kindness when all he had shown her was hatred. How far was he willing to go? As his resolve faltered for a second, he quickly recovered it. He would go as far as it took, and it didn't matter who else got hurt as long as his sister was safe.

Stephen

Stephen rode slowly forward toward Eneva's cabin. Though he knew what he was going to confront Luna about, it still confused him, and the exact words hadn't come to mind quite yet. As he reached the small familiar house, he rode around the back to where he knew Luna's window was. He knocked until he was greeted by Luna's sleep-filled face. She pushed back her disheveled hair and lifted the window.

"What are you doing here?" she asked in surprise.

"We need to talk. Get dressed and come out here," he demanded after noticing she was still in some sort of nightdress.

She pulled the window down, not so gently, and drew the curtain back to its proper place. After about twenty minutes, Stephen began to wonder whether she was coming out at all. She had never taken this long to get ready. After another five minutes of waiting, she finally reappeared at the window. Her hair was braided down both sides, and she wore a tidy jumper with the tight undersuit she usually wore. Leather boots completed the familiar outfit, and all in all, he never would have known she had been sleeping but half an hour ago.

She pulled the window up, and Stephen expected her to leap over the sill as he knew she could, but he was wrong. Luna came over the window clumsy and wobbly.

"Are you okay? You seem a bit…um…unsteady."

"I'm fine," she retorted to his concerned look.

"I need to know exactly what happened last night. It's important that we find out who's issuing these threats," Stephen stated. "Who did you talk to last night?"

"I really don't know. His voice sounded familiar…but he never took off his cloak," she answered with a puzzled look.

"Do you remember what he looked like?" Stephen asked, trying to make sense of things.

"I thought I told you. He was wearing a black cloak and gloves and boots. They were all black," she exclaimed, slightly exasperated.

"How do you know that it was a man?" Stephen asked, trying to find out as much as possible.

"Because I'm smart," she retorted sarcastically. "No, because he sounded like a man and was really strong. But his voice was familiar." Suddenly, she stopped and looked at her boots. "No, it couldn't have been…"

"It couldn't have been who?" Stephen now urged with interest.

"Daniel. It's just the voice sounded so much like…"

Stephen looked at her in disbelief. "That's ridiculous, I know he's been a little unfriendly, but that's no reason to think—"

Stephen paused and thought for a moment. "Although we have been told to watch him lately," Stephen finished in confusion.

"Watch him?" Her voice told him she was curious.

"I wasn't supposed to say that, so forget I did." He remorsefully slapped his forehead.

"Well, you said it now, so I can't just forget. Why are you watching him?"

Stephen looked at her questioning face and crossed arms and knew he would end up telling her one way or another. "He has been reported to leave a lot in the evening and be gone... sometimes for a whole day. He has been acting oddly. His reasons for absences don't always add up."

Luna looked at her boots. "I-I'm sorry, I know you guys were pretty good friends." Luna looked at him sympathetically.

"I still can't believe he would go as far as threatening people."

"It probably wasn't him," Luna added. "We can't be completely sure." She reassured him before walking around to the door of the house. As he watched her go, he hoped what she said was right.

18

Luna

Luna stared up at the rough roof of the makeshift shelter above her head. It felt good to finally be on their way on this adventurous mission. It had been delayed for a whole two weeks after the whole hubbub with Daniel. Daniel disappeared the day after Stephen confronted him, and she had not been successful in finding out what had transpired. Stephen had seemed distracted and gloomy ever since.

Slowly, she had been able to do her agility courses and bow-and-arrow practices easily again, and they had all prepared carefully for the trip. Although she had told Madai that if she didn't want to come, that was fine, Madai had insisted that she wasn't going to miss out on anything, so Eneva had agreed to take care of Zoe. When Eneva had been let in on the secret of Zoe's existence, she had been surprised but soon fell in love with the little girl. She enjoyed spending time with her. And Zoe loved to "help" with baking.

They had been following the map that the man had given her for two uneventful days. At first, they were on the regular trail to Talenia, which was more heavily travelled, but they had now left that trail and branched off to the east. This trail was faint and weaving, and it was apparent that few knew about it. They set up camp off to one side and felt fairly secure in the nook among the deep grasses. Right now Stephen was on watch and then it would be her turn, and Johan was third in line. After the last trip with Madai, they had realized that she wasn't capable of staying awake for a night watch. It was good to have one more nightwatcher.

A sharp whistle caused Luna to sit up stiffly and snap on her belt. Shaking Madai awake, Luna hurried to the side of the tent. Looking out at the top of the shelter, she wondered what was happening. The whistle was an alarm they had all agreed on.

Madai sleepily asked, "What's going on?"

"I'm not sure," Luna whispered back.

Suddenly fire engulfed the pine branches laid around their camp. Fright tugged at Luna's heart as she slipped out the back of the shelter followed by Madai. Suddenly she saw several figures surrounding their position. Leaning close to Madai, she whispered to her the danger. After barely getting the words out of her mouth, they were charged from all sides.

"Run!" Luna yelled before a hand clamped over her mouth. Struggling fiercely, she kicked and elbowed, but she was no match for the man behind her.

Kyle

Kyle tuned over with a groan on his hard mat. "If they're planning on keeping me as a permanent tenant, they could at least give me some comfortable lodging," he grumbled to the dreary walls, which were his only companion besides the small water bucket in the corner. He was glad that they had finally given him food and water and had stopped the constant interrogations.

The worst part of his incarceration was the extreme boredom. What was there to do? The small copy of the book, which had been in his pocket on that day when he had left Sandar, had by some miracle been overlooked by the guards. He spent every day, night, and lots in between thanking the Lord of the Book that he had been allowed this one small treasure. Looking on the bright side, it did give him an opportunity to really study the book as he never had before. He tucked it carefully back in the small depression under his mat and stiffly got to his feet.

Eagerly, he stood by the barred gate of his cell, listening to the approaching stomping boots. The small portion of dried meat and old bread was none too appealing, but in light of the circumstances, he found that he felt very thankful for it. His stomach growled as he waited in expectancy.

It was also an opportunity to talk to someone. In this bleak, lonely prison, even a guard was a welcome sight. The cells on both sides and the one in front of him were empty. As terrible as it seemed to wish it, he almost thought it would be nice if someone else could be arrested to accompany him in this lonely place.

"Good morning." The gruff voice that shook his longing thoughts away startled him. It was not the usual guard who brought his food.

"G-good morning," he stuttered slightly in surprise. The dark-cloaked figure seemed familiar, and as Kyle looked closer, he realized it was the man who had been in the castle the day he had been captured.

"I've come to talk to you about the mixlings who helped you."

Irritation surged through Kyle. Would they never stop interrogating him? "Look, I have been questioned over and over, and I know nothing!"

"That's why you're still a-l-i-v-e." He drew out the word with a sneer. "However, I'm not here to question you. I'm here to inform you."

"Inform me?"

The tone of the guard's voice was anything but kind or comforting. "I've come to inform you that the mixlings who helped you no longer exist." And with that, the man turned and walked away.

Kyle watched in a daze. "No longer living?" The question came out as a whisper and burned his ears. Had he heard right? The mixlings who had risked their lives for him were no more.

Stephen

"Seriously, Luna, that's not helping anyone." Stephen looked at Luna in agitation mixed with amusement.

She was still trying to untie herself, and he had to admit her skills weren't impressive. "Why are you just sitting there?" she hissed angrily at him.

"Even if I was to get loose, they're watching us. We don't have a chance. Besides, to escape, you need proper training and a good head on your shoulders..."

"I would pay you back for that comment if I was untied," Luna grumbled with a scowling look toward him.

"Oh, I know. Why do you think I said it?" He really was laughing now. Laughter could also be heard from around the campfire, which was a good ten strides away.

"Looks like they're plenty distracted. If you're so good at untying yourself, then why don't you?" Luna asked him.

Slowly, Stephen began to reposition his hands, carefully twisting one and then the other. He could tell Luna was surprised when he held up his freed limbs and started working on releasing her. Soon they were running shoulder to shoulder toward the woods. Just as they reached the edge of the trees, they came to a halt. In front of them were a dozen or more beetles.

"We don't leave our camp unguarded." The lead guard grunted, still out of breath, behind them. "Now turn around and walk this way."

The command was clear, and they both hurried to obey. Unfortunately Luna went a little too fast. As she turned, her boot caught on a protruding twig, which sent her sprawling. One of the beetles, misinterpreting the movement, charged, and its gleaming horn caught her in the leg. Immediately, the guard began to scold, but it was too late. Stephen bent down to examine the wound. It was a smooth cut as long as his hand, starting from a little below the knee. He could tell that Luna was holding back tears from pain, and he wondered what to do.

"Do you have medicine for the pain?" he asked the guards who seemed as concerned as him.

One of them came back with a small bottle and a roll of bandages. Stephen took the offered medication and began to treat the cut. He realized he wasn't extremely proficient and must have lost some of his practice. Some of the faces Luna was making made him feel that he was being too clumsy. As he wrapped the clean white cloth around and around, he wondered what had happened to Madai and Johan. Maybe they would send for help. The medicines Luna carried were in her bundle where they had tied the mice. He finished bandaging the cut and helped Luna to her feet. Then he offered an arm for her to lean on. However, just as he suspected, she did not accept it but walked with a limp on her own.

She is really stubborn, he thought to himself.

Not long afterward, they were tied again with a new tightness to their posts, and Stephen couldn't help but realize Luna didn't even try to reposition herself as they tied her. When they had gone, she rested her head on her shoulder and seemed to fall asleep. Stephen did the same but could not accomplish the falling-asleep part. Was this where it would end? They had just started their journey. He wondered how they had found them. The trail was well hidden and unknown to most. Hardly anyone at the resistance even knew that they had started their mission. The guards, who had been kind in their own rough way, soon fell asleep by the fire.

As Stephen watched the flickering flames play shadowy figures across Luna's face, he thought of a similar fire so long ago. It had been a camping trip. He had begged and begged his father to go, and at last it had been allowed. It was the best week of his life, by himself with some of his friends and one of their dads. It had seemed so grownup-like, to be only eleven and away from home for a whole week. He blocked out the memories that followed, but now they came rushing back. The moment of running home, excited to relate his trip to his family; breaking through the clearing and seeing his house—burned to the ground. He had run to it and began calling for his father, mother, brothers, and sister, but no one answered. After staying there at the ruins for more than three days, a man came to him and told him that while he was gone, his family died in the fire. Devastation set in as he realized everything he had lost.

A noise jerked him back to reality, and with a start, he realized his face was wet with tears. With a burst of anger, he kicked his post. Why did he let those thoughts come? When they did, they always seemed to take over. A counselor from the resistance had told him he should thank the Lord of the Book for the good times he had had with his family and not to dwell on his loss. But whenever he thought of the good things, the bad things came too: the time he lied to his mom about the missing cookies he fed to his beetle, the time he broke his sister's favorite toy, the time his father told him he had to wait to have his own mouse, and he had gotten so angry. They were all a jumble of regret, and he hated to know he had no second chances to set things straight, to tell his mom who took the cookies, to tell his sister who broke her favorite toy, and to tell his dad that it was okay, he would wait.

With his anger, he began working on the ropes that tied him. Even if they couldn't escape because of the beetles, he might at least be a bit more comfortable. More than once, he reminded himself to thank Carl for teaching him this trick. It had often come in handy. It was difficult, but soon his rope dropped to the ground, and he sank to the forest floor and leaned against his post.

Looking toward Luna, he wondered what her story was. Why did she live with her uncle, and what happened to her parents? Picking up a small stone that lay by his feet, he threw it with all his might and followed it by another. Boredom was definitely a part of tonight. Suddenly, he heard a rustling sound heading toward where he had thrown the pebbles. That was when it dawned on him: the beetles were following the noise! Quietly but quickly getting to his feet, he roused Luna.

"What are you doing? You know we can't escape," she mumbled sleepily.

"Well, we all know I'm the brains of the operation," he retorted smartly while untying her hands. He knew he would probably receive a friendly punch for that comment later. As he released her, she began rubbing her wrists.

"So what's the plan, genius?" she whispered nervously, glancing toward the sleeping figures by the fire.

"We throw pebbles that way, and we run this way," he stated calmly. "But we have to be very quiet."

"Wow, I'm really impressed!" she exclaimed with exaggeration. "Let's review things a bit. We don't have our bows, arrows, or mice, and if you haven't noticed, I don't think I'm going to be winning any running races anytime soon."

Stephen noticed her voice was sarcastic but also longing. "They didn't bring anything from our camp, so we just have to get our weapons, which are over there." He pointed in the direction of their familiar bows and arrows leaning against a tree. "We have to try to make it to our camp…and I'll help you run."

Luna looked at him doubtfully but shrugged her shoulders as an okay.

As he turned to leave, Luna stopped him. "We should ask the Lord of the Book for help." Her voice was soft but sincere in her request. He too had been thinking that, but it was easier for him to ask in his mind than out loud.

"Dear Lord of the Book, please help us so we can get away and find the city and help the queen and her son. They need your help too. I don't know where they are or what they need, but comfort them somehow and help us be successful in this attempt. Thank you for watching out for us and for giving me the opportunity to be a part of the resistance. And keep my uncle and Nio safe. Amen."

Luna gave him a little nudge, which he decided meant it was his turn.

"Dear Lord of the Book, thank you for everything you've done for us. Bless these rebels who have taken us captive in some way. Teach them about you. Please help us get out of here. Amen." He had decided it would be good to bless the rebels since they had, in their own way, been kind. "Okay, let's go."

Luna nodded in agreement, and from there, everything started to move fast. Stephen handed her a handful of pebbles and instructed her to keep throwing them. Then he set out for their bows, arrows, and waist belts. Everything went smoothly, and they were soon armed and ready to run. A racket of raining pebbles hailed down on the opposite side of camp, and they were off.

Stephen noticed Luna was just barely keeping up and also saw that the cut was bleeding through her bandage again. He took her arm and ignored the slight resistance she gave. Running wasn't easy, but they soon reached the edge of the forest. Just as they were entering the trees, a rushing sound behind them brought them up short. Heading straight for them was the army of beetles. They had not been fast enough, and it seemed the guards were not going to make it in time to stop the attack.

They both drew their bows but knew that two dozen arrows would never be enough to battle the army that had quadrupled in size.

"Run!" Stephen instructed Luna and gave her a push in the right direction to encourage her.

As soon as she took off, he was right behind her. But navigating a piece of woods they were strangers to, in the dark, with agile beetles behind them, was not easy. The next scene took place in a daze, and Stephen watched in rising panic as Luna tripped on a root and went sprawling. He realized that by the time he got there to help, it would be too late. He watched as Luna pushed herself up, and the beetles ran toward them. It seemed he wasn't moving, and everything else was moving without him. He told himself to run faster, but no matter how much he tried, he couldn't. He couldn't do anything, and the inevitable was about to happen.

19

Luna

"Dear Lord of the Book, help us!" Luna cried out. How it had come to this end eluded her as she looked around and saw the thundering army of shiny beetle horns coming right at her. Even though Stephen lurched in her direction, she could see he wasn't going to make it. Suddenly, a shrill whistle broke through the resounding noise of onrushing destruction. As Luna turned, still half on the ground, she could see the back of a youth who seemed to be a rebel by his clothing. He was standing with arms stretched forward in front of the now hundred or more beetles standing docile, waiting for another command. A short tweet and hand motion sent them all in the other direction.

As Luna stood, she was surprised to hear the youth say, "We'll have to hurry. It won't take the guards long to redirect the beetles."

Not questioning, she followed the youth and Stephen toward where they had been ambushed at their camp. As she ran, she felt the throbbing pain in her lower leg where one of the beetles had earlier dealt its blow.

Luna and Stephen were surprised to recognize the youth when they all stopped to rest in some tall grasses. He was Thomas, the young rebel whom Luna had helped with her medicines after Zoe had been kidnapped in Talenia.

"Remind me, Thomas, to take beetle training lessons from you when we have more time," exclaimed Luna as they wound their way through the complex undergrowth.

When they reached the burned-out camp, they were uncertain as to whether they would find their missing companions, but their fears were soon abated when Johan and Madai came out of some nearby bushes.

"We weren't sure if you had also been captured or not!" Luna exclaimed in relief.

"While they were struggling with you two, we managed to get the mice out before they got to us," Johan answered."

"Let's go!" Madai whispered nervously, and no one objected.

Luna glanced down at the now pink bandage around her leg. The pain had intensified over the last four hours of traveling. Stephen had offered that they stop and take care of the wound, but she wouldn't hear of it. She hated holding anyone up, and besides, all injuries hurt. Their pursuers had not given up easily, and it had been one terrible hour of doubling back and leaving false trails.

Luna turned to the rebel who rode by her side on a deep-gray mouse. "Who trained the beetles? The only ones I've ever seen obey so well are Eneva's…"

He looked at her curiously. "Actually, as a matter of fact, we don't train our beetles. We—or should I say, they—steal them."

Luna remembered Thomas's quick explanation to Stephen of how he had never really enjoyed being a rebel, and for some time, he had been trying to leave. It was difficult to escape once you became a rebel. They considered anyone who left their ranks a traitor, and most did not escape alive. His father knew he had left but had stopped the others from following him. Thomas had recognized Luna and Stephen when he ran across the guards' camp that night and decided to repay her kindness to him. He still had a splint on his leg and walked with a limp. Thomas had seen this as his chance to join a different cause, and their unexpected ally had been very helpful.

"Hmm, so that's where all the resistance beetles go," Luna said musingly, not wanting to pry.

"Luna!" Madai's call drew their conversation to an end.

"Yes?" she answered.

"Come here a moment."

Luna rode past Johan and caught up to Madai and Stephen. "What is it?"

"I was just going to ask you if we're setting up camp now, or in a few hours?"

Luna examined the black sky. In another two hours, it would be light again. "If Stephen agrees, and if you guys aren't too tired, I think we should ride all through the day, at least until we are too tired to go on. If they decided to track us further, it could be a big risk sleeping in the daytime."

"That's exactly what I would have said," muttered Stephen.

"R-i-g-h-t," Luna sarcastically drew out the word.

As she and Madai looked at each other, they burst into laughter for no reason, much to the annoyance of Stephen. Happily, Luna breathed in the cool, fresh nighttime air. It felt so good to be somewhat safe and on their way. And now they were a group of five, following the map the tiny man had given to Luna, looking for a city made of glass.

The Castle of Icelair

"What's the good news?" The king's humor was its usual self, and he was not known to be amusing.

"Well, uhmmm—"

"I'm afraid that doesn't qualify as an answer, and as all of my subjects know, I only like good answers." The king examined his nails, his elbow resting on the icy throne's armrest.

"The resistance representatives have been taken care of," The rebel leader seemed to tremble in the king's presence.

"They are in the work order?"

"Yes, sir."

As soon as the king gave a wave of his hand in dismissal, the rebel leader needed no second bidding. Rushing out, he wondered where he could hide before the king found out the truth of the escape.

Luna

Luna drew back the bandage slowly, gritting her teeth in pain. She had volunteered to get water for the camp and had stopped to wash her wound. Digging into her carrying bag, she soon found her jar of medicine and some clean bandages. Dipping her hand into the clean stream beside her, she let the chilled water spill over the cut. Clenching her teeth, she determined not to make a sound. As she bandaged it, she tried not to notice how red it was. Some beetles carried a toxin on their horns, which could cause a nasty infection. She was confident her medicines would do their job.

Wrapping the new white cloth tightly around her leg, she contemplated the days behind her. Two days had now passed since their escape from the rebels. Thomas had been happy to supply them with all the information he knew about the rebels and their intentions. He had told them how they had started the fire, captured Zoe, and had orders to capture Luna and Stephen. They had been hired by an inside contact with the resistance, someone posing as a resistance member but working directly for King Elsiper. Luna shivered slightly as she remembered the description Thomas had given. Who could it be? Could it really be Daniel? Or maybe Janet was giving information to the rebels?

She found it hard to believe anyone in the resistance force could be working for the evil king.

Getting to her feet, she filled the two acorn buckets and made her way back to camp. With every step, she felt the cut shoot a hot streak of pain up her leg. When she got back to camp, she noticed everyone watching her walk up.

"Thought you might have gotten lost there for a second," Stephen stated with concern.

"I'm fine." Luna sighed and joined Madai by the far side of the fire, catching her breath. "What you making?" she asked, truly curious of the small seedlike berries through which she was pushing a fish bone.

"A bracelet." She smiled at Luna. "You want to make one?"

Luna looked at the bracelet with admiration. "I'm afraid my lack of patience doesn't allow for that kind of concentration," she said with a tinge of sadness. She excused herself remorsefully. "But it looks neat."

With that, she pulled out her copy of the Great Book and began reading it by the light of the fire. The stories were so fascinating. They could hold her captivated for hours.

Stephen's voice called her out of the exiting encounter of the Lord of the Book and his people in the desert. "Luna, I need your opinion on the map."

Standing up a little painfully, she joined him, Johan, and Thomas.

"Don't you have enough opinions?" she asked, raising her eyebrows at Johan and Thomas.

"Yes, but one more is always nice!" Stephen encouraged. "Tomorrow we're supposed to cross this part here through the rocks. Do you think we should go around them or through them?"

Luna stared at the map laid out before her. "Well, there's always the possibility of creatures or other rebel bands in the rocks. However, going around them could lead to some sort of dead end. As you can see, all the other parts of the path are marked as open sand, but this piece has nothing but rocks for miles on either side. It would take a long time to go around. And in the open, it's almost more dangerous."

"That's about as reasonable as it gets." Stephen nodded in agreement. "Okay, so I'll see everyone at daybreak."

Stephen

"Here we are, my brave followers!"

Stephen tried to make humor out of the despairing sight in front of them. Huge gray walls of rock loomed almost as high as they could see. Their flat peaks loomed above them, and jagged paths ran across their majestic sides. Deep shadows stood between them. The path looked smooth enough. For a moment, his mind wandered, imagining what sort of creature might be responsible for the smooth trail they were about to walk on. He thought for a moment about rain. In a situation like this, rain could be very dangerous. The sky was clear and sunny. He shook his head, dispelling the chill that passed over him and nudged his mouse forward.

"Well, I guess in this case, we shouldn't have wasted our time planning," Luna said quietly, looking at the towering gray walls.

Stephen shrugged his shoulders. "I guess it's straight ahead."

After an hour of walking, the path began a steep incline. Soon they were exhausted, and none of them objected to a break. They sat on a ledge to rest, looking up at the high walls above them. After a few minutes, they began to feel chilled, and Thomas suggested they continue on before they caught a cold.

"You're right, Thomas," agreed Stephen.

Slowly they continued their climb through the narrow cut in the rocks. Luna, who was leading, suddenly stopped, and Stephen almost collided with her.

"Listen!" she quietly commanded, looking expectantly around her.

A sort of whimpering sound drew all of their now attentive ears toward a dark cave almost directly above them on an overhanging ledge. Voices also drifted down to their tilted heads.

"Who is it?" Luna's curious voice whispered at Stephens's side.

"Whoever it is, we should leave them to themselves," Stephen said firmly and continued walking, only to be pulled back by by Luna.

"We should see if they need help," she said, concern in her violet eyes.

"Are they asking?" he said, trying not to be harsh but eager to get on the way.

A baby's weak cry broke into their busy whispers.

"They have a baby," she insisted.

"Lots of people do. Come on! Don't worry about them. They'll be fine. Besides, we don't know who they are. They are probably rebels. They know how to take care of themselves," he reassured her, giving a gentle push on the shoulder toward the trail ahead. He noticed her reluctant look toward the sound once more before she continued up the path.

Stephen looked over his tired band of travelers. They had been leading the mice most of the day during the sharp climbs. A couple of the mice were weak from lack of food, so they carried the packs for them too. The five of them had divided Madai's load up a few hours back when she had sprained her ankle on a loose rock.

Waiting for Luna to catch up, Stephen offered to help. "Can I help you with one of those?"

"No, thank you. I'm fine."

He waited for her to pass. If one of his small band was too tired or got sick—they could be delayed for quite a while, even with the aid of their medicines. He had noticed that both of the girls had been going slower in the last few hours, which wasn't so unusual for Madai, who wasn't used to this kind of trip, but Luna had trained so much; she was the last one he had expected to be lagging. Even though he wanted to ask her why, he decided not to, knowing that she did not like being treated any different than the others in the group.

Looking at the now clouded sky, he hoped the storm that was brewing would wait. It was dark gray and seemed to close in to the points of the jagged rock mountains all around them. He had also begun to feel a chill in the air that wasn't there earlier.

"We should keep going till we get through these rocks, or we could get caught up in the storm," he advised with an authoritative voice, and no one argued. Sighing, he put one foot in front of the other and tried to focus on more monotonous things as he followed the bleak gray path in front of him.

Luna

The rain began as a light mist late in the twilight of the evening. They all donned their leather rain covers over their cloaks to help them stay dry. Luna tugged her blanket and cloak up further toward her chin. She was cold. Soon the rain intensified, and the path became slick and dangerous. They mounted their mice again as their four feet were more secure than two.

"Be on the lookout for some shelter!" Stephen announced to the worried group.

Luna knew, as well as any of them, that if the rain continued in these steep and narrow trails, they could suddenly be washed away without warning. They desperately looked for a ledge or cave, but all of the sides of the rocks were straight and smooth. It seemed like hours passed before Thomas called out, "I see it! There's a cave ahead!"

A loud crash of thunder drowned out his words. The next blinding flash of lightning illuminated a small cave up ahead on a ledge. They looked for some path that might take them there, but the darkness and the rain made it nearly impossible to see anything. There was a tall plant near the ledge, and Thomas was already chopping at it with his ax.

"If we can topple this plant, the mice should be able to climb up," he stated eagerly.

The water was knee-deep and rising, so Mitzie needed no encouragement to tackle the climb. She gripped the plant stems with her nimble toes and scurried to the top with ease.

They entered the cave tentatively, looking in the nooks and crannies to make sure the cave wasn't already inhabited. A small gray knee-high spider reluctantly left the shelter after several prods with arrows and the waving of a blanket. Madai shivered after it was gone.

"I really do not like spiders!" she exclaimed.

"Well, at least it left without a fight," Luna answered. She knew that some spiders would put up a terrible fuss, but this one had been quite cooperative despite the rain.

The cave was small but adequate. There was enough space for both tents, and they built a fire in the mouth of the cave. Temperatures had dropped drastically, and none of them had been prepared for that. Luna and Madai were sharing blankets and cloaks to pool their warmth, but both of them agreed that it wasn't quite fair since there were three of the boys in the other tent, and none of them would be alone during guard shift. Luna laughed at this and pointed out that Madai would get double blankets when Luna left to guard.

All of them were glad that Madai had come; she had shown her excellent skill in cooking. They probably would not have eaten so well if she had been absent. And she always cheered them up when things looked bleak. Madai had been a good friend.

They put up the tents and set up heat reflectors near the fire, one for each shelter, but it had done little to cut the chill in the air. Luna could hardly wait till it was her turn to stand guard so she could sit by the fire. They had all been so surprised when the sounds of rushing water were replaced by the soft pitter-patter of snow. Stephen had warned them they might be here for a day or two as he looked worriedly into the silent wall of falling white. They had never been so far from home base. And winter was coming faster than they had anticipated.

As she resisted pulling all the blankets to herself, she thought of the baby's cry back at the turning point in the trail. Stephen hadn't counted on it snowing. Maybe if he had, he would have helped them, she thought. *What if they don't have blankets or food? What if they need medicine? That baby didn't sound healthy*—the thoughts ran on and on till Luna heard a knock on the shelter post.

As she slipped her cloak around her now cold shoulders, she pulled back the door flap and relieved Johan from his post. The fire was comforting but brought back more guilty thoughts of the baby in the cave. Was that baby by a warm fire? Did her family know how to make a good fire? Trying to calm her thoughts, she pulled out the little book, which she loved so much, and began reading in the firelight. But as she turned every page, a straggling thought of remorse found its way into her mind. Luna read in misery as she thought of the fate of the less fortunate.

Luna's head jerked with a start. Had her eyes just been closed? She couldn't remember. She hated that feeling when she couldn't remember if she had been sleeping or not. As she readjusted herself, she winced in pain. Looking down at her leg, she realized it was slightly more swollen than it had been before. Walking earlier had certainly not helped it. Pulling her small bottle of medicine from her belt, she decided it was necessary to apply it. Unwrapping the bandage halfway, she poured the burning liquid over the now bright-red cut. Clenching her teeth, she watched as it bubbled and foamed across the wound. Rewrapping it, she sent a quick prayer toward the sky, asking for it to get better. Thinking it not a good idea to risk falling asleep again, she stood and went to wake Thomas for his shift. Seven sequenced knocks on the post brought Thomas out groggy-eyed and hair a mess.

"It's my turn already?" he mumbled.

"You're lucky! I should have woken you an hour ago," she whispered back, trying to make him feel better about sitting in the dark on a cold night by himself. Smiling at the prospect of warm blankets, she retired to her shelter. Not long after lying down, the same nagging thoughts came back. *Is that baby warm enough tonight?*

20

Stephen

"Everybody up!"

Stephen called good and loud, rousing his sleepy companions. He could hear the bright birdsongs that drifted down from the deep-blue sky. As he walked outside, he was greeted by Thomas.

"I'll catch a little more of that stuff you call sleep while you guys get breakfast," he mumbled drearily, reentering the shelter Stephen had just vacated.

Noticing the water buckets were not filled yet, he took them and headed toward what had been a smooth dry trail when they started out. He carried a light tune as he broke the ice atop the glistening stream along the lower side and filled the buckets with the freezing liquid. The snow had surprised them all, but he realized with joy that most of it was melting. Maybe they wouldn't be here as long as he had thought. Hopefully, if everything went well, they could leave by tomorrow morning.

When he got back to the camp, the worried looks on his friends' faces alarmed him. "What's wrong?" he asked cautiously.

"Luna's gone."

"What?" he asked. He honestly thought he had heard wrong.

"She left this." Madai handed him a note.

He straightened the crumpled piece of paper and tried to make sense of the scribbly writing.

> I couldn't get the cries of the baby we passed on the trail out of my mind. I couldn't just sleep in my shelter and ignore the fact that so near to us there were people who could really need help. I'll be back before we can leave.

Stuffing the note in his pocket, he took some food and a blanket then mounted Lightning and started out, calling instructions to the wordless people in the camp behind him as he left. Irritation tugged at him as he started down the precarious icy trail.

—∘∘◦❋◦∘∘—

Luna

Luna set the whimpering baby back into his mother's arms.

"Thank you," the young woman gratefully and sighed.

Luna surveyed the warm crackling fire and the reflection structure she had built. Then she looked over the small rebel family. A young mother with four children was their complement. She told Luna that the band had left them there and promised to come back within the week, but they were already late, and she had not been prepared for the cold snowstorm.

Her oldest was a youth of about fourteen, who seemed to watch his mother with concern but, not knowing what to do, did nothing. Luna had instructed him on how to keep the fire going. Then finally she said good-bye.

"Thank you…for everything." The woman again showed her gratefulness, holding out a slightly trembling hand.

As much as Luna wanted to stay and help more, she knew she needed to get back, or the others would come looking for her, if they hadn't already. She thought, with a twinge of dread, of what a scolding she could expect from Stephen. As she left the humble little dwelling, she sighed in satisfaction one more time before heading out into the cold again.

Stephen

Two hours of floundering through the icy-cold snow had made Stephen's already grouchy mood ten degrees worse. Although Luna's bent figure hunched over her mount was a welcome sight, it only made his anger flare more for the moment. Anger was in fact a way to cover the concern he had for her. Before, he had always thought she could take care of herself, but lately, she was moving slower and acting strangely.

"Where have you been?" he asked with controlled anger as soon as she was within hearing distance.

"I left a note," she mumbled apologetically, looking away.

He noticed her flushed cheeks and that the leg she had cut was not in the foot loop. Usually they didn't use the seat for the mice, but the uneven terrain that might be expected on this unknown trail called for it.

"You left a note? That's your..." He left off in slight exasperation, searching for the right word to convict her of her wrongdoings. "That's your explanation?"

She raised her head in a bit of defiance. "Those people needed our help, and we just left them there. It's a young mother and four kids. One of them is a baby, and they had no fire. I just couldn't sleep because I couldn't stop thinking of the baby in the cold." Her explanation came out in a passionate rush.

"I told you to let them be! It could have been someone dangerous!" Stephen tried to keep his resolve.

Luna sighed. "Look, Stephen, the whole reason we are on this mission is to help people. Remember the Lord of the Book, we need to help in every way we can, whether it's a campfire or exposing a secret city and a wicked ruler."

Stephen looked at her, and though he understood her point, he showed no agreement or disagreement and turned mutely to resume their trek back to camp.

Stephen looked at the trees above. Their iced tips contrasted nicely against the clear blue sky. After she had returned the day before from her journey to help the stranded rebels, she had seemed a bit depressed. When the two boys and Madai decided to go look for edible herbs and go hunting, she had uncharacteristically decided to stay put.

"Luna," he called, walking toward the now cold campfire.

She now emerged from her shelter, a questioning look on her face. "Yes?"

"Oh, I was just wondering if you were up for a contest of shooting arrows, seeing as everything is under control here." He looked at her quizzically. Usually, it was like her to jump at the chance and try her best to beat him (which she had yet to do). Stephen noticed that although she agreed, it was less heartily than usual.

After three rounds of twelve shots, Stephen winning twice by two and the last time by one, Luna suggested a change in game. "Maybe a game in bookliness?"

Stephen had no objection, although he did know it was a game she could win at. They would pick a small passage from the book, and first to memorize it would win a point. However, if a mistake was made, they would forfeit two points. After setting their bows and arrows where they belonged by the shelters, the two walked to some larger pieces of wood scattered at the cave's edge, books in hand.

"I hope you have better luck at this game than the last," Stephen stated with pretended seriousness.

"Be careful what you wish fo—"

Stephen turned quickly as her sentence was abruptly cut off. He noticed her face seemed flushed, and her smile was no longer there. "Luna?" he asked with concern.

Slowly, she raised one hand up to her head, looking down to the ground.

Luna

Luna lifted her hand to her head. Suddenly she felt hot and then cold.

"Luna?"

Stephens's voice sounded far away and unfocused. The pain in her leg suddenly reminded her of its nasty look that morning. In fact, it had been the whole reason she hadn't gone on the hunting trip, which she actually really wanted to do. *Pull yourself together.* The thought was the only one in her mind as she tried to take control of the situation. As she raised her head to evaluate the distance to her destination, she saw her surroundings begin to spin.

"I'm fine," she managed, trying to convince her now concerned friend.

"No, you're not." Stephens's voice sounded urgent but like it was coming from nowhere.

As she tried to focus on his face, she suddenly couldn't find it. It seemed like it was there one second and then gone in a storm of bright static. Suddenly everything began to fade, and as much as she tried, she couldn't get it to come back.

"Luna! Luna, listen to me!" The sound of Stephen's voice seemed to linger, and she could hear it but couldn't locate the source

"I-I can't…" Suddenly, she struggled to stand, and everything faded into blackness.

Stephen

"Luna! Luna! Listen to me!"

Stephen looked urgently at Luna's blank face. Her flushed cheeks suddenly lost all of their color. She seemed to be looking at him but not seeing him.

"I-I can't…"

Without warning, her hand dropped from her head, and she fell. Catching her was not hard, but what to do next was a mystery to him. Carefully, he laid her limp form on the ground.

"Luna, this isn't time for jokes!" he scolded, but he knew she was really unconscious. "What am I supposed to do?" he asked himself.

As he turned to stand, his eyes rested on her right leg. Suddenly, everything fit into place. Her next-to-nothing enthusiasm in things she had previously enjoyed, her lagging behind on the journey, and that day her boot had been out of the riding strap. Afraid of what he would find, he reached out the back of his hand and laid it against her forehead. The heat he found there told its story, and the gravity of it chilled his heart.

Two days had passed. Stephen, Johan, Thomas, and Madai sat around the campfire, drearily thinking on what to do. Luna's fever had gotten worse. She now lay in the shelter tossing and muttering as she had since she had gone unconscious.

"We should pray again," Madai interrupted the gloomy mood.

They had been praying often because of a story in the Great Book that told of someone who had been sick, and when their friends and family prayed for them, they got better. Madai went to check on Luna. She rinsed the cloth and put it back on her forehead.

"She's still unconscious."

Everyone stared into the orange flames in concentrated sadness. How long would they wait? What should they do? Stephen was angry with himself that he hadn't recognized trouble sooner.

"We should soak her leg again," Madai suggested as she put on a large pot of water to boil.

Luna

Blackness surrounded Luna as she opened her eyes. Her head beckoned to be allowed to rest on her crude pillow as she pushed herself up on her side. Why was she in her shelter? Last she remembered, she was walking with Stephen toward the edge of the clearing. Suddenly, she remembered the strange feeling of falling. Glancing around, she saw Madai's sleeping figure.

"Madai? How long have I been sleeping?" she asked tentatively, shaking her friend awake.

"Luna! You're awake!" Madai's excited squeal was accompanied by a hug.

"What happened?" Luna mumbled, putting a hand to her head in pain.

Madai looked at her with sympathy. "You fainted. You had a fever from an infection in your leg, and then you were unconscious for three days."

Luna gave a wry face. "I guess that's why I'm so hungry."

They both laughed.

"I think your fever's down." Madai congratulated her after feeling her forehead.

A firm knocking came from the outside of the tent, interrupting their giddy mood.

"What's going on?" Stephens's groggy voice floated in to the two girls.

"She's getting better!" Madai half-exclaimed, half-sighed.

Stephen poked his head in the tent door and smiled at Luna. "How are you feeling?" he asked.

"A little better, I think, although my head still hurts," Luna replied.

"You had us all worried. I'm so relieved to see you're back with us," he said with feeling.

"So am I." Luna sighed. "I think I need to sleep some more though."

The morning sun sent sparkles of light through the opening in the roof of her shelter. Luna stared reflectively at the bright spots. The others had greeted her enthusiastically before breakfast and told her several times of how they had passed the last three days and also how they had prayed to the Lord of the Book for her to get better. As she thought of the journey ahead, she felt very glad to have such good friends. They would wait a few more days for her to rest before resuming their travels. Luna dozed off again, content knowing that the Lord of the Book would be watching over them.

Luna smiled up at the beautiful sunshine above her, surrounded by the clear blue sky. It was more comforting to look up than down these days since they were still in the mountain range. The climate had been awful. She remembered the horrible storm in which she had gone to help the rebel family almost two weeks ago. Since then, one day would be freezing and the next sweltering. The good thing, however, was that the cut on her leg was healing. And she was regaining her strength a little each day.

In remembrance, she flexed her foot. They had waited another week after she regained consciousness before resuming their journey. Most of those days, she and her companions had told jokes and stories to pass the dreary hours. As her leg improved, so had the conditions outside their small camp. In that time, the snow had melted, and the trail had mostly dried.

They started off with new enthusiasm. As the hours passed, there was always that same old gray trail in front and the tall jagged rock mountains on the sides.

Suddenly, Madai's excited voice brought her down from her mouse and over to join her happy friend. "Look! We're almost back to regular terrain!"

Luna shaded her eyes with her left hand while still holding Mitzie's reins in the other. In the distance, the ground was no longer gray but brown and green! Between there and where they were, there was a rather deep valley where they would not be able to see the encouraging sight for many hours, possibly the whole day. After discussing it, they all decided that it would be best if they kept going the entire day and even into the night so they could reach that land by morning. That night, after traveling the entire day and late into the night, Luna went to bed feeling content that they were almost out of the valley.

As the sun rose, Luna groaned and covered her head with her cloak. "Why does he have to always wake us up so early?"

"I know! I could sleep another hour at least!"

She was greeted with a grumble of agreement from Madai. They soon got up and began packing their things after a threat from Stephen to take their shelter down with them still in it. Soon they were on their way up the steep side of the valley, almost back to regular land.

Stephen

As they neared the rise, Stephen couldn't help but break out whistling. Finally! They were leaving the gray terrain that had been affecting all of their attitudes so much! His cheerful thoughts were abruptly shattered when his fellow travelers stopped stiffly in their tracks. In front of them was the smooth, even terrain they had anticipated, but not ten feet from them was a moving column of the large creatures they all knew as *ants*.

The ants were glossy black and brown, with gleaming eyes and twitching antennae. They were only half the height of the mice, but their army was large, and they could move fast. The venom that they could inject into their victims was deadly. Stephen could hear the clicking of their curved mandibles as they cut away leaves from the plants along the trail. An ant could sever an arm or a leg quicker than you could say scat!

Fear gripped Stephen as the closest ants quickly turned to face them. The mice twitched their tails nervously and began to dance around. The ants began to circle their position, twitching their antennae and clicking louder. Some climbed the rocks behind them, cutting off any route of escape. There was no going forward, no going back. They turned their mice outward, forming a tight circle.

"Any ideas?" Stephen asked quietly, hoping his voice wasn't as quivery as he felt.

There were hundreds of ants, as far as you could see, a massive trail of moving black-and-brown.

"Luna?" he hissed.

"What?" Fear was not in her voice, although her face betrayed her anxiousness. "I'm sorry," she whispered.

Madai surprised them all as she spoke up. "We need to make a fire."

"A fire?" Johan asked.

"Something that makes lots of smoke. They read a chemical smell. See how they all follow the same trail? My grandfather once told me that if you make smoke, it confuses them," Madai explained shakily.

Stephen looked around the small circle they had created. "What can we burn? There's no wood here."

"Well, we can burn one of the blankets," offered Luna.

"I only have one match left." Johan suddenly ruined their short moment of hope.

"There's no way we can start a blanket on fire with one match," Thomas stated pessimistically, looking over at the blanket Madai was quickly unfolding.

"Hair," Thomas put in quickly.

Stephen noticed as a look of dread passed over the girls' faces, but they knew it was true. With no other kindling, hair just might work.

"I guess it will grow eventually," he heard Luna mumble as she handed her knife to Madai.

He watched as the two girls took turns cutting each other's braids.

"This had better work." Madai breathed.

With a short, fervent prayer, Johan struck the match and, with the hair, created enough of a fire to light the blanket, which soon turned into a blaze. He waved it around him, creating a cloud of smoke. The ants scattered in confusion, and the five comrades allowed their anxious mice to scamper away from the milling ants. The panic in the army of ants seemed to spread outward from the center. The closest ants became frantic, and the others, confused by their fellow ants' behavior, ignored the scampering mice bearing their riders.

Shortly after they reached the end of the mass of scattering creatures, they all came to a screeching halt. There in front of them was a river. Stephens's thoughts ran rampant as the possibilities hit him. The river was much too big to swim across and stretched for as far as he could see on both sides. He also knew that when the ants came to order, they would unite to protect their hill, which lay not too far downstream from them. He could see the raised mound in the distance, a trail of black marking its location. Beyond that, the twin boulders marked on the map loomed high above the trail.

Following a suggestion from Madai, they all knelt to ask the Lord of the Book for guidance. As they took turns, Stephen felt the fear in the air change to a calm that only the Lord of the Book could provide.

Surrounded by ants

21

Luna

"I know it's not the right direction, but I think we should go upstream, away from the anthill," suggested Luna.

"You are right," agreed Stephen.

Luna and the others listened carefully as Stephen gave instructions. "Try to be as quiet as possible so as not to attract the ants' attention. If worse comes to worse and there is no other way, jump in the water…they won't follow you in. But then get out as quick as you can and get dried off. I am sure that water is dangerously cold."

"Let's hope it doesn't come to that," Luna said with dread in her voice. "I am not one to go for a swim at this time of year."

The others nodded grimly as they looked across the wide river of frigid rushing water. It was dangerous indeed.

They began their trek upstream in silence, all of them looking nervously over their shoulders toward the ant army. It appeared that the majority of the ants had returned to their tedious job of carrying cut pieces of leaves into their underground storehouses. Though the small troupe of travelers passed quite close to the line at one point, none of the ants seemed to take note of their passing. Luna suddenly realized she had been holding her breath for far too long, and she felt a little dizzy from lack of oxygen. She tried to breathe slow, even long breaths and soon felt her head clear. Wow! This was too tense! As they went around a curve in the river, she began to feel a little better. They couldn't see the ants anymore.

What she could see though was that a tree up ahead had fallen across the river. It was a huge tree. It would take some work to get up on top of it, but she was thankful that they wouldn't have to try to build a boat or swim across. Everyone set to work without a word, tying ropes and vines together and using a hook made from fish bones to scale the tree. It took about twenty minutes to get the whole group up. With some coaxing and pulling, the mice followed. Crossing the river was the easy part. The tree was so wide, Luna couldn't even see the rushing water below. They felt exposed as they crossed the wide open area.

Luna thought for a moment about birds. *No, I won't start that!* she said to herself, shuddering at the thought.

As she climbed down a sloping tree branch, she looked down tentatively. *Why ever did he give me this assignment?* she asked herself. It wasn't that she was complaining, but her knowledge as far as outside life was concerned was indeed somewhat limited. Even though she had been accepted by this whole group, sometimes Luna couldn't help but feel a bit left out when they joked and talked about things she hadn't experienced.

Although out of loyalty to her as a friend Madai had come along on this mission, she had confessed innumerous times that she was much happier and comfortable keeping house and fulfilling a girl's responsibility at home. Madai may not have had the adventurous spirit that Luna had, but she was able to be of assistance when it came to cooking or making camps a comfortable place to be. She could make anywhere seem like home.

As Luna watched, she had to smile as Thomas urged Madai on with gentle words after Stephen said something upsetting. Luna had noticed Stephen wasn't exactly a sensitive person in public.

Jokes and jabs came easy for him, but sometimes communicating true feelings could be difficult.

Every day now she wished she had confronted Janet outright and asked her what was wrong. She probably had a very difficult family situation. But then maybe Janet would have turned on her again. It seemed to be her way of defending herself. As the thought of family crossed her mind, it was accompanied by a wave of homesickness.

All four of them, two on either side, had to hide a smile as Madai lowered herself onto a swaying branch with a slight grimace, teetering all the way. The mice scampered down as if it were nothing. They seemed to have no fear of the water or of falling. Their tails swayed as they used them to balance. Soon they were all across and on solid ground again, sending up prayers of thanks that they had been able to flee their predicament with no permanent damage to their complement. They found a small cove at the base of a tree and began to set up camp as the sun was going down. The large tree roots protected them from the wind.

That night, as Luna stared up at the top of her shelter and listened to the even breathing of her companion, she couldn't help but turn her thoughts once again to Janet. Was she feeling lonely right now? Despite all the mean things that Janet had done, Luna couldn't help but feel sympathetic. But then maybe Janet was a spy.

An elbow on her side woke Luna a good time before she wished to be awoken. "Madai!" She groaned, slightly annoyed.

"Sorry, I can't get comfortable. This ground is so hard!" Madai said apologetically.

"I know what you mean, but I had already gotten over the stage of blocking that out…," she mumbled as sleep left her.

Not long after, Luna was lying wide awake, and Madai seemed to be in a deep sleep, but to be sure, Luna whispered softly, "Are you awake?"

"No, I'm not," Madai replied in an equally quiet voice.

"Why do you think Janet was so mean?" she asked and then, when Madai ignored her, said, "Then how can you answer if you're not awake?"

She had to giggle at Madai's answer. "I'm Madai's conscience… sent to tell you that she is asleep and wishes not to be bothered by complicated questions."

"Madai!" Luna exclaimed, poking her on the side.

"What do you want?" Her friend sighed, finally rolling over, feigning irritation.

"Why do you think Janet was so mean?" Luna now repeated her question.

"She was probably insecure. I mean, maybe she thought that people would like you better or something silly like that. Can we talk about it tomorrow?"

"I guess," Luna mumbled, still puzzling over her friend's answer.

Had she in some way said or done something to make Janet feel that way? The question rephrased itself a million ways and followed her dreams all through the rest of the night.

Stephen

"And that's how we met," finished Stephen, waving his hand emphatically in front of him as he rode.

"Oh, you tell a different version than the one I heard!" said Luna.

Stephen looked in her direction as she made her taunting remark. "Really? I'd like to hear your version then."

Everyone laughed as Luna began to relate the night they had met Thomas. "See, we were tied to this stinky mushroom, helpless, and then I had the bright idea to untie the two of us… so we started running and then this army of beetles was about to attack us. Then the beetles actually held the bad guys off while we ran away because I told them to." Here, she stopped as everyone started laughing.

"I think you both got it wrong!" exclaimed Thomas as he began to weave a completely new version of the tale.

Johan and Madai had not been there for the exciting events and had yet to hear the truth of it, but the fake stories kept them in good humor and had passed much time on the dreary trail. Stephen diverted his attention from Thomas's version of their encounter to the low sun in the sky. After another long day of riding, they were all looking forward to reaching their destination, which, according to the map, was anytime soon.

A chirping sound in the bushes brought all their attention back to reality. Stephen watched as Madai and Luna were off their mice in a leap.

"Oh look! They're baby quail!!" he heard Luna exclaim in that squeaky voice girls used when they were excited.

He had never seen Luna quite so excited since that first day when he had seen her shooting in the clearing. The fluffy chicks were about shoulder high and looked at them curiously as they crouched in the grass. They appeared so sweet and fluffy; he himself was curious.

"Hey, maybe we could keep one as a pet?" Luna was petting a yellow-and-brown-spotted chick.

"No! Don't even think about it!" Stephen exclaimed, looking at her incredulously.

What was she thinking? Seriously! A baby bird on a trip like this? No way!

"The mother can't be far," Stephen reminded her cautiously. Even though they were timid and gentle birds, one could never be sure a mother bird would be gentle if she felt her young were in danger. After they had all admired the small birds (even the boys), they remounted and continued their journey. Although the girls' constant chatter of "How cute!" and "They're so fluffy!" and "I can't believe he could resist keeping such a cute creature!" was annoying, Stephen felt content. Smiling to himself and shaking his head slightly, he sighed with a deep sense of satisfaction. His traveling companions were turning out to be a pretty neat group of friends.

Since the encounter with the small quail, Stephen was happy with the progress his small band had made. They now had reached the end of the map's description and were due to run into the city at any time. The sun was getting very low in the sky, and he wished to make camp. But there was a good two hours left before dark, so the general vote was to keep going. As they rode with purpose through the little traveled forest, his mind began to wander as it had lately taken to doing.

The finding of the quail had brought back old memories, which had been buried a long time ago. He remembered one cold spring morning when his older brother had come across a quail nest. Benni had taken him every day to watch the smooth brown eggs until one day they hatched. He smiled as he remembered the unforgettable feeling it had given him to watch the delicate creature poke its not so tiny beak through its hard shell and then emerge wet and new, ready to follow its mother to find food.

The small trail through the thick grass seemed to be getting narrower, and the grass brushed against the sides of the mice with increasing frequency. It was late afternoon, and the sun beat down on the tops of the grass. It seemed hot and stuffy as they wound back and forth on the narrow trail. Stephen was abruptly brought to the present when Madai's mouse suddenly stopped and thumped and rattled its tail on the ground in warning. The other mice froze in their tracks, and a foreboding filled Stephen's heart. The mice had a sense about predators that people didn't have. No one moved for what seemed like an eternity. There was a faint rustling sound in the distance, and he couldn't decide from which direction it came. Only the twitching whiskers of the mice moved as if they knew the danger and were somehow communicating with one another.

Stephen thought he was prepared for anything when suddenly he found himself flat on his back. His mouse had leaped from under him in terror as the shadow passed above. There was a loud rustle and a thud—and he heard a mouse scream its last. He turned in alarm as he heard Madai scream.

"It's a fox!"

All of their mice had fled and left them. Stephen cautioned all of them to gather together and remain silent as they crouched and waited with hearts pounding to hear whether the predator was still close by. They heard the grass rustling and then silence. Did everything have to be a dangerous adventure? It wouldn't be so bad if it was just Daniel and him, as in old times, but now, with so much at stake, he resented the danger more than ever before.

As the sun crept ever lower in the sky, Stephen felt a growing urgency to do something. He could see nothing but tall grass surrounding them and the occasional cricket passing by. If they continued on, and the grass betrayed their presence again, they could become prey to the fox themselves. If they sat and did nothing, the fox might return to where he had last seen or smelled them. He finally decided that once it was dark, they would continue on and try whistling for the mice. He wondered which of the mice had become a meal for the fox. He hoped Luna's mouse had been spared. He had noticed how, for her, Mitzie was more than just a means of transportation. He thought of his own sleek-black mouse. He was young and spirited, and his black fur glistened in the sun. His underbelly was a soft reddish brown. It had taken a lot of patience to train him, but he was quick and nimble on his feet. Stephen said a prayer for the mice and listened to the evening wind brushing the tops of the grass. The coolness of the approaching evening made him shiver. He hoped that by now the fox had found other hunting grounds or had satisfied his hunger elsewhere.

---◦◦◦❖◦◦◦---

Luna

Luna held one arrow ready in her bow and felt somewhat reassured by the presence of the other eleven in her quiver. The thought of how close the fox had come to pouncing on them made her tremble. Her legs were beginning to ache from her crouched position. It was hard to control the urge to run each time the wind caused the grass to rustle. She closed her eyes for a moment and took a deep breath. She mustn't let her imagination get the best of her. She was worried about Mitzie. They had all heard a mouse scream in a way that could only mean it had lost its life to the fox. Mitzie had been a friend to her, as well as her trusted mount. Her eyes filled with tears, and she shook her head to clear away the unpleasant thoughts.

At last darkness began to come as the sun set, and the pink clouds faded to gray. The moon was full and lit the tips of the grass with its ghostly light. They finally stood from their cramped positions and warily began to walk slowly through the tall grass. The trail wound back and forth, and in some spots, seemed to disappear completely. They carefully slipped through the narrow places trying not to disturb the grass on either side. After about an hour, Luna decided to call to Mitzie. She whistled long and low then a high tweet. They all stood listening but heard nothing. She continued to call to her every ten minutes, her hope slowly fading to sadness. Maybe Mitzie had been the mouse that the fox had captured.

———∘∘∘◦❧◦∘∘∘———

Stephen

Was it his imagination, or did he hear something behind them? Stephen put his hand on Johan's arm. They all paused, listening intently. There it was again—an unmistakable sound. His heart began to pound loudly in his ears. Should they hide in the grass or stay put where they were? They waited but nothing happened.

"Let's go," Stephen finally said.

They all continued, but their earlier joviality had been replaced by a nameless dread. He felt a huge weight of responsibility for his companions' safety but felt helpless to protect them from this sort of danger.

The trail finally widened, and they were able to move faster now. They were glad to be able to move freely, if not without fear. They must be nearing the city, Stephen reasoned. It had been hours since they had first thought so. Again, the sound in the grass behind them startled Stephen. He turned to face it, motioning for them to continue. He put an arrow in his bow and waited quietly. Relief flooded over him as Mitzie's familiar nose peeked out of the grass.

"Why, you silly mouse!" he scolded gently as he approached the nervous creature.

She allowed him to take the reins but was hesitant to leave the cover of the grass for the open trail. "I know how you feel!" he said as he stroked her behind the ears and tried to calm her. She finally consented to follow, and moments later, it was a joyful reunion between Mitzie and Luna.

With renewed hope, they continued on their way. As they finally came to rockier terrain and left the deep grass, the valley opened up before them. The moonlight illuminated what lay ahead, and the sight they beheld caused them all to gasp in wonder.

22

PYRAMIDIS

Luna

Luna held Madai's hand in excitement! They were really there! It had taken so long that she wasn't really sure she believed that they had really arrived. They had travelled the whole day and begun to despair of ever coming to the end of their journey. They looked for a hidden place, away from the trail, to set up their camp. It would be best to enter the town in the daytime to arouse as little suspicion as possible. After all, there were many mixlings in Pyramidis. Maybe they could just blend in with the natives and do some hunting for information.

Luna groaned as she opened her eyes. How had morning come so quickly? It seemed that she had just closed her eyes a few minutes before. She lay quietly for a moment and then remembered that they had finally arrived at their destination. It was cold, and the fire had gone out. She dressed under the covers and put on her blue cape and boots, reluctant to leave the warmth of the blankets. She shook Madai and left the tent. She wished she could start the fire, but they would be leaving as soon as the camp was packed up. Stephen had already taken his tent down, and Johan mumbled groggily to Thomas to fold the blankets. Two more of their mice had joined Mitzie during the night. They were skittish but unharmed.

Luna smiled as she watched Stephen stroking his black mouse fondly. "I guess he followed us," she said brightly.

"Yeah…I didn't think I'd see him again," he answered, a bit self-consciously.

She could tell he was pleased. Johan and Madai's mice had not returned. Thomas's brown mouse was rough-coated but very hardy. He ate the seeds they had set out for them voraciously.

By sunrise, they had set out for the entrance of the city. They were walking through a tunnel of greenery. Small glass ornaments that were painted different colors dangled from above. Luna examined them almost with fright as she saw the strange objects inside them, which they were made to honor. Most of them were pyramids. Some were owls while others resembled the letter *E*.

As they emerged from the tunnel, they all stood in dazzled surprise. There in front of them was a huge tower. It was the shape of a pyramid, three-sided and glistening in the sun. It was truly majestic! On its front, it held the slightly protruding object of a fitted smaller pyramid with a circle at its center. At its tip was a plaque: pyramidis, and underneath the pyramid there was an inscription in block letters balanced on a gold curved beam: THE GLASS PYRAMID OF STRENGTH.

As they passed this strange monument, what they beheld was beyond their wildest dreams. There were leagues of workers, all dressed in blue uniforms. They wore a small pyramid- shaped badge below their right shoulder, and they were all working on building or cleaning glass buildings.

On either side of what seemed to be the main street were fancy houses—all made of glass and rare metals. There were people cleaning the windows while others were paving the sidewalks, and still some others were sweeping the roadway.

Luna watched as two young girls walked by, giggling as they carried heavy loads of seeds and vegetables. They all entered what seemed to be a factory. Then she recognized what had bothered them from the beginning: All of the workers in the blue uniforms were mixlings.

Stephen

"Ask her."

Stephen urged Luna forward. He watched as she timidly tried to get the attention of a young girl.

"Excuse me, do you know what time it is?"

The young girl stared at Luna as if she were a beetle. Then she turned and walked away without as much as a word.

After trying several more times, he told Luna to give up. "Something isn't right about this."

"Why do they act like we don't belong here—" Thomas was cut off by a commotion behind them.

"There they are!"

They all turned in fright to observe about twenty gray-uniformed officers headed their way, and they didn't look friendly.

"Let's go!" Stephen called to his stunned companions.

They took off running down the main path. As they were cut off again by another group of guards in front of them, Stephen again yelled directions, "Split up! We'll meet back later where we camped!"

Although he didn't want to admit it, he had a feeling this one would be hard to get out of. Racing down an alleyway, he didn't need to look back to know about the league of pursuers behind him. As he came to a T in the road, he faltered in a moment of indecision and then took the left side, but when he realized it was a dead end, it was too late to turn around. Cornered, he turned and watched with rising panic as his pursuers closed in.

23

Luna

Luna rode hard toward where she could see Stephen being cornered. Putting her fingers to her mouth, she let out a shrill whistle. The group of guards that was nearly upon him turned around to locate the whistler. That moment of indecision gave Stephen the time he needed to escape. As the guards had their backs turned, he ran through their midst, reaching her within seconds.

"Nice timing!"

Luna smiled at his compliment. Pulling him up behind her, she wasted no time in turning Mitzie and heading for the main gate, soon losing their pursuers. As they rode, Luna listened, amused, as Stephen made excuses for his predicament.

"Where'd your mouse go?" she finally interrupted him.

Without warning, he whistled a piercing shriek, calling his mouse.

"That was my ear," Luna grumbled as he jumped off.

He mounted his own mouse, and they continued toward the gate.

—◦◦○╾◉╼○◦◦—

Carl

Carl moved the small ornate vase back to its previous position. "Why did it still not look right?"

Finally, in exasperation, he averted his gaze as he collapsed into his comfy chair. Ever since his wife—no, he would not dig up old memories. But were they really that old? Fifteen years was a long time, but not long enough to forget, to forget the love, the hope, and most of all, the fear and pain. Luna brought back a lot of these memories, and she now entered his mind, troubling it further.

His feelings toward her were also strange, similar to that of the vase; he contemplated this as he let his gaze once again run back to the small brown object atop his otherwise messy desk. He wanted it there, yet it didn't belong, or did it? How could he once again bring order to his life? Everything was falling apart—the rumors of a spy, the mission to the glass city. His mind seemed to wander from one thing to the next, too distracted to settle on any particular topic.

And maybe he should tell her his secret. No, he couldn't. She would be angry, and he couldn't face that right now. Disdainfully, he stood up and headed to bed. But before leaving the room, he took the vase and buried it under a pile of clothes atop some books. If only he could so easily bury other disturbing thoughts.

Stephen

"How does it look?"

Stephen watched as Luna did a half-spin in the new blue uniform. They had broken into a small staff facility, which they had seen others come out of dressed in the blue uniforms. As he watched, Thomas and the two girls inspected their new outfits. He hoped Johan would hurry. He had gone back into the woods another way to leave the mice near the camp. He would take them into the woods and create a type of fence to keep them contained. Although they came when whistled to, it would not be good to lose them. Luna seemed rather reluctant to let Johan take Mitzie, but in the end, she allowed it.

Stephen looked down at the shiny black boots he had put on. He inspected the pair of dark-blue pants and long-sleeved shirt of matching hue. The only distinctions of color were the black stripes that ran down the side of the pants and down the arms of the shirt. A simple belt completed the uniform. The girls' uniforms were similar: a full skirt over blue tights in place of the pants. The lot of them looked like they had just walked off the streets of Pyramidis. All they were missing were the small pyramid pins. But Thomas had wisely suggested the idea that perhaps those might only be given when a job was assigned. They searched the facility, and they found nothing other than all sizes of uniforms.

"Well, we look like them all right," Madai exclaimed, examining her uniform in a large piece of glass propped against the far wall.

"Okay, so let's get started. We need to find out the layout of this city and somewhere to stay the night," Stephen instructed. "As soon as Johan gets back and changes, we'll get going."

"Hey, look!" Thomas exclaimed, drawing Stephen's attention from a tower he was examining. There, in front of them, stood a huge glass building that seemed to be under construction. "We could find a place to stay somewhere in there. Maybe no one would notice," Thomas offered hopefully.

A soft hello caused Stephen to turn around, expecting to find Luna or Madai with some objection to the other two's eager suggestions. But to his surprise, an older couple greeted him.

Dressed in blue, they looked a little different from the rest of the workers. He examined the odd pair with discernment. The lady, who he assumed was the man's wife, was slightly taller than her husband's slight form. The man was very skinny, and his blue-green eyes were adorned with round glasses. A thick but neatly trimmed mustache gave his already intriguing face character. His wife was a bit taller and not quite so slight. She had a kind, motherly face and blue eyes, and her brown hair was pulled back into a long ponytail. He took in all these features in a swift glance and smiled, hoping for a friendly response.

"Hello! We are happy, very happy to welcome you to our town. You must be new here?" the man spoke with confidence and held out his hand in a friendly gesture.

Stephen looked at them, slightly astounded. They seemed so familiar to him, but he had never been in Pyramidis before. No, he must be imagining things. "Thank you! We just got in, and well, it's nice to see a friendly face." He caught himself clumsily after a sharp jab in the ribs, which he assumed Luna had delivered.

"Have you all been assigned a place to stay yet?" The lady's voice was sweet and kind as she looked at them caringly. "Why don't you all come over for dinner?" she said.

The man interrupted before Stephen could muster an answer. "Well, let's go!" the man said enthusiastically.

Stephen noticed Luna's smile at the way the man spoke passionately, making gestures with every sentence. He himself almost smiled as he remembered how his father had made exaggerated gestures like this man. Although the couple was welcoming and cheerful, they also seemed a bit sad and tired. He watched their backs curiously and wondered about the evening ahead. He felt a bit wary. At first, no one had spoken to them, and now a dinner invitation after only a few minutes in a uniform. This was a strange place indeed.

———∘oo⦿oo∘———

"It's delicious, but I couldn't eat another bite!" Stephen smiled at their host's hospitality.

They had prepared a delicious meal of bean and quail egg. The girls had eaten delicately, but he noticed the couple's satisfaction with the boy's appetite. Stephen let his mind wander for a moment to their two sons: the older was named Aaron and the other Isaiah. It brought to mind his own brothers, Benjamin Aaron and Earnest Isaiah. He was only two years younger than Benni and four years older than Earnest.

"You look a lot like our other son." The mother's soft, sad voice brought him back to the present.

"Your other son? Where is he?" Stephen asked curiously to make conversation.

"He didn't come with us when we moved here," the father answered before his wife could respond.

"Where did you live before here?"

Stephen turned his head toward Luna, who had asked the question.

"We...we lived in small house on the outskirts of Sandar, in the woods," the man answered, slightly faltering. He seemed suddenly sad and turned away. He cleared his throat and said, suddenly brisk, "Well, enough about us! And where have you all come from? Your accent is different from most of the mixlings we have met here."

Stephen and Luna exchanged looks over the table.

"Ummm. We are from Sandar...we are here looking for a friend who hasn't been seen for some time," answered Luna cautiously. She was suddenly uncertain about telling strangers too much.

Stephen was far away in thought. Maybe he really did recognize this couple. After all, they were from Sandar, where he had grown up. No, that couldn't be possible! He couldn't even let himself think that. Looking away, he tried to push back the now troubling thoughts.

"Are you okay?" The lady's voice broke into his mind.

Are you okay? Are you okay? Are you okay? The question shouted itself into his mind, carrying him a million hours away, years back. He was running in the yard. He was showing his mom what he could do, but the somersault went wrong. "Are you okay?" she had asked, picking him up with care and tending to his scraped knee. How had he remembered that? He had been like six or seven years old.

Suddenly, turning in his chair, he addressed their now worried looks. "Wha...what are your names?" he asked, almost afraid to hear the answer.

The couple looked at him strangely but not unkindly.

"Aaron and Tatiana," the father answered softly.

"And your last name?" Stephen dared not hope, but now that the idea had formed, it began to seem clearer.

"Malines. And your name, son?" Aaron asked, suddenly sounding afraid.

Stephen swallowed hard before answering, "Stephen Joshua Malines."

The sound of a dish falling on the floor startled all of them. A look of wonder spread over the face of Mrs. Malines.

Kyle

Kyle woke from a shallow sleep as he heard the ruckus coming toward him. He let out a silent groan as his least favorite face greeted him at the bars of his cell.

"Sleep well?" The king's voice was sarcastic and somewhat annoyed. "I'm sure you're wondering why we're here." He gestured loosely to two guards, as well as his companion whom Kyle recognized as the same man who had brought him to the castle with that awful message. "As we've all noticed, you don't do us much good rotting here in our dungeon, so we've decided to offer you a position."

Kyle looked back at the cruel faces with caution. "A position?"

"An honest position, if your conscience is bothering you again." The king sneered in amusement. "Since you enjoy the mixlings so much, you can go and work in their town."

"Talenia?" Kyle was surprised. Why would they put him somewhere where he could leave anytime he pleased? Maybe it wouldn't be so bad after all.

"No! Not Talenia. Somewhere that will contain your troublesome self. You will work as a guard there, patrolling the city, but one mistake, and don't misunderstand me here"—he paused as if for dramatic effect, and Kyle did have to admit it worked; he hung on every word, almost dreading the end of the sentence but also waiting expectantly—"if you make one mistake, you are finished!"

The king left nothing unsaid in his cruel face or choice of words. As the small group retreated, Kyle watched their armored backs in consternation. Although it would be great to be a real guard, what would this place be like? This thought followed him through the rest of the day. How his life had taken such a drastic turn of events! First, he had been nothing but a messenger and low worker in Sandar, then Elsiper's prisoner in Icelair because a mixling had helped him in a moment of need. And now he would soon be a real guard in a town of mixlings that he didn't even know existed. He wondered about it—Talenia was the only mixling town he had ever heard of.

Luna

Luna watched with curiosity as the whole scene unfolded. First, they were eating with strangers and then the family was a jumble of happy hugs and tears. Luna knew it was only a miracle—a gift from the Lord of the Book—that Stephen had found his family. After sitting there, sort of on the outside and uncertain, she stood quietly and motioned for Thomas and Johan to do the same.

At the door, she instructed them softly, "There are still a few hours of daylight. If you're up for it, maybe you should go carefully"—she stressed the *carefully* part—"and look for anything that could be useful in our search."

"Sure thing!" Thomas gladly agreed.

"I could go exploring, just to find out what the town's like." Luna was surprised to hear Madai's voice behind her. Noticing Luna's concerned look, Madai quickly explained herself, "Well, it looks like Stephen's going to be kind of busy, so I figured maybe I could make use of the time."

Luna noticed that they were eager to be on their way, and after receiving some assurance that they would be careful, she waved them on, and they slipped quietly through the door. Luna went as if to rejoin Stephen but stopped. Stephen was sitting across from his newfound parents. They were laughing and talking, exchanging old stories.

A wave of sadness hit Luna with extreme force. She noticed that for her, there was no lost family, no shared memories. Her Uncle Matthias had been like a father to her and Nio, the perfect little brother, but it was difficult to know why her parents had left her. Was it because they were afraid of the hardship of raising a mixling—because they had not even been willing to try? Because of the color of her skin, eyes, and hair, her own mother and father had been willing to leave her on a doorstep in the middle of the night, like an irresponsible owner abandoning a helpless beetle.

Startled, she realized that tears had spilled out of her eyes, and she retreated to the outdoors to be by herself.

"Hey."

Luna jumped with a start as Stephen's soft voice distracted her from her thoughts.

"Are you okay?"

Luna avoided his gaze as she tried to hold back tears. His family reunion had disturbed her more than she thought possible. She stared out over the now dimming city lights as she leaned harder against the smooth glass wall behind her.

"Yeah, I'm fine," she said, trying to sound convincing.

"Somehow, I don't believe you," Stephen insisted, and she knew he was right.

Stephen

"You're missing your family?" Stephen asked Luna.

"It's been a while."

Luna's answer brought back memories of himself missing his family, but he had never really had the hope of seeing them again. He tried to comfort her in some way. "Maybe someday you will find your family too."

Her answer surprised him in some way. "I don't even know if they're alive. I don't even know who they are."

He had never thought of who her parents were. He had assumed somehow that she had a relationship with them, that maybe they visited her. "You don't have any idea who they might be?" he asked, interested.

"No. I remember being dropped off somewhere, but that's it. It might not have even been them. I don't even know if they wanted me."

Stephen understood her feelings. It was true that many pure-blooded parents saw mixling children as imperfect. In fact, often they didn't even regard them as their children but as mere mistakes. How could anyone think so? He was glad his parents had not been in the lot with hers.

"Did Carl mention any time when he planned for me to see my uncle again?"

Her question brought him back to the approaching night. "No, no, he didn't mention anything." Stephen wished that he had.

"What will happen now?"

Again, her question caught him off guard. "What do you mean?" he asked uncertainly.

"Will you stay here with your family?"

He met her violet eyes although he could hardly see them in the gathering dusk. "I don't know," he answered softly. "I hadn't really thought about it."

And although he could offer her nothing more for reassurance, he felt in his heart that even with his newfound joy, he would continue with the resistance because it was what he felt was right to do.

Eneva

Eneva paced back and forth in anxiousness as she heard the drumming of the rain on the roof. Zoe had dozed off an hour ago, and Eneva hoped she would stay asleep. At first she didn't hear the knock on the door but soon realized it was a different sound than the even pounding of the huge raindrops. Opening the door, she was extremely surprised to see Eric.

"Eric! What are you doing here?" she shouted above the roaring of the storm.

"It's the silkworms…"

The rest of his sentence was lost in the storm.

"Something's wrong! I don't know who knows more, you or the strategy engineer's wife, Linda…"

Quickly, Eneva bundled and scooped up the sleeping girl, wrapping her in a blanket and rain cover. "Let's go," she said hurriedly as she pushed past him into the raging storm.

An hour later, Linda and Chritian, the strategy engineer, along with Eneva and Eric, were in the barn with the silkworms.

They all realized it was going to be a long night, but somehow it didn't really bother Eneva.

Stephen

The exploring the team members had done earlier in the evening hadn't yielded much information other than the basic layout of the city. Tomorrow they had hopes of finding some clues as to where they might find Queen Anara and her son, Elihu.

"Okay, so we're all clear on the teams?"

Stephen checked that everyone had heard right. Although he was extremely excited in finding his family, he had made it clear to everyone that he had no intention of skipping out on his regular duties. They would not let Carl down. They would find the missing queen and the heir and take them back to the resistance to set everything straight. They were gathered in one of the two bedrooms that had been vacated for their use, and although they were tired, the excitement of the mission kept them all from yawning.

"Wait. So those three are going to go explore the east side of the city while we go over the north?"

Luna exasperated him with yet another question. Sighing, he reached out a finger and began explaining the map over again. "Look, we are here—"

Luna's laughter interrupted him.

"What's funny?" he asked, trying to be patient.

"You've explained it four times already, I think we got it."

He noticed Luna's half-smirk and realized he had been treating them like children. "Sorry." He sighed. "I just want this to turn out right."

He looked around at their attentive faces and knew that if it was possible, things would go right. They all bowed their heads and asked the Lord of the Book to be with them while they were on their mission.

"If we have him on our side, how can we fail?" stated Luna.

"You're right, Luna," Stephen said in appreciation. "Well, okay, I'm off to my roost." He grunted, pushing himself up from a sitting position. Thomas and Johan followed his lead, and he closed the door softly behind them.

Judging by the lights that were turned off on the first floor of the cozy house, his family had already gone to sleep. Catching himself, he resaid the words in his mind, *his family*. It had been so long.

After climbing into the soft bed, Stephen stared at the even glass roof. His mother had told him that the sun would wake him early shining right through it. He also contemplated the strange story his parents had recounted to him. Apparently, that day so long ago had been like any other when suddenly a league of soldiers arrived at the door. They demanded that they pack a few possessions and follow them immediately. When his parents refused, the guards took them by force, listening to no pleas, which they gave in plenty for their two absent children.

His sister, Roseanna, had been at a friend's house that beautiful morning. Only five years old, she did not know the danger her family was in. His parents had eventually convinced the guards to stop by the neighbor's house where she had been allowed to go play earlier, but when they got there, it had been in cinders, nothing left. They had told him that they had already been taken. When they arrived in Pyramidis, they were included in a work detail. They located the neighbors a week later and were reunited with Rosie. From there, they had slowly made a new life for themselves in Pyramidis.

The thing that bothered Stephen was that he asked his parents if they were being held captive here, but they assured him that one year after they arrived, the authorities told them that if they wished, they were free to leave after they paid back their debts. Then it had been explained to Stephen that his father, wanting a beautiful home for his wife and children, had already taken out a loan, which he intended to pay back with his work at the local school and food factory. But such a dream had not yet come to reality even after six years. Apparently, his benefactors charged him for the gift of loaning, and even though he paid a goodly amount of precious stones and other goods to them, he still had half to pay. But even worse, his parents were comfortable here and had no wish to leave.

As all the thoughts tumbled through his head, he couldn't help but wonder—why? Anyone could see that the life here was not near as nice as it had been in the woods near Sandar. His father worked two jobs; and his mother, one in the morning while his brothers and sister were at school. As too many different possibilities for his life ahead crowded his mind, he unknowingly fell into a deep, peaceful sleep, the first of which he had had in several months.

The Castle of Icelair

As soon as the king saw the messenger in the doorway, he burst into joy. "Yes! I have been waiting for this day. The resistance thinks they can send spies into my city? Ha! I would have loved to see their leader's face when he heard about their capture! We must celebrate! Tell Mikol and my sister that we will have a special banquet. Oh yes, we will have roasted quail!"

Suddenly, he glanced down toward the messenger after hearing no responsive joy. "Are you not pleased? Did you not want this too? Yes, of course you did! A raise in pay! You deserve it!"

"Yes, sir, very glad," the cloaked figure finally managed to acknowledge the speaker.

The guards lining the hall looked at him curiously, for even if their king did not see it, they could see he was not in the same mood as their leader. The messenger soon excused himself, clumsily retreating into an adjoining chamber.

"Hiding from someone?"

The voice made him jump, but he calmed himself as soon as he realized it was only Mikol.

"Can you talk to him? Please? Make him understand!" The messenger held his cloaked head in his hand as in exasperation, he realized Mikol knew nothing of what he was talking about.

He paced the room nervously and then pulling off his hood, he stopped in front of Mikol, his eyes pleading. "I didn't catch them! They got away. They're loose in Pyramidis, and the king thinks I've caught them. He's going to celebrate! Did I mention he thinks I've got them?" Red in the face and sweating, he sagged down into a nearby chair. "Please, can you explain it to him?"

He looked pleadingly at Mikol, who was bouncing his one-year-old daughter on his knee, making her giggle, a sound that annoyed him.

"I'm afraid my brother-in-law is not an understanding person, my friend. I, for one, intend to celebrate capturing the resistance representatives!"

And with that, he hoisted little Bell up on his waist. After leaving the room, he poked his head back in, and with a small smile, he said softly, "I suggest you do the same if you want to keep your head on your shoulders."

24

Madai

Madai, Thomas, and Johan had been searching for the last three hours with no turn of events. The winding streets and beautiful glass buildings were a maze of confusion, and no dungeon was to be found. The three of them were tired of their excursion and wondered how it was fairing with Luna and Stephen.

Madai stared in front of her. They had already passed this part of the city three times. "Thomas, why do we keep going in circles?" she asked, almost exasperated.

"We're not, are we?" he countered.

A commotion in the distance caught their attention.

"Guards, holding a prisoner," Johan informed them in whispers.

They moved off behind a building and watched as about twelve guards approached with a young youth in their midst, securely tied and bound with ropes. "From Sandar," Thomas whispered the obvious, which could be told by the youth's clothing and stature. The small group passed, looking around them every few seconds as if to make sure no one would see where they were going.

The three resistance members watched in fascination as the guards came to the wall of the biggest glass building, and one of them tapped a pattern on its sheer, glassy outer shell. The door opened into a huge dark forbidding room. The guards entered with their prisoner. The strange thing was that the door seemed to have opened on itself. Madai tapped the rhythm over and over in her palm, willing herself not to forget as they left the area in haste.

Luna

Luna walked carefully between the market stalls. Everyone seemed to be there, selling their goods. She had noticed many more shoppers entering a store nearby, which seemed to sell produce. She remembered that morning when Stephen had said good-bye to his parents for the day; they didn't want to let him out of their sight, much less out to roam the town. When Stephen asked them about the dungeon, they seemed frightened and assured him that they knew nothing of one.

Out of nowhere, a young man was standing there in front of them, exclaiming about not having seen Stephen for quite a while. He seemed to be in his twenties or maybe thirties. Luna noticed he was lightly built but had probably overdone it on the sweets somewhere along the line. He had glasses and looked slightly ill-kept.

"Nea'n!" Stephen greeted him warmly. "What are you doing here?"

"Well, I was offered a better life away from my parents, and I took it, and look around you! Have you ever seen a prettier city?" Nea'n was certainly impressed with his surroundings. "Why don't you two join me for lunch?"

Luna noticed that Stephen looked to her for an opinion, but not wanting to decide, she pretended to be interested in a vegetable stand. The vegetables did seem to have a peculiar quality. Back home, a bean her uncle brought from the market would fill a whole pot! Here the beans were half the size. *It would probably take two beans to make a pot*, she thought.

"So I guess we're going to lunch!" Stephen's whisper brought her back to their present situation.

They followed Nea'n to a large housing complex. After four flights of stairs, Nea'n invited them into his small quarters. Luna noticed that although the residence wasn't poor, neither was it fancy. It consisted of four small rooms: a kitchen, a bedroom, a center room, and a bathroom. In the center room, there was a large glass window that looked out over the courtyard. He had a long white couch against the far wall and a matching single chair and desk on the other side of the room. A small glass table with supporting marble stone pillars decorated the center of the room. Other than these simple furnishings, the room was bare and plain.

"Take a seat!" Nea'n invited, motioning to the couch.

Luna and Stephen moved to comply and sat neatly on opposite ends. After a few minutes passed in awkward silence, Nea'n brought out their lunch. As Luna's plate was set before her, she examined the food in curiosity. A lump of what seemed to be mashed bean accompanied by stiff bread and some sort of shriveled green veggie stared up at her. "Looks good!" she said, trying to sound excited.

After a shared look, she and Stephen bowed their heads in unison. Luna concentrated on the prayer, repeating in her mind every word Stephen said and meaning them with her heart. When they were done, they were both surprised by Nea'n's question.

"Why did you guys do that?" he asked, clearly puzzled.

"Well...well, don't you pray before you eat?" Luna asked him, trying not to sound criticizing.

"Pray? Oh, pray! Didn't anyone tell you guys?"

Luna noticed Stephens's curious look. "Tell us what?"

"We don't have to pray anymore! Look, the book doesn't say anything about it. The copiers made an error. All the defective copies were collected three weeks ago and burned. Thankfully, I have a new one."

Luna accepted the small book handed to her. Tenderly, she wiped the thin layer of dust off its nameless cover. She noticed it was slightly thinner than her own. "And what happened to the copiers who made this 'error,'" she asked.

"I think they were punished for trying to inflict unnecessary rituals on the people. They were no longer allowed to work as copiers of the book."

"What happened to them?"

"Uh, I don't know."

Nea'n's disinterest gave her concern. She herself did not believe that references to prayer were not in the book. Of course they were! There was no way... Contemplating this, she swallowed another bite of the food, which uncharacteristically still lingered on Stephen's plate, as well as her own.

"The food is...good. How is it made?" she asked in attempt to make conversation.

"Oh, that food is wonderful! The factories pack it in airtight pouches, and it is way cheaper than the other stuff. And it's clean too. The stuff from outside could have bugs or dirt in it. This has been sterilized. Some of it is made from special chemicals, designed to look and taste like the stuff people used to eat, but it is made with vitamins, so it's much healthier than the old food." Nea'n was happy to supply the information.

Over the next hour, Luna smiled and attempted to look as if she were enjoying herself. But in reality, she was far from it. She felt very uncomfortable with these strange new things that seemed to be part of regular life in Pyramidis.

Stephen

"Well, that was interesting," stated Luna dryly.

Stephen had to smile at the wry look on Luna's face that accompanied her statement. "You know, he didn't used to be that way." Stephen tried in some way to excuse Nea'n's behavior.

"Uhmm, I don't really know...," she responded with a quizzical look.

He remembered she hadn't been around for that epoch of the resistance. Stephen began to explain, "Well, the strategy engineer, Christian, he and his wife originally had three sons. There was Mikol, Nea'n, and you know, Johann. They lived and worked together for a long time until about a year after I joined the resistance. Mikol visited one of the Icelair festivals. He had the looks of a pure Icelairian and therefore fit in nicely. When he didn't come back for a whole year, Mikol's parents grew deeply concerned. Then one day Mikol sent a messenger to tell them he was getting married—to the king's sister!

"They were invited to the wedding and went but were treated with disdain, although all tried their best not to show that they sensed it. After the wedding, Pearl, Mikol's wife, took measures to slowly cut off Mikol from his parents. Christian and Linda have a grandchild but have only seen him once in four years." Stephen paused to make sure Luna was following.

"And Nea'n?" Luna asked, clearly enthralled with his story.

"Nea'n unfortunately began hanging around Pearl and her parents, who encouraged him to follow in his brother's footsteps. They kept telling him that he really should be out on his own and learn how to live away from his family. All we heard was that they offered him a better opportunity. And slowly, day by day, Christian and Linda received less and less communication and, after a while, were no longer even sure of his continued existence. Well, the rest is history. Somehow he ended up here in Pyramidis."

As they continued side by side toward the house they were staying, Stephen contemplated everything that had happened, all that he had seen and heard. It seemed that people here in

Pyramidis were so caught up in the glass buildings and artificial ways of life that they had forgotten about the importance of their freedoms and even of the truth of the Great Book. Why had his parents made no more effort to search for him? Yes, they were happy to see him, but why hadn't they returned to look for him in Sandar? These questions bothered him as they continued on.

25

Luna

"Shhh, don't make a sound!" Stephen hissed in her ear.

He was aggravating to her sometimes. Obviously, she wasn't going to stand up and holler! Johan and Thomas were on the other side of the building, waiting for a signal. They were going to go into the mysterious building the others had discovered earlier that day. The waiting seemed to take forever, and she had to restrain herself completely from asking Stephen what he was waiting for. Finally, after what seemed like hours, Stephen raised his hand, signaling that it was time to go.

Slowly, the four made their way to the towering glass wall. Luna watched in wonder as Thomas opened a secret door in the wall with ease, tapping on the glass a code with his fingers. The inside of the building was nothing less than intimidating. Although the light was extremely dim, it was enough to see the polished black walls and the gleaming tile floor. It was a huge room, bare on every side.

"Over there," Johan whispered, pointing to a small red door at the far side of the empty space.

As Stephen made his way over, Luna, Thomas, and Johan all faced a different direction, bows in hand in case of an unwanted interruption.

Surprisingly, the red door opened easily, and they entered into a long hall. Luna was surprised to see there were no doors on either side of the hallway. They walked on, tense with anticipation. Still Johan and Thomas faced backward, careful to watch for any guards who might interrupt their unauthorized visit. At the end of the hall, there was a staircase. Luna stared down the winding steps and shivered at the engulfing dark at the bottom of it.

"Let's go," Stephen whispered, pushing her forward.

"You go ahead," she resisted.

"You scared?"

Luna noticed the sarcasm but decided to ignore it and waited for him to take the first step.

"Wait!"

She was pushed against the wall as Thomas yanked Stephen away from the steps.

"What are you doing?" Stephen hissed, picking himself up and brushing off his uniform.

"The steps are rigged." Thomas pointed to the place Stephen had almost stepped. They all turned to see what Thomas was looking at. He was right.

Stephen

Stephen watched in curiosity as Luna knelt to examine the trap. Thomas explained that it was a technique often used by the rebels when protecting something of value. The lighting in the building was so dim that no one else had seen the thin rope strung across the first step. He watched as Luna traced it up to a beam, which was above them, fastened to the ceiling. It was attached to a number of gears and mechanisms. None of them wanted to try it out and hear what kind of alarm it was or see what kind of defense it offered.

"I'll cut the rope. You hold the top half, and we'll tie it to the side beam," commanded Luna quietly.

Carefully, Thomas took the rope and sustained it while she did the rest of the handiwork.

"I guess it's a good thing you came along, Thomas. If you hadn't seen that, we might not get another chance at this."

"Glad I could be of service," he replied, bowing slightly.

Luna was trying to be helpful as well. She insisted they were not going to go raid the dungeon without her, and she made the point she might be useful. However, Stephen had refused to take Madai, and Madai looked relieved.

The four crept cautiously down the steps until they reached the bottom. At the end, it was damp, eerie, and dark—but finally, the dungeon. Stephen could hear water dripping somewhere in the dark tomblike place. Down the main hall, there were five cells on either side and, between each, another passage way.

"We'll spread out. Locate any prisoners, but don't let them out. We don't know who they are or know what kind of alarms could be rigged. We'll have to consider carefully before acting. If you get lost or find something, signal on your whistle," Stephen instructed his band of explorers with authority, and they moved to obey.

Heading down the first off branch, he saw it was like the main hall, with five cells on either side, only thankfully, no more halls branching off. After checking each one, he was disappointed to find no prisoners.

Making it back to the main room, he contemplated what would happen if they didn't find the queen. After the second corridor, he was again disappointed to find no one. Suddenly, he heard the short tweet of the whistle. In only a few seconds, the four of them had gathered in the third hall on the right side. Johan stood there holding his whistle triumphantly.

"There's nothing here," he heard Thomas's criticizing voice echo against the walls.

"There's nothing in any of them," afirmed Luna.

"But look!"

They all turned to the empty cell that Thomas was excitedly gesturing to.

"I see it!" Luna exclaimed in eagerness.

Then Stephen saw it. In the corner of the cell was a block of flooring, and around it sparkled a soft light. "A hatch." He smiled as he tested the door. It opened easily.

They all advanced into the cell and pulled up the door slowly. Below, they could see at least fifteen cells, and all of them held prisoners. In the midst of them, to their dismay, strolled a blue-uniformed guard.

"The sleeping medicine…," Luna whispered, drawing from her belt a small flask. Her idea seemed good to him, and he accepted the short arrow she handed him. His aim was beautiful, and the arrow hit the man's upper arm perfectly. It would do no lasting harm. They watched in satisfaction as he looked in surprise at his arm and then sank into immediate slumber.

"Let's go!" Stephen commanded and began down the shaky ladder.

———∘∘∘❦❧∘∘∘———

Luna

Luna followed Stephen down the ladder with trepidation. Although she hated causing anyone pain, their mission was important, and she was glad for the small supplies of medicine her uncle had provided her with. He had also given her the knowledge to make the medicines if necessary, and already, this knowledge had served her well.

At the bottom of the ladder, she waited impatiently for Thomas and Johan to finish descending. After she watched

Stephen talk to one of the prisoners, she was surprised he gave to order to let them all loose. The ring of keys hung on the guard's belt. They pulled him into a cell and placed him on a bed.

"Sleep tight," Luna said, smiling.

One young man, whom they had liberated, began to lead them, and Stephen motioned for the others to follow. He led them through a maze of hallways, passages, and doors—and then they saw it. At the end of the last hall was a short ladder leading down into a separate room, and in a large furnished cell on the far wall was a lady. She looked to be in her thirties and very beautiful. The dress she wore reminded Luna of the ones Nio described from the festival and the royal people who lived there. Her hair was a beautiful pale gold and fell around her almost white face gently. Her eyes were blue, so deep and soft.

"Who are you?" exclaimed the lady with a look that seemed full of joy and disbelief.

"I'm Luna. W-we came to get you out of here," she answered, stuttering slightly, still unable to believe they had really found the queen. "You must be Queen Anara?"

"Yes, yes, I am."

"So glad to finally meet you." Luna smiled at the lady's sweet face. *How could anyone lock her up?* "And your son?"

"He's not here. They have taken him away to a work camp." The queen looked sad.

"It's okay. We will find him…but now we must get you safely out of here." Luna smiled encouragingly and took Anara's hand.

Luna jumped when Stephen touched her arm. The dungeon was making her nervous.

"Come on!" he said urgently.

They made their way up the first ladder and back through the maze of hallways. As they turned down the last dark hallway, the young man leading them tripped over a rope that was only a little above the uneven floor. Suddenly, a piercing, screaming siren broke the air.

"Run!" their guide yelled.

Luna looked back in time to see Stephen grab the queen's hand and pull her after them. As they reached the main room again, they saw only Thomas and Johan with a few stragglers. They were all running every which way trying to find somewhere to hide. Several had climbed the ladder and were making their escape through the higher dungeon. As Stephen climbed the ladder, their guide pushed Thomas and Johan up first, followed them, and then reached his hand down for Luna. She reached up to take it, but then she saw the guard coming from the tunnels they had just vacated.

Moving out of the way, she pushed the queen forward. "Go!"

The queen hurried the best she could, but Luna could see time in the cell had not left her with much strength. Luna attempted to shut her ears to the still wailing sirens and watched in satisfaction as Queen Anara made it to the top with Stephen.

Luna reached up her hand to follow her companions, but as she stepped onto the first wrung of the ladder, she was pulled back. She unwillingly let out a scream as she was pulled into the tunnels by the guard behind her.

Stephen

Stephens's heart seemed to skip a beat as he heard Luna's scream. Johan and Thomas were hoisting the trapdoor back into place.

"I'm going back for her!" he tried to explain to his unrelenting friends, who were trying to seal the trapdoor.

"No! They took her into a tunnel. There will soon be many more guards! It's too dangerous. We need to get the queen out of here! We'll have to come back later!"

He realized what they were saying was true and reluctantly pushed the queen ahead of him as they all hurried toward the top of the stairs. But even though he was distracted by their rapid flight, his thoughts were on his captured companion.

Luna

Luna struggled and pulled against the strong arms that held her. She could see very little, but she did recognize the dark maze of tunnels that she had just run through with Stephen and their guide. When they finally reached the end of the tunnel, her captor turned her roughly around against the wall. Luna gasped in recognition.

Kyle

Kyle leaned on the sturdy post behind him. It felt so good to be out of the cold damp cell, which had been his home for the last several weeks. He had been transferred to the dungeon early that morning after two weeks of training above ground. Once more, he examined his pert uniform and remembered the words it had been delivered with: "Careful with it now, lad, these things don't come cheap." The man had said it as he handed Kyle his new clothes. It consisted of a long-sleeve shirt and comfortable pants, both black with little décor. Only a gold line ran down the sides of the pants and likewise down his arms. It also came with an over vest, which was a dark gray color. He fingered one of the round gold buttons on the vest and thought how smart he looked in the glass with his perfect-fitting cap to complete the outfit.

The guards back in Sandar had also worn uniforms, but not anywhere as fancy or sharp-looking as the one he wore now. He smiled to himself to think of how the guards back home would envy his fancy position. Although he was a regular-ranked soldier/guard, he still felt amazing being just that. He had noticed the city itself was magnificent. *Pyramidis*—even the name was majestic! He stood on the midlevel of the humongous building, which he had been informed was the dungeon. He was told not to allow anyone to enter or leave unless they were officials. That was easy enough.

Suddenly, a screaming siren broke into his distant thoughts. Rushing headlong, he ran through the door and hurried to the staircase at the back of the room. His instructor had told him what to do in this kind of an emergency. As he reached the staircase, he paused halfway down and turned to the glass wall at his side and knocked a code that opened a door to another staircase. The instructor had told him that this would take him to the main room of the dungeon. As he reached it, what he saw was chaos. People were scrambling up the ladder. Maybe they were prisoners! Right behind them was a tall girl with golden hair. As she began up the ladder, he quickly pulled her down and then dragged her toward the cells. When he turned her around, he found himself face-to-face with the mixling who had helped him when Kaylee had been hurt!

As she faced him, he could see shock register on her face. "What are you?" Her question was left unfinished, but he could guess the rest.

"There's no time for talking right now!" he hissed.

Putting his hand over her mouth, he pushed her toward the tunnels on the far side of the room. In less than a minute, many other guards would join him. Frantically he pointed to some crates at the back of the room behind one of the empty cells. She did not need to be told twice, and not a second too soon, she ducked behind the stacked crates.

"What are you doing in here?" demanded a gruff, angry voice from behind him, which brought panic to his heart.

The words of the horrible king ran through his mind: *You mess up just once, and you're finished.* "I...uuhhh...came when the siren started...I thought I would check back here for anyone who might have come this way...," he stammered with uncertainty.

The guard looked at him for a moment and then grunted angrily. "Stay on this level awhile before you come up, in case anyone comes through here. We're going to search upstairs."

As soon as he had gone, Kyle breathed easier. Even so, his hands shook, and he tried to ignore the horrible feeling of dread that came over him. How was she involved in a dungeon raid in Pyramidis? And he had been told that she and the other mixling were no more.

"What are you doing here?" The girl's pointed question made him jump.

"What am I doing here? More like what are you doing here?" he demanded angrily. "I thought you were dead." Immediately, he recognized his error when he saw distrust cloud her face.

"I asked first."

He noticed the underlying icy tone present in her question.

"I'm a real guard here now," he stated, "and you could really mess up my job. You know I've been in prison for the last several weeks because of what happened in Sandar? If I mess up here, I don't know what will happen. The king said I'd be finished." He was unable to keep fear from his voice.

"Did you tell them about us?" she asked. "My uncle told me he had you deliver a message for the resistance when you went to Icelair."

"No. I told them nothing. The king wanted to know who you were, but I knew that would be the end of Mr. Matthias if I mentioned where you lived."

"You've been in prison, and you didn't tell anything about me or my uncle?" Amazement tinged her voice. Then in a change of mood, she continued, "So now you start working for the bad guys?" Her voice was accusing, and he cringed inside.

"They're not all that bad," he tried to defend his new comrades.

"Not all that bad? I can't even live with my family because of what…you guys are doing."

He noticed her slight hesitance as whether to address him as part of the "you guys," but she overcame it after a glance at his uniform.

"So since they're not that bad, why didn't you turn me in?" she asked, her tone slightly softer.

He stared at her, trying to answer her question in his own mind. "I…uuh…look, I will be eternally grateful for what you did for Kaylee. You saved her life, and I've wanted to repay you and your friend. This is my way of saying thanks, but as soon as you walk up that ladder, you're on your own. I can't afford to be noticed again by the king. I'm sorry, but I have to stay alive somehow."

"Well, that may be true, but the Lord of the Book is the real answer. If you depend on Him, things may change in time," she said as she started up the ladder.

She seemed to hesitate slightly at the top of the ladder. She held her bow and arrow poised for action. Before she disappeared from view, she turned back with a sentence that hit him hard. "I thought you were different." And then she was gone.

He contemplated the words over and over, and mixed feelings arose. He thought about the time he had delivered the message for Mr. Matthias, the many interrogations in which he had kept the secret of Matthias's involvement, the Great Book and what it had meant to him while he was in his cell. Why did she say she thought he was different? Puzzlement made his head hurt, and he thought regretfully how good it had felt to be different, to be serving the Lord of the Book by showing his love and mercy to others. But by telling her what he had, he had in a way betrayed her trust. He felt that somehow he would never again be involved in the mysterious group she seemed to be a part of, and that made him feel sad.

———∘∘∘❖∘∘∘———

Eneva

Eneva bounced Zoe on her knee as she sang a funny tune and smiled at the little girl's giggles. Zoe was so cute and lovable. A frown touched Eneva's face for a moment as she thought briefly of the time when Luna would again take over her care. "But I guess if she lives with me, I'll still see Zoe," she reasoned, happy once more.

Her mind wandered to the adventures of a few nights past when Christian, the strategy engineer, and his wife, Linda, and she had spent many hours at Eric's, saving his silkworms. She had been so glad that nearly all of them had lived. It turned out that the shed had flooded, and the worms, which were contained in their stalls, had become extremely cold. They had built a fire and warmed the shed, drying each soft worm with towels and shoveling out the accumulated water from the stalls. Her eyes wandered above her door to the gauzy scarf Eric had given her as a token of appreciation. It was a violet color mixed with reddish streaks. As she continued amusing Zoe, her mind kept wandering from one happy thought to another.

Luna

Luna rubbed her arm in indignation. It had been a bit hard getting out of the dungeon and avoiding the guards. It had taken her much longer than she had planned, and she was beginning to wonder how this day would end. She noticed in dismay the darkening sky and quickened her pace toward Stephen's house. It was strange, calling the house Stephen's house. Although she was happy for him, it also brought back sad reminders. How she wished she too could find her long-lost family, but was it even possible? Even if her family were alive, would they even want to know her? Hadn't they dropped her off at some unknown doorstep in the middle of the night?

As she recognized the now familiar white glass door in front of her, a burst of energy entered her steps. She approached and knocked tentatively, wondering who would answer. Stephen's worried face greeted hers. His anxious frown was soon replaced with glad relief.

"Hey, I'm back!" Luna exclaimed, trying to see whether he was mad at her for being caught, or if he was just glad to have her back.

"I was so worried!" his sincere response warmed her heart, and she gladly entered the warm room beyond the door he held open for her.

Stephen

Stephen was very relieved that Luna had made it out of the prison. He had worried about the events to come the rest of the day and wondered how they would possibly get back in after their escape with the queen. He lay in the dark room, tossing and turning. He just could not get to sleep. Suddenly, the urge for a drink of water was too great. Slipping past his sleeping brothers, he made his way to the kitchen. A bucket of water sat by the door with an dipper hanging over the side. After locating one of the palva pouches his father had crafted, he quenched his parched throat.

"You couldn't sleep either?"

The soft voice behind him made him turn sharply, coming face-to-face with the queen.

"Aahhh, your highness...umm...my lady..." He tried frantically to find the correct title for the lady of stature in front of him.

"Call me Anara."

He couldn't help but notice her slightly red eyes. It looked as if she had been crying.

"Can I get you something, my lady?" He recognized his slip in name too late but didn't bother to correct it.

"No, no, I'm fine. Did you know there was nothing I, or anyone else, could do to stop them?"

The question seemed strange and out of place to Stephen. "To stop who?" he asked, puzzled by her question.

"The soldiers…they were everywhere." She seemed to be in some other time or place and was, in a way, talking to herself.

"When they attacked your village?" He tried to play on her train of thought, which reminded him of the diary. Remembering it, he wondered if he should show it to her.

"Yes, when they attacked the village. You know his father always told us we would always be safe." She looked at him as if relieved that someone knew what she was talking about.

"Please just wait a second," he instructed her quietly before bounding neatly to his room and retrieving from deep within his pack the small weathered book. Upon returning, he held it out to her as if in some way it might help her troubled mind. She took it in an almost reverent manner, smoothing its rough cover with her delicate white hand.

"Laraan, she always hated to write so…"

He was surprised that she recognized the book so readily. Didn't a queen keep herself separate from her servants? But then again, the diary had said they were more like a family.

"What happened to her?" he asked, curiosity tugging at the back of his mind about the mysterious character who had kept an account of events even in those terrible times.

"I'm afraid she was one of the few who didn't make it out of the village." The queen sadly stared at the first entry in the book as tears filled her eyes. "She was so loyal. If it hadn't been for her, I may not be here today."

Stephen was tempted to press further but knew it would not have been respectful.

"When the soldiers first came to the village, I was in the garden with Elihu. On gardening days, I was never dressed in my usual garments. It happened that, that day, Laraan's sister, Diana, had arranged a tea party for the ladies. It was custom that they dress up. I had planned to go but was to arrive late on account of helping Elihu with the garden. There were advisors who came that morning, and they said we should all stay inside. The others argued with them. What could we do anyway? There was no place to go. We thought we were safe there.

"All of a sudden, soldiers came, and they said they had orders to execute the queen. Everyone was terrified. The men demanded to know who the queen was. The ladies in the tea room all claimed they were the queen. There were six of them, but they knew they couldn't delay for much longer.

Laraan was in the cabin she shared with Diana. The soldiers burst into the cabin, and they assumed she was the queen because of her dress. She let out a cry that she would not leave without her son and took off running for the castle. The guards took this to mean she indeed was the queen going after her young prince. While they chased after her, the rest of the servants did their best to hide Elihu and me, but it was of no use. Laraan was executed, and they took the rest of us here as prisoners. I was sure I would soon be identified. Then a guard recognized me from the royal family. But this guard had been a faithful servant to my husband, so he commanded them not to kill me but to imprison me and take my son to a work camp. His orders were the second time that day my life had been saved."

She stared down once again at the weather-beaten book in her hands, slightly out of breath. "We can find him. We need to find him," she added.

Stephen looked at her sadly. She returned his gaze and then looked at the floor, deflated. "It isn't possible, is it?" she asked.

"There are too many guards, and if we did find him, we could never get him away from the city." Her gaze was pleading with him to reassure her, and he tried to quiet his heart against the warnings she had just given. "If we work together, there is a good chance we can find your son and save the kingdom."

He smiled at the beautiful queen and hoped with all his heart that he would not disappoint her.

———∘∘◦❊◦∘∘———

Stephen

Another day had passed. They had carefully scouted out two more camps but still hadn't found the prince. There were only two left, and he felt that time was running out. Surely someone would begin to get suspicious soon. Stephen lay in his bed, staring up at the glistening roof above him. It felt so rich and cool living in the tidy house his parents owned, but what if what the former prisoner had told him was true? His heart skipped a beat as he thought back to his warning. Apparently, whoever began to know anything about the secret motives of Pyramidis disappeared, and they disappeared for good.

The man who told him had related that he himself had been in a group heading out of town, supposedly being moved to a new job, when they had been stopped by guards. Everyone else in the group had been taken. Only he had been detained and taken to the dungeon where he had remained, all because he had asked a few questions around town about the inner workings of Pyramidis.

Stephen tried to calm the worry he felt for his family. He and his friends had unwittingly endangered his own family. What if they were next? They had also asked a few questions and were new in town. Now they were also hiding the queen of Icelair—a dangerous thing for sure. They would be looking for her. She was a very valuable prisoner. Also, the man said something about the city being built for Sandarians and Icelairians to live in. Why would they want to live in a city full of mixlings? All of the workers in Pyramidis were mixlings. Things weren't adding up. He tossed and turned, trying to will sleep to overcome all of his worries.

A firm knock sounded at the window on the east side of the room. With a groan, he pushed his warm covers off and held back a discontented shiver as his feet touched the chilly floor. As he pushed up the window, he was surprised to see one of the messengers from the resistance.

"What are you doing here?" he asked.

"I was sent to follow you and deliver a message if anything happened…like what happened this evening."

Stephen stared at the speaker, wondering if he had heard right. "You followed us? You've been watching us? Who sent you? And if what happened?" Still not believing, he was stunned to see Carl's membership stone settled neatly in the palm of the messenger.

"He has given me and a group of three other members the authority to take Luna back to the resistance camp should things become dangerous, which even you can see is happening."

Stephen hesitated. Yes, things were getting pretty dangerous. The possibility of a hidden plot behind the beautiful city and now the extra threat of being recognized since the prison raid, not to mention how Luna had been caught in the prison. If it hadn't been for Kyle… The messenger must have seen his hesitance.

"You do see it's dangerous for her here. Carl wants her safe, and I think that's one thing we can agree on."

Stephen fought the urge to argue. The messenger who had been chosen to deliver the message was not one of his favorites; in fact, they had often argued, and more than once, things he hadn't done had been put under his name.

"She needs to come back with me whether you like it or not," the messenger still insisted.

"Why? What's with Carl? He's firm and businesslike one minute and then the next he sends a messenger to follow us to take her home when things get rough...it just doesn't seem like him. And since when does he protect resistance members from danger?" The mission wouldn't be the same without Luna.

"Oh yes, and one other thing, Madai is supposed to stay with the queen."

Stephen, who had been staring at the windowsill, now lifted his head sharply. "Stay here? She's supposed to be Luna's companion." He met the messenger's cold glare.

"Look, I'm telling the truth. She needs to stay with the queen."

Stephen sighed. "Why couldn't things just go smoothly for once?" Turning back to the late-night visitor, he sighed once more. "I'll tell her."

The messenger gave him a relieved look then turned to go. "One more thing. Carl doesn't want her to know the reason, so make something up."

Stephen began a sputtering response, but his conversationalist was already gone into the dark night. Once more, he stared at the glass ceiling, but his mind was now on other thoughts. Why was he forced to lie to her again? He hated lying but especially to Luna, and especially after what had happened last time. It was a long time before he finally drifted off to a restless sleep.

26

Stephen

"Hey, Luna, can I talk to you about something?" Stephen started out tentatively.

"Well, I'm guessing you're going to talk to me about it sooner or later, so what is it?"

Stephen hesitated at her happy face. His news was sure to spoil her mood.

"Uhmm, you need to go back to the resistance camp."

"Why?"

He was surprised at her calm composure, even though there was heavy puzzlement in her voice. "Apparently, there was a messenger sent after us to bring you back to work with Key or something. They didn't give me much detail." He avoided her gaze, almost afraid she might see through him.

"Oh."

Her voice was strangely quiet, and Stephen felt horrible as he saw she looked like she might cry.

"Is Madai coming?"

What would she say when she found out that she would be going alone? "Carl thinks she should stay with the queen."

It wasn't possible for Luna to look gloomier; he was sure of it.

"When do I have to go?" Her question was barely audible this time.

"Right now."

A not-so-friendly voice broke into their conversation. Stephen turned to glare at the familiar face of the messenger. Couldn't he leave well enough alone?

"I'll be ready in a few minutes." Luna's timid voice broke the awkward, unfriendly silence.

As she disappeared into the glasshouse behind him where her things were, he addressed the messenger, "Why are you here? We decided I would tell her."

"You did tell her, I was just making sure you didn't delay."

Anger boiled within Stephen as he stared at the insensitive face in front of him. "You had better make sure she makes it back safely!" Stephen added firmly.

"Oh, don't worry. There has also been a change of plans. We talked it over, and we all agreed it would be best if we take the queen and Madai with us too. If she is found here, it endangers the rest of the mission. Have you located the boy yet?"

"We have narrowed his location down to two work camps on the south side of Pyramidis. We hope to go tomorrow to check them out."

"Good. Here are some clothes for the girls. We will be under disguise until we leave the city and are well on our way back." He handed a bundle to Stephen and instructed him to have the three of them ready in half an hour.

Luna

Luna was relieved that she wouldn't be returning alone with the four strange men. She put on the rough men's clothes and looked into the glass mirror, laughing at the image that she saw there. "Who are you?" she said to her reflection. Madai joined her, and they both laughed at the "men" of slight build who looked at them from the glass. Anara came into the room awkwardly.

"I can't say I've ever felt so strange," she said, smiling shyly from under the hood of the heavy cloak. "These boots feel so clumsy."

"Here, let me help you tuck your hair into this brown cap," Luna offered.

When they were done, they all looked in wonder at how the clothes had transformed them into three tall thin men.

Stephen

While the girls prepared for their journey, Stephen continued talking with the messenger who had come and changed everything in one night.

"What's the real reason Carl wants Luna back?" Suspicion floated in his mind like a dark cloud waiting to burst.

"You know what you need to know," came the short reply.

"Carl has always trusted me. I'm sure he wouldn't mind you telling me the real reason." Stephen looked curiously at the messenger.

"I shouldn't be telling you this, but she's related—"

Stephen flushed as he heard Luna's approach behind him. He felt uncomfortable having Luna walk in on a conversation about her. As he glanced at her strained face, he realized in relief she had not noticed.

"Well, I guess this is...uhmm...good-bye..." She faltered.

"I'd just say it's until next time," Stephen replied with a sad smile. "If it is the Lord's will, we should be back soon with the boy." He tried to sound reassuring. "Wow...you look so different," he added, looking at the trio before him.

He shook hands with Madai and the queen and then he paused for a moment before briefly hugging Luna. "We will be praying for you to make it safely," he said as they mounted their mice. He watched the small group as they rode toward the city gates. He felt a pang of sadness as they rode out of sight. He would miss them.

Luna

Luna stared up at the rough ceiling above her, so different from the one she had slept under only a week ago. So little time had passed, and yet it seemed it was years ago. Traveling with the new group of men had been difficult. They disagreed about everything and, for the most part, kept their distance whenever possible. They refused to think a girl could have anything "intelligent" to add as far as trail-planning went. Luna's mind wandered to the two unnecessary detours they took the day before, which had cost them hours. They had almost been attacked by the ants again when the men did not heed her warning and nearly walked directly into their path.

Luna and Madai felt very insecure with these new leaders of their group. They didn't seem to care if they got them back safely or not. Luna flopped to her side, trying to find a less-aggravating position. She tried to push her worries to the side. Tomorrow they should be out of the dreary cliffs and back to wooded territory. She would look forward to that. Anara was not as strong as she and Madai, but she didn't complain. She worried about her son a lot, but even so, she tried to remain cheerful despite the cold and difficult journey. Luna was glad that the weather had been more cooperative than on their previous trip. Finally her thoughts trailed off, and she drifted into a restless sleep, dreaming of danger and nameless shadows.

—∘∘○──○∘∘—

Stephen

Stephen paced back and forth in his room, trying to calm his unsettled feelings. The last four days had been regular routine with nothing out of place in the beautiful but menacing city. In fact, that was what made him so uneasy. He was expecting some sort of reaction to the disappearance of the queen from the prison, and yet nearly a week had passed with nothing to indicate that anyone had even noticed. He also missed Luna. He hadn't realized how much he had been used to her being around, and now it was just Johan, Thomas, and himself. He missed her cheer and optimism.

He thought about tomorrow. They had already packed tents and supplies to last for several days. They would be going to the last two camps to look for Elihu. These camps were further out of the city and would require an overnight stay to have sufficient time to explore them. If they wouldn't able to find the prince, they wouldn't be sure what they would do next.

—∘∘○─○─○∘∘—

Luna

"Zoe!"

Luna squealed happily and engulfed the little girl lovingly in her arms. The baby girl's smile warmed her heart and made the aching in her chest lessen, if only a little bit. After hugging Eneva and thanking her profusely for taking care of her charge while she was away, they put their packs in the rooms where they would be staying and sat for a few minutes enjoying the warmth of the fireplace. Finally they put on their cloaks and reluctantly headed off toward the familiar cabin. The messenger had wanted them to go straight there with him, but she had taken all she could take of his arrogant attitude. After reassuring him for a fifth time they wouldn't get lost, he had finally agreed and left.

Even though Luna appreciated the familiar sights of the resistance base encampment, she still missed her companions whom she had left back in the glass city. As they rode down the familiar path, she was startled to realize that the messenger was following them at a distance. It irritated her that he couldn't even trust her to do this one simple thing. She didn't even know this messenger's name. He said she didn't need to know when she had asked, an unfriendly character for sure!

As she approached the cabin door, she had to remind herself not to be angry with Carl for recalling her. He must have had a good reason. As she entered, she was surprised to see only him there. He came forward to meet Anara. He was pleased that they had made it back without incident. After a few minutes of small talk, he dismissed the queen and Madai and turned to Luna awkwardly.

When they were alone, he spoke, "It's good to have you back. Your uncle was worried about having you so far from home…and so was I." He paused as if to study her reaction.

She felt puzzled.

"I...uhmm...hope you aren't angry. I know you all weren't finished with the mission." He paused, looking at the floor, and looked like he wanted to say more, but abruptly, he turned to the window and cleared his throat, running his hand through his hair. "Now that you're back, I would like you to continue training Key. He did pretty well in his trials but could use some personal attention when it comes to archery, which I know you're good at. My messenger has delivered a full report on your progress from Stephen. Good work. I'll see you in the morning here at sunrise…to give you instructions on Key's lessons. That's it."

Luna had to restrain herself from gaping. He had called her two weeks' journey back for some special attention at archery training? Trying not to show her frustration, she nodded in respect then left the cabin without uttering one word.

Carl

Carl watched Luna's straight back retreating back down the path on which she had come. Why couldn't he talk to her? He had meant to tell her, but when the moment came, he just couldn't find the words. Another time so similar to the present rushed into his conscience. Another stubborn-willed person, someone he had wanted to talk to but he likewise had been unable to. Then the decision to forgo any other possible pain by leaving something he had not realized he had loved so much until it too was gone. It had been too late to change those former events, and as much as he wanted to, he knew that it was in the past, until now.

And now Luna was here—the only person in the universe who could pull down the walls he had built up around his heart for the past fifteen years. And even as he saw the danger, there was nothing he could do about it.

Stephen

Adrenaline rushed through Stephen as he slipped out the door, closing it gently after Johan and Thomas. Bravery was not the correct word to describe their feelings, but he and his companions were determined.

"We will find him," he reassured himself in a low voice as they disappeared into the breaking dawn among the shadowy buildings.

27

Luna

"That's good, make sure your wrist is even with the bow hand," Luna instructed her archery pupil. She sighed in satisfaction as the arrow hit the center of the target with a gratifying thunk. "Okay, that's good for today. Meet you here at sunrise tomorrow?"

She was happy with the agreeable nod he gave her and turned to pack up her arrows. When she was done, she neatly swung the sheath over her back without misplacing a single arrow and then picked up the small bucket with the pastries in it for the strategy engineer's family. Eneva had asked her to deliver them when she was done training, and Luna had been only too happy to accept. It was dull with nothing to look forward to in the house. And with Stephen so far away, it was hard to concentrate on anything. She missed his companionship and the adventures they always shared.

The mystery of why she had been called back still troubled her. She was tired of having to think one thing over and then the other, weighing the motives but not trusting any of her theories no matter how plausible. The trail she followed was well known to her and required little concentration, which allowed her mind to wander as she rode along.

Suddenly, she stopped Mitzie. Voices drifted through the thick bushes ahead. Setting down the bucket of pastries, she tied Mitzie to some blades of grass and edged forward, trying with every muscle in her body to control the sounds around her and remain undetected.

"I'm busy! I can't come at the moment."

Another voice answered the first, "The king is in a horrible mood. He requests your presence immediately."

The first voice, which sounded familiar, raised in tone. "All the more reason I can't come. People are starting to get suspicious, and I still need this position in the resistance."

"It's a bad idea not to come when he asks for you," countered the other voice. "Remember he has your sister!"

"Oh, I hate that man!"

"Careful what you say! He is the king, you know!"

Luna inched forward, trying to ignore the uncomfortable crouching position she was in. Now only a thin wall of grass separated her and the speakers. Carefully, she created a parting with her hands, unable to stop the sharp intake of breath that thundered in her ears. She breathed a thank-you prayer as she realized the two in front of her had not heard it. A million thoughts crowded her mind as she tried to make sense of the scene in front of her. The one who was requesting the presence of the other she did not recognize. By his features and clothing, he was obviously from Icelair. The other, however, she had seen many times. She closed her eyes and shook her head. Why? This confirmed her suspicions. When she opened them, she was still watching the same person: Daniel.

The path was treacherous and seemed that it had been abandoned for quite some time, but Luna was determined to keep up. It seemed the messenger had convinced Daniel of the necessity of his presence because soon after, he had set off at a neck-breaking pace. Luna was extremely curious about where he was going and why. She noticed that he looked back every few seconds as if worried someone might see him.

"Always a bad sign," she mumbled to herself. She tried to stay far enough back so that there was little chance that he would see her. As the hours passed, she began to feel restless. Where was he going?

A shiver ran down her spine, as much from fright as from cold. She began recognizing the forest; they were getting close to Icelair. She stationed herself neatly in a small cove-like place sheltered by grass on all sides, where she could still get a good view of the castle door on the other side of the bridge. She watched with rising anxiety as Daniel entered the castle. Then there was nothing else to do but wait for him to return.

Luna rubbed her upper arms quickly trying to generate heat. Why had she not brought her cloak this morning? Well, the reason why was because it was wet from being washed, but it would have been dry by now, and she would have been grateful to have it around her now almost-numb arms. She glanced apprehensively at the lowering sun, which was only a small gleam of yellow in the sky. She wrapped some dry grass around herself, hoping it would keep her from freezing. She decided she should wait until Daniel's return. Since she had gone through so much risk already, it seemed wise to gather every piece of information there was to gather. Soon, however, her resolve gave way as the sun set, and she decided to leave.

She gathered her bow and arrows and turned to get her mouse. She jumped back in surprise as she came face-to-face with Daniel.

"What are you doing out here?"

Luna recognized the anger in his voice but also the slight undertone of fear.

"I-I was…" She stopped, embarrassed, not quite sure how to continue.

"Spying on me?" His voice was accusing now.

"I guess, I was….bored, so I followed you. I saw you on the trail as I was passing…and I just followed you. There's not much to do these days. I didn't know you were on a secret mission." She hoped that it was a believable excuse.

"What do you think secret means?" he growled back, no longer attempting to keep his anger hidden.

"I'm sorry. I didn't know it would bother you so much..." She stopped, out of words.

"Well, it does. The last thing I need is a girl snooping around, ruining things for me."

"I'm sorry. I didn't mean anything by it." She paused, searching for words to confirm her innocence. "Daniel...I'm not sure why you hate me so much, but I want you to know, if you ever need a friend..." Her voice trailed off. "I know it seems that I've come between you and Stephen...but it was never my intention."

He stared at her a moment, shocked by her unexpected apology. For a minute, it seemed that his face softened but then he turned abruptly, and he left a warning over his shoulder, which chilled her heart. "I'll be watching you."

Luna doubted that there was indeed a mission involved. She was sure that it was strange that Daniel had gone into the Icelair castle, and the conversation she had heard didn't make sense. She had never heard of the Icelair king "summoning" a resistance worker. What was it the other man said about the king holding Daniel's sister? Now, that would make a person more cooperative when it came to doing things that they might not do otherwise. She tried to quiet her fears as she hurried through the woods toward the cabin. She knew now that he was the mysterious, threatening stranger who had warned her not to go on the mission to Pyramidis, and now it worried her deeply. She couldn't imagine that Daniel was evil through and through; after all, he was Stephen's friend. She wished Stephen was here. He would know what to do.

Fatigue engulfed Luna as she finally stumbled up to the cabin door. In dismay, she observed a heavily packed mouse cart with two mice. Carl would probably be busy. After righting her hair and composing herself, she entered the familiar room. She was surprised to see some very important leaders of the resistance gathered in a serious meeting. When she inquired, they told her that Carl was busy talking with someone in the back room. Luna sat down patiently on a chair near the door and tried not to feel awkward.

Daniel hadn't come here first and spread some rumor about her, had he? As much as she tried to quiet her nervousness, it caused her to fidget in her chair.

She jumped up as the door to the back room opened, and the last person she had been expecting to see walked out.

"Uncle Matthias!" she cried joyously as she jumped up to embrace him.

Although he hugged her tight, she couldn't help but realize that he seemed strained.

"I-I'm in a really big hurry, but I'll be back...someday." He paused, looking down sadly at her. "Luna, soon Carl will explain some things to you, things that will probably clear a lot of questions up for you. Try not to hold a grudge for those who have hurt you. It was for your own good. He never meant to hurt you...only to keep you safe. Some people have a hard time showing how much they care."

"What do you mean, Uncle Matthias?" Luna asked in complete puzzlement.

"Be patient. In time you will know. But until then, you need to trust in me and in the Lord of the Book. Everything will work together for good. You just wait and see." He tried to be reassuring as he hugged her good-bye, but it did not help her. As he left, she felt more alone than ever and very puzzled by his words.

28

Luna

Luna sat down with a sigh at the familiar meeting table. In the puzzlement of her uncle's quick departure, she had delayed telling Carl about Daniel. The night before, she had asked him some questions about their suspicions about who the spy might be, and he had told her that he had scheduled a meeting for the next afternoon in which that very topic was to be discussed. He added that if she wished, she could ask other members her questions. This made her uncomfortable, seeing as she had never liked public speaking, and she tried hard not to show her nervousness.

Carl finally welcomed everyone to the meeting and began speaking. "I know you all are anxious to know what this meeting is about. As a matter of fact, we are here to discuss the increasing rumors that there is a spy among us." He paused and observed the knowing nods that went around the table. "There has been information leaked on several occasions, and upon investigation, we find that, by some means, word of resistance plans and strategies is getting out, even though only the most trusted are privileged to such information."

As Carl continued talking, Luna let her mind wander to her friends in Pyramidis. She wondered what they were doing right now. She thought about how exciting it would have been to help find the lost prince.

"Luna?"

She looked up quickly, meeting Carl's patient gaze.

"Uh...yes?" she asked somewhat uncertainly since she had not been paying attention.

"You said you had something to ask about the spy?"

"Uh...maybe you should let everyone else have a turn first," she said slowly. She checked herself as her mind fought to wander off again. She would not be caught off guard a second time.

"What will happen to the spy when you identify him or her?"

Luna turned her head in the direction of the speaker. He was a taller man, probably somewhere in his thirties. She had never noticed him at the meetings before. His question, however, was interesting: what would happen to the spy if he was caught?

"The spy will receive just punishment. He has caused no little trouble in the settlements of the resistance. He will most likely be executed, although that will be decided by the higher committee when we know who he is."

Shock ran through Luna's body, although she tried to conceal it. She couldn't help stuttering as she sputtered out her next question, "I-is that final? I mean is there any possibility that the spy would be allowed to live?"

Carl stared at her quizzically. "I'm afraid that would be the most just punishment. After all, he has caused the death of several resistance members. Do you know something about the spy?"

Luna felt her pulse quicken as she met his now piercing gaze. "I-I was just curious."

The others hid a smirk or two and then returned to the topic, investigating it on every logical level and aspect. Although Luna tried to follow the conversation, near panic gripped her every time she met Carl's sharp violet eyes, which seemed to keep returning to her seat at the table.

—◦◦◦❦◦◦◦—

Stephen

Stephen sat straight up in his tent. His gaze quickly swept over the dim scene of his comrades sleeping nearby. Although they were in a safe location, something had woken him up. What could have awakened him? Maybe it had just been a dream. Stealthily, he crept out of his tent, being careful not to disturb Thomas, who was sleeping almost directly in front of the tent opening. As he stepped outside, he suppressed a shiver as he walked around the small clearing.

They weren't in the woods but had cleared away a spot in what seemed to be an abandoned construction site. As he walked the perimeter of their campsite, a face in the grass not three steps away caused him to gasp and nearly fall backward. When he again regained his balance, he faced a short, stocky man in guard's clothing who looked over his shoulder every few seconds nervously, as if expecting some scary creature to materialize from behind the rubble.

"Uh, hullo, me name is Deran. I be here to give advisement."

Stephen immediately recognized the broken accent and the strange features of the individual in front of him. He remembered his father telling him of a third city that had once been in existence between Icelair and Sandar but had been eliminated when they refused some imposed laws against mixlings. He had described an odd accent, almost a different language, and they were of short stature with reddish hair. Maybe some of its people had survived, like so many others who seemed to every day defy the evil wishes of their enemies.

"My name is Stephen. You kind of startled me there, sneaking up like that," he clumsily tried to excuse his unsteady appearance.

The man seemed not to take note of his excuse but began to speak quickly, though he stammered. "Y-You must get family out of dis place. It be dangerous soon. People be taken other places and not come back. You need leave before happen. You come with me tonight. I leave tonight."

Stephen stared at the man, a bit dumbfounded at the warning. It was not the first one he had received concerning the topic. His thoughts went to his family. He had told them that they should highly consider leaving the area, but his father had refused, telling him that it was all superstition.

A shudder ran down his spine, and this time, it wasn't due to the cold. "I-I'm sorry, but I can't leave. I'm on a mission right now, a very important one that could stop all of this. We are looking for someone important, but I thank you for warning me," he finished, giving the construction site a brief scan with his eyes.

Even with the maps they had acquired, the city was like a maze and became more complicated every day. The man nodded and continued, "I warn you good. If you be on a mission, do it quick. Who you be looking for?"

Stephen paused, uncertain whether to tell the man or not.

The man looked at him with such a childlike expression and trusting eyes that Stephen finally relented. "A boy…he has golden hair, and his name is Elihu."

"Ahhh…it be the prince you want?"

"Yes. Do you know him?" Stephen queried in surprise.

"Yahh. Sure I knows. All us knows! They be keeping him down below in camp two. All us knows he be a good boy. He be kind to all that knows him. Why you look for him?"

"We are trying to get him back to his mother. And if he can get back to Icelair and take the throne, we will have no more of evil Elsiper."

The man clapped his hands and grabbed Stephen's hand, pumping it up and down with childish enthusiasm. "Ohhh! That be a good day! That be a good day!" He suddenly stopped and looked around as if remembering that he was supposed to be hiding. "I sorry you be busy. I be on my way. I wish good luck to good friend."

And with that, the strange man disappeared into the shadows. Stephen stood there, trying hard to decide whether what had just transpired was indeed a reality or just a figment of his imagination. It would take another day travelling to get around to the far side of Pyramidis to camp two. At least, they finally knew where to look.

Luna

Luna rode steadily on her mouse toward Talenia as she had for the whole day. She was constantly glad for the overhanging vines and grass on either side of the path, which protected her from the overbearing heat. Carl told her that she could find the main head council there, who was in authority over him and in charge of punishments and sentences concerning resistance betrayal. He seemed puzzled by her inability to confide in him, but she was afraid to let the information out without assurances that Daniel wouldn't be killed. Finally, the welcome gates of the city greeted her weary gaze. The guards let her in when she showed her membership stone, and Luna hurriedly made her way toward the place Carl had described.

Riding through the neatly marked streets in Talenia, she held the hard-to-read map close to her face and tried to decipher the directions in the dimming light. Slowly, she directed her mouse through one turn after another and finally heaved a sigh of relief as she reached the simply decorated door she had been looking for. She knocked a bit timidly and then entered shyly when the door was opened, leaving her mouse tied to a post that had been put there for that purpose.

She was slightly surprised to see that the head council was already gathered. A tall man addressed her kindly, "Hello, we have word you are here to talk about the spy."

"Well, yes…in a way…," she scrambled for words. "Okay, I have an idea who the spy might be, and I'm willing to help trap him or find him on one condition." She spoke hurriedly, hoping they would hear her out before making decisions.

"Go on," the man who had greeted her pushed on impatiently.

"My condition is that you modify the punishment. I don't want the spy to be…killed."

She could tell the council members were very surprised by their astounded looks. She hoped they didn't mistake her compassion for misplaced loyalty. She knew she could never face Stephen if she were the reason Daniel had been killed. She couldn't even think of such a thing, though she knew others in the resistance were almost blinded by their loyalty and would hand over anyone for such a crime without a thought. The council members seemed to be discussing her request, debating in whispers, and Luna watched in nervousness as every once in a while they cast her a worried glance then went back to their whispers.

Suddenly, the possible consequences of this visit hit her. What if they resorted to force to get the information they wanted? Highly improbable but possible. Or what if they thought she was in league with the spy? These disturbing thoughts made her all the more uneasy.

"We've come to a decision," the leader finally addressed her.

Luna looked at him hopefully.

"First, you realize that if you withhold information from the resistance council, and that very information causes harm to other members, it is the same as collaborating with the spy yourself. If you do know who it is, it is of paramount importance that you give us that information before someone else comes to harm. It is customary in these situations to have a trial for the traitor in question before deciding whether or not to execute him, although the nature of his crime has already spilled the blood of several resistance members, therefore weakening his case severely. We will grant your request if you are able to deliver him to the clearing outside of Talenia by sunset the day after tomorrow. We'll be waiting for you. You may go now."

Although Luna wanted some proof of their honesty, she didn't dare ask for fear of them changing their minds. As she left the house, she thought hard on how she would contact Daniel. If she didn't deliver the first time, well, there was no knowing what measures they would take to catch him if they found that she couldn't help them anymore.

Stephen

The sky was getting brighter, and caution told Stephen that danger was near. He attempted not to show his concern so openly, but he couldn't help his tapping foot and repeatedly glanced behind him. After what seemed an eternity, the road was finally clear. Stephen walked in front with Johan and Thomas close behind. Stephen ushered his two companions off the road into a tight alleyway while pointing out the barricaded road.

"We need to get through there," he mumbled, scrutinizing the roadblock. "Thomas, you're with me. Johan, stay behind us and keep watch. Whistle if there's trouble. Wait a few minutes and then catch up, okay?"

After giving these final instructions, he quickly removed his weapons then nodded to Thomas to do the same before he ducked into another alleyway a little closer to the blockade than the first. He loaded two thorns with the sleeping potion and gave one to Thomas.

When Thomas joined him, he stepped out into the open, attempting to be casual and unconcerned as they approached the two guards who were watching them quizzically. He pulled one of the standard maps out of his pockets and began to ask the closest guard directions; Thomas asked the other for the time. As the guard leaned toward the map, Stephen grabbed his left wrist, and the tip of the thorn punctured his skin.

"What?" said the guard as he looked at his wrist in alarm.

He suddenly slumped forward, and Stephen wrapped his arms around him and pulled him into the bushes. Thomas was likewise pulling in the other guard who had gone down without a sound. They carefully removed the bow and arrows from the guards and hid them under some leaves. Stephen and Thomas exchanged their blue uniforms for the black-and-gold guard uniforms and tied the men to two small trees.

"Good thing they're our size," Thomas commented.

Stephen looked around before leaving the cover of the grass. They went back into the alley to retrieve their bows and arrows. "Cover me," he said as he walked toward the small booth the officers had erected.

He needed to make sure there was as little room for the guards to warn someone as possible. He carefully tied the door shut and then wound the remaining part of the rope around some branches and dandelion stems nearby. He was counting on them, trying to open the door before sounding the alarm. He knew that as soon as they continued, their time would be ticking, and only a miracle would help their plan go without a hitch.

"Impressive." Thomas smiled at him as he walked away from the now secured shack.

"Is that a true compliment or sarcasm?" Stephen laughed, giving his friend a playful shove as they headed into the camp.

Stephen helped Thomas down the steep slope that looked over work camp number two. He himself was having a hard time balancing on the almost straight up-and-down hill they were descending. As they neared the fence, he didn't have to say anything to Thomas or Johan for both of them to move below the protection of some tall grass, which grew close to the fence. As they ducked under its safe cover, he turned to fix it carefully to conceal them. He was almost pulled off his feet when Thomas gripped his shoulder in excitement.

"There he is!"

Stephen turned to look through the fence and saw a young boy of about twelve; he was bent over a younger boy who seemed to be about eight or nine. The older child had an even build, which was neither slim nor chunky. Stephen watched as he brought a dipper of water from the bucket by his side to the younger boy's mouth while cradling his head in his free hand. His long golden hair fell over his eyes as he bent diligently over his companion. After setting the dipper down, his pale hand reached to smooth back the coal-black hair of the sickly child. When he was done, he laid his "patient" gently back to the rough ground below them.

"Are you sure?" asked Stephen.

"I'd bet my life on it," Thomas replied. "I've seen him in the woods many times when they were living in that secret compound."

"You!"

The shout startled all of them.

"We need more water over here!"

The boy stood up wearily and picked up his pail, heading toward the caller. Before he disappeared from sight, he cast one more worried glance to his fallen companion. Stephen contemplated the scene as they sat in the grass waiting for their chance. The boy had shown such responsibility. He had acted as few adults would have in his situation. Stephen had also noticed the dirty scratches on the child's cheek and arm, injuries that he had seemed not to mind. As time passed, he felt his mind whirling with plans on how they were going to get the little prince out of the compound.

"Johan will create a distraction, as if he were trying to get in through the front gate. I will intervene and take him into custody. Meanwhile, Thomas, get Elihu and his friend out the back through the fence. See over there where there is a space? You'll have to give them cover while they get under," he addressed Thomas directly. "Create a distraction if necessary. Tell the boys to hide in the grass, and when it gets dark, we will get out of the area. We'll all work our way back through the grass to where they are waiting once the excitement is over."

Stephen went over the attack plan one more time. As he looked at his friends' hopeful faces, he sent one last prayer heavenward.

Thomas

When Johan rattled the gate, two guards started toward him, but when they saw Stephen pull Johan's hands behind his back and tie them, they went back to their rounds, assuming he had things under control. Stephen opened the gate and pushed Johan in ahead of him. Thomas walked in behind Stephen and went off in search of the boy.

At first, Elihu wasn't sure whether to trust Thomas when he told him they had an escape plan. He flatly refused to go without the other boy.

"It's okay," Thomas assured him. "We planned on taking both of you. But you are going to have to get him out under the fence while I try to block the view of what we are doing. Once you are on the other side, go into the grass and lie down. Don't move. We will come for you as soon as we can. It may not be until after dark."

Elihu nodded, looking around the yard.

"We already got your mother out and safely away from the city."

The boy looked at Thomas with amazement. "My mother? I was afraid I would never see her again."

"She has already returned to resistance headquarters by now. We just need to get you there too. Then we can get you back on the throne where you belong."

Elihu seemed to grow in stature as he looked around with new determination. "It's almost lunch hour. Everyone but one guard will be going inside. That will be our best chance," Elihu said with confidence. "I will go around to the bathrooms with Timmy and wait until they are inside. If you can distract the guard, we'll go under the fence."

"Okay. Here we go," said Thomas as he walked back toward Stephen.

Stephen

Stephen untied Johan's hands and tried to look natural. Johan was young enough to pass for a camp worker, and he wore the regular blue mixling-worker uniform, so he blended in well. He picked up a broom and began sweeping the area behind the buildings. Stephen watched Thomas talking with Elihu on the other side of the large yard. Finally, Thomas turned and strolled in his direction. He stopped and told him that the plan would go into motion as soon as everyone went in for lunch. All they needed to do was distract the one guard who remained in the yard.

How much better if they could put him to sleep, thought Stephen. He loaded one of the small hollow-tipped arrows as he leaned against the wall to conceal his actions. The sharp blast of the lunch whistle made him jump, and he nearly dropped the arrow.

"Johan, go to the bathrooms and stay there until the guard is out," he commanded.

Johan walked quickly toward the gray building and disappeared inside. He stood behind a door, hoping he wouldn't be discovered.

All of the youth filed into the building, leaving one guard at the main gate. The doors closed, and Thomas and Stephen walked slowly toward the gate talking among themselves, trying to look like they were having an everyday conversation about life at home. The guard stepped out of the gatehouse in a friendly manner.

"When did you two get transferred here?" he asked curiously.

"Oh, this morning," Stephen answered. "Seems like they are always moving us somewhere."

"Yeah, isn't that the truth!" the guard countered.

"Say, I wonder if you can help me with one of my arrows?" Stephen asked. "One of those thorn tips just keeps falling off. He pulled out the arrow, and as he handed it to the man, he poked his arm. "Oh, man. I'm sorry. I am so clumsy today."

By that time, the man was already slumping over. Stephen and Thomas took him into the guard shack and propped him on his chair against the far wall. It looked like he had dozed off on duty.

"Sorry about that," Stephen said as he adjusted the man's hat and closed the door. He ran to the bathrooms and called to Johan and the two boys. "Come on! We need to hurry."

Stephen lifted Elihu's friend into his arms. The boy now seemed to be only semiconscious. Elihu scooted under the fence, and Stephen helped him pull the other boy after them. It was a tight squeeze. Johan rolled under, and between the two of them, they got the sickly lad into the grass.

Stephen looked with respect at the tall slender pine needles woven together into a formidable fence. The needles were intimidating, but they were also part of a beautiful creation, and he ran his finger across one in admiration. Johan grabbed a branch and smoothed the footprints away behind them. They made their way into the deep grass and slowly made their way as far from the fence as possible. Stephen and Thomas took turns carrying the boy as they slowly circled around toward the front barricade where they had first come in.

Stephen hoped the guards were still asleep. The sleeping medicine could have worn off by now. Since the plan had gone much easier than planned, there was no need to wait for dark. The sooner they could get away from the camp, the better.

Stephen walked ahead to see if anyone was at the main gate. It appeared that they were in luck. The guard shack was still closed, and no one was in the area. He slipped into the clearing where they had left the sleeping guards. They were still immobile. He quickly removed the black uniform and put on his blue one then took the other uniform for Thomas. When Thomas changed, he took the black uniform back and placed it near its owner. He carefully cut the ropes and removed them from the men's hands. With any luck, they would wake up and think that a joke had been played on them.

They slipped into the alleyway and made their way back toward the house where they had stayed the night before. Stephen thought back to how kind the people there had been to offer them shelter even though they had no reason to. In fact, they had been pretty much strangers. Stephen put his cloak on the sick boy and set him on top of his mouse. He asked Elihu to walk alongside the mouse to steady him.

Finally, after what seemed like an eternity to Stephen, they reached the small house where they had spent the night. The evening sun was painting the clouds various shades of pink and gold, and darkness was coming fast. Stephen noticed that the front door was ajar. He knocked loudly and called out, but there was no response. The door opened easily, and they paused uncertainly before stepping inside. At first glance, everything seemed about how they had left it in the morning.

Stephen walked cautiously to the kitchen. A bucket of water was spilled across the threshold of the backdoor, which stood open. As he turned to examine the rest of the scene, a steady uneasiness crept over him. A chair was overturned, a rug crumpled. It looked as if something had transpired in their absence. In fact, it almost looked as if their hosts had been forced to leave.

"We should be on our way as soon as Johan and Thomas get back. They went upstairs to look for the lady of the house," Stephen said quietly.

He had hoped that there would have been time to let the boys rest and recover a little before taking them on the journey back to the resistance camp.

Johan and Thomas didn't keep them waiting for long. When they walked into the room, Stephen's uneasiness intensified as he listened to their report. Something was wrong.

"They're not here. And we don't think they left willingly," Thomas said in a low voice, holding up the jacket that belonged to the lady in a trembling hand.

As he turned the velvet-green garment over, Stephen felt something was very wrong. There, across the soft fabric, ran a long-jagged tear. He remembered in remorse seeing the lady wearing that very jacket earlier that morning as she said good-bye.

They packed up their things and took some food from the kitchen. Stephen left a note of thanks and enough money to pay for the food twice in a drawer in the kitchen. He also borrowed two cloaks from the man's closet to help disguise the boys. They were a little big, but it was most important to hide the blue jumpsuits used in the work camps. He wondered if the couple who had fed them and offered them their home were sitting in the dungeon right now, and if it was because of them. He shook his head sadly.

They planned to stop at Stephen's parents' house to say good-bye. He hoped that no one knew they had been there. What if? No. He wouldn't worry just yet. It was now completely dark. They strapped their packs to the mice and helped the boy get up on Lightning. Elihu climbed up behind him and wrapped his arms around his friend to keep him from falling. Stephen took the reins, and they began making their way through the dark deserted alleyways. It was a good six hours later that they finally arrived at Stephen's parents' house. All of the lights were off. Stephen knocked, his heart hammering in his ears.

Finally, when he was about to give up, a window opened. It was Roseanna, Stephen's sister.

"Stephen! Why are you here so late? You need to go quickly! The guards have been looking for you. If they see you here, they will take Mama and Papa away!"

"Can't I even say good-bye?" he asked sadly.

"No, you should go. They were here just an hour ago. You need to get out of Pyramidis! I will tell them you came. I love you, Stephen."

"I love you too, little sister. Give my love to Mama and Papa."

With that, they stepped away from the house and began their journey home. When they reached the main entrance to the city, Stephen noticed a new large sign:

***** ATTENTION ALL RESIDENTS OF PYRAMIDIS *****

From this day forward, the king has decreed that all personal copies of the Great Book be exchanged for the new copy. A conspiracy within the scribes was discovered, and false information has been found in the ancient copies. If any individual fails to comply with this latest decree, he/she will be detained indefinitely.

Signed,
The Higher Council

Stephen stood for a second, staring in complete awe at the notice. How could that be possible? Errors in the ancient copies? What Nea'n had said was true. They really were changing the writings of the Great Book. He hoped no one would stop them and check for copies. At first, the prospect of being caught with the current copies of writings from the Great Book frightened him. But then they had broken so many rules, they would be detained indefinitely for sure if the guards caught them; thankfully that was not in his current plan.

29

Eneva

Eneva adjusted the stools around her table one more time. As she started toward her room, she smoothed yet another wrinkle from the table. Everything had to be perfect. She was expecting Eric and his mother any minute now. She wondered why they were late. Maybe her sundial wasn't functioning properly. She had cooked for the last two hours for her visitors and fixed her hair at least three times after putting Zoe to sleep. She sat down nervously in her rocking chair.

The sharp knocking at the door made her jump. Hurriedly, she leaped up, almost knocking into the small glass lamp on her night table. As she passed the mirror, she checked herself one more time. When she opened the door, she was surprised to see only Eric's mother.

"G-good afternoon...," she stuttered. "Won't you come in?"

They lady glanced briefly around her small quarters then answered in a voice as sharp as her knock, "I suppose I will."

Eneva watched her with curiosity. She stepped into the room with her head held high and looked over the quarters as if she was inspecting a dish after a small child had attempted to wash it.

"You're interested in Eric?"

Eneva stared back at her a little dumbfounded and not quite sure how to respond. "I...uh..."

"Well, let me tell you he has very high tastes." She said the word *high* in a way that disgusted Eneva. "Anyway, I came to tell you that he had a different dinner date with the daughter of a good friend of mine." She paused, watching Eneva's face carefully.

"I see," Eneva said softly, trying not to look at the irritating lady. "Well, tell him I said hello."

Eneva spoke in a soft voice, trying to keep her frustration under control. At that moment, Zippy, her pet beetle, came tip-tapping into the room.

"Oh my!" The lady gasped, looking at Eneva with a look that could be described as horror. "How can you bear to keep such an animal inside?"

Eneva squared her shoulders and, with only a hint of challenge, proposed her own question. "Oh, I'm sorry. Are you afraid of pets?" She portrayed her best surprised face.

"Don't be ridiculous! I'm not afraid of such a tiny creature as that. What's its name?"

Eneva paused only a second. She wasn't sure it would end well if this lady attempted to call Zippy; he had a habit of overreacting to people calling his name. But then without hesitation she answered, "Zippy."

Eneva watched as the lady bent slightly down then called in a sweet voice, "Zippy! Come here, Zippy!"

Eneva started to call out a warning before realizing she was too late. She should have warned the lady that if you talked to Zippy in an excited manner, well, he reflected it with his own excitement. The little beetle ran ecstatically at the lady and ignored her screeches as he ran in circles around her, trying to get close. Eric's mother, in her attempt to get away from him, stumbled against a decorative acorn chair and then fell backward onto the floor, tipping a bucket of water in her hysteria.

The beetle, considering the task completed, climbed atop her, begging for attention. At this, the lady writhed wildly, shaking her hands in a futile manner and screaming. The little shiny beetle wiggled and squirmed on her stomach in delight at the attention. Eneva only allowed herself a few seconds to enjoy the scene before hurrying to her rescue.

As she helped Eric's mother up, she had to hold back her mirth at the sight of such sophisticated disorder. Eric's mother's hair was half-undone, and the back of her dress sopping wet, not to mention the muddy beetle prints on the front of the green silk attire. In attempted gracefulness, she took her wilted hat with a jerk from Eneva's hands and made an effort to put her hair back to some order.

"I do believe it's time for me to—"

"Mother! You came early!"

Eneva had a shocked look as Eric walked through the door.

"Mother, what has happened to you?"

Eric's mother's eyes spat fire. "Never mind, son! We'll be leaving now."

Eneva had almost lost her dinner appointment once and wasn't about to lose it twice. "Oh, but you haven't eaten yet, and dinner's all ready."

Eric's mother turned quickly, almost losing her balance a second time. "Nonsense! I am not staying to eat dinner like...like this!" She finished in anger and frustration.

Trying to hide her smugness, Eneva made a generous offer. "Don't worry. I can let you borrow something of mine."

Eric smiled a bright smile and comforted his mother as he led her toward a room Eneva gestured to. "See! Didn't I tell you she was just wonderful?"

Eneva couldn't help but smile as she heard his comment, and that smile lasted for the rest of the evening.

Luna

"Okay, I can do this," Luna whispered to herself, breathing deeply.

Stepping out into the path, she pulled the hood of her cloak lower around her face. It took a good while to reach the place she knew Daniel would be. He was there tanning a mouse skin.

"Daniel," she demanded in a strong voice.

He turned quickly. "What are you doing here?" he challenged.

"I've been thinking. Things with the resistance haven't been quite what I expected. Let's just say, I'm looking for a new job. I have a hunch you might have need for some extra help. So if you're interested, I'll be in the clearing off the eastern lake, noon tomorrow. Be on time, or I'm leaving."

With this, she turned and walked out of the range of his tent before he had any time to answer. She didn't want him to have time to answer. If he did, well, there would be no reason for him to go to the clearing. After putting it off as long as possible, she had to do it, and she now prayed desperately that it would work. She quickened her pace as she made her way to Eneva's house. She was looking forward to an uneventful evening with Zoe.

Luna swatted once again at the persistent gnat. It was such an annoying thing, not harmful but about as big as half her fist, and it seemed intent on flying in her face—constantly. Anxiousness tightened around her rib cage, and she stopped for a second, wondering if she could really do this. Daniel wouldn't be expecting her for another twenty minutes. As she headed toward the place, the council members had agreed to meet her; she wondered once more about the doubts she fought the whole night before. Suddenly, voices stopped her in her tracks.

"Everything as planned?" said the first voice.

"Yes I followed her myself. She should be here to alert us any minute. I talked to her yesterday evening, and she seemed convinced he will show."

"Let's hope so."

"I really wish we didn't need to use her like this. She thinks we're going be lenient. I'm not sure how she'll take it when she finds out we're planning on going through with the execution. It must be someone that she is friends with."

Luna's breath came quicker as she tried to concentrate. They were talking about her! And Daniel! They weren't planning on keeping their side of the bargain at all. All they wanted was to catch the spy, and who they lied to didn't matter. She called herself all kinds of dumb as she hurried toward the clearing. What she was about to do could put her position in the resistance in jeopardy. But she was the one who had lured Daniel to this place. She had made a mistake, and now it was her responsibility to correct it. She hurried into the clearing, trying to fight back her tears of disappointment.

Daniel turned to her angrily. "You're late."

She looked back at him, attempting to get up the courage to do what she must. "You need to leave...now."

"What is this? Some sort of prank? You know I'm a busy person. I don't have time to play your games—"

"This isn't a game! It's a trap!" Luna interrupted him urgently. She backed away in fright as Daniel took two quick steps toward her.

"You have some explaining to do."

"There isn't time! Look I...I got you here to be caught by the resistance, but they weren't supposed to hurt you. But they lied to me, and they're going to kill you," she said in a rush.

She saw red anger come to his eyes, and his jaw clenched. When he heard a branch crack behind him, Luna saw the anger leave Daniel's eyes, and a fearful look replace it.

"Give me your cloak." Her whisper was barely audible even to him. She watched as he turned her request over in his mind. Then slowly he removed his cloak. She did the same.

"Put it on," she whispered, handing him her own violet cloak.

"You're not going to?"

She read the dumbfounded look on his face. She took his hand and led him toward the far side of the clearing where the grass was dense. "I will go out the other side, you go through here. You won't have much time."

He looked at her, an unbelieving look in his untrusting brown eyes. "They will punish you," he said.

"Yes, I know." She turned to leave and then laid her hand on his shoulder. "Daniel."

His piercing brown eyes stared into her violet ones.

"The Lord of the Book is able to help and forgive you if you will just ask him. You can always change, and if you ever do, Stephen and I will be here to help and forgive you too. Now, go!"

Just then, a voice broke the stare that went between them. "You're surrounded. Stay where you are! Good job, Luna."

With that, she walked to the middle of the clearing. Standing confidently, she bent her head for a brief moment of prayer before she burst through the perimeter of grass.

Luna felt the tall grasses whipping at her face as she pushed ahead at the quickest speed possible. She knew now that the council wished to execute the spy. She hoped that they would wait for a trial like they had said. She didn't fancy being hit by a stray arrow. The long black cloak made it hard to run, and she stumbled several times. When she felt she had given Daniel enough time to get a good distance from the clearing, she slowed her pace.

"You're surrounded, and you're wasting your time trying to escape."

Luna recognized the young council member whom she had negotiated with as he stepped confidently into view. She kept her head down, the cloak concealing her face, but he came and stood directly in front of her.

"I'm afraid you've lost, and now you will pay for everything you've done to the resistance."

With a shiver, Luna knew that the people she was dealing with might have a good cause, but there was room for evil even in the best of places.

"I'm sorry to inform you, you've chased the wrong person," Luna stated evenly, trying to keep the nervousness from her voice as she raised her head and removed the hood of the cloak.

"Luna?" The council member took a step back in surprise.

"You lied to me, Jared," she accused, holding her ground.

"Where's the spy?"

"You just missed him. If you would have kept your side of the deal, I would have been glad to keep mine."

Jared's eyes blazed with anger. "You let him go? You had no right to do that!"

Jared's voice rose as he now advanced toward her. Although fear knotted itself in her middle, she tried not to show it.

"You were going to kill him. I had every right to do what I did. We had a deal, and you didn't keep your end!" she responded.

"You traitor!" he yelled.

"We are supposed to be helping people live out the words and teachings of the Great Book! If you would have killed him, you would be going against every teaching there!" she countered. "You or we would no longer be an example but just another form of wrong with a different name!"

Luna checked her voice level as she noticed it was rising almost as much as Jared's. "You have no idea why he is doing this. I believe the king is holding his sister as a hostage," she said in a calmer voice.

"You have made a big mistake, Luna. We make the rules, not you. He will have to pay for his crimes regardless of his reasons for being a spy. Why do you care so much anyway? Are you in league with him?" Jared's voice had changed to a menacing accusation. "For all we know, you are a spy too."

She stood facing him with wide unbelieving eyes. "If I was a spy with him, I would have never led you to him. And my only mistake was that I believed that you were honest," she stated precisely and with striking clarity, which seemed to unnerve Jared.

"If he causes another member to be killed, it will be on your conscience, Luna. We'll be watching you, and we will have to decide what your punishment will be."

Luna watched Jared's retreating back. Confusing as it was, she was rethinking her actions. It would have been so much easier to hand Daniel over. She would have been celebrated for catching the spy, not to mention trusted. Now she was an unspoken outcast, one who had betrayed the resistance in the worst way possible—by helping their enemy. And Daniel seemed to still hate her. She wished, as she had so many times in the last few days, that Stephen was there.

"If he were here, he would know what to do," she said quietly.

Carl

Carl paced the cabin. His heart weighed heavily as he thought about the occurrences of the past couple of days. The council had come and informed him that Luna knew who the spy was but that she was adamant that they not execute him. In fact, some of the council members were worried that she was in league with the spy. This was indeed a disturbing rumor. He wished that he had told her the secret that burned in his soul day and night. Maybe then he could talk to her, and she would confide in him. But now it was more likely that she would be angry and upset. Oh, how he wished there was an easy answer.

Daniel

Daniel stared blankly at the blue cloak he held in his hand. This was what? The third time he found himself going over the events that had so recently taken place? His theory that girls were impossible to understand had been proven once again. Why had Luna captured him then let him go? Why would she care if he was killed or not? He had never said anything kind to her, and yet she had looked at him with eyes full of care and compassion. She was so much like his sister that it made him angry. He had tried to protect Diana and care for her, but he had failed, and now she was in some unknown cell, a hostage to an evil and selfish king.

A memory suddenly came to him; it had been so, so long ago. He and his little sister, he must have been twelve or so, and she about three years younger than him. He remembered how they had explored the woods much to his father's dismay, building forts and playing with bows and arrows. Then his mother had died of a sickness no one knew how to cure, and two days later, his father disappeared, leaving a note behind about seeking his fortune elsewhere.

Daniel had been so sad, and he felt that his childishness had been his father's reason for abandoning them. He had turned these feelings of guilt into anger over the years. How could the Lord of the Book forgive him? He had done so many bad things. He had kept all his pain to himself and, in his anger, had inflicted it on others. Why would the Lord of the Book care? Why would Luna and Stephen care?

A tear came to his eye, which startled him back to the present. He hadn't cried since that day. Angry at himself for reliving the past, he stood abruptly and threw the cloak hard at the dresser by the wall. It fell unscathed behind it, hidden from sight for the time being.

30

Luna

Luna stepped into the camp circle and realized the meeting was bigger than she had expected. The clearing held every resistance member she knew and quite a few more. She moved toward where Eneva was sitting but was intercepted by a stranger she didn't recognize. He directed her to a seat in front of the crowd. Misgiving tugged at her mind. Something wasn't right. She sat down stiffly and waited for the meeting to begin. To her surprise, she saw the head members of the council she had visited in Talenia come to the front with Carl.

Carl had a look of someone who had just lost a loved one. His eyes brimmed with tears as he looked at the ground about a foot in front of her feet. She recognized Jared, who stood directly in front of her. He held his hand out to someone behind him, who supplied it with a rolled-up piece of paper.

"Family of the resistance, we are gathered here today to proclaim the decree agreed upon and signed by the high council of the resistance."

Luna looked around at all the upturned faces. Her nervousness made her heart pound faster.

"We hereby thank you, Luna, for your services in past missions to the resistance, but for charges of aiding the enemy, you are hereby to be expelled from the resistance. Any member of the resistance caught discussing any project of the resistance will join her. And this includes all family members—in particular, her father, Carl, or her uncle Matthias. We bid you farewell."

Luna looked at the man dumbfounded. Had he just called Carl...her father? She was expelled? Just like that? No, this couldn't be happening. She noticed the crowd was breaking up, and the strategy engineer and his wife were headed her way.

"We're so sorry. Maybe someday you'll be reintegrated. It has happened before." The couple stared at her apologetically. She nodded and left them, her mind numb with disbelief.

Pushing her way through the crowd, she didn't stop till she was right in front of him. "Carl? You're my father?" Her voice came out too loud.

"Look...I can explain."

"You can explain how you left me on Mr. Matthias's doorstep in the middle of the night? Or how I came to the resistance, and you didn't say anything about who you are?"

Carl looked at her briefly and then at the floor. "I didn't want to lose you. I lost your mother, and I couldn't properly raise a baby girl."

For a moment, Luna relented and noticed the man's sadness, but her strong feelings replaced the moment of silence. "You wouldn't have lost me by telling you I am your daughter!"

He met her eyes for a moment, grief etched in his face. "If I would have let you know, we would have been family again, I couldn't risk...losing someone I cared about again."

"You didn't want to tell me because you didn't want to care about me?"

"No! It isn't that! I didn't want you to get hurt!"

Luna looked at him, trying hard not to cry. "Hiding from people doesn't change who they are. It only changes who *you* are."

And with that, she turned and stumbled off into the forest. She ran until her legs could carry her no more. Finding a small cove among the thick grass, she made camp in the middle of the forest. Exiled and alone, she lay on the thick bed of grass and pine needles, hoping answers to her situation would come before morning.

Stephen

He cast a worried glance back to the frail form that lay in the makeshift cart he had built for his mouse to pull. The boy, unlike his friend, the prince, had showed little improvement. However, it was promising and uplifting to all of them that soon they would be back to the resistance base. He had missed Luna. He wondered if she had missed him too. He wondered how she had done for herself in the resistance without him. The happy thoughts of reaching home once more quickened his pace.

Luna

Luna glanced apprehensively at the still dark sky. For some reason, it was easier to leave early under the cover of darkness. She turned to where Eneva was hugging Zoe good-bye. She noticed her now good friend wipe a tear from her eye. Luna herself had a hard time holding her tears back as she received Eneva's warm good-bye hug.

"You should keep fighting for Eric. You two are good together," Luna said quietly before she mounted her mouse and started off into the breaking morning.

Now, Zoe, the mysterious pet who was left to her by the old man, was her only family. She would go to Talenia and try to start a new life there. She felt wooden and hollow. All of her tears had not washed away the hurt of the night before.

She had been on the trail for nearly an hour, and the sun was near to the horizon. The light on the path ahead of her was dim, and she had a hard time deciding which branch to take.

"Lost?"

The smooth voice made her whirl in the mouse seat, almost waking Zoe. She gasped in surprise and fear.

"And so this is the banished one?"

The man was unfamiliar to her, and his face was cold and evil.

"What do you want?"

"Nothing too big, I assure you. I hear the resistance has dumped their loyal follower."

"No need to remind me," she put in sarcastically.

"You could join us."

She stared at him aghast. "Never."

"And why not? The resistance leaders think you have."

"Well, they are wrong. I just didn't want to see the spy executed. So if you don't mind, I'll be on my way."

"Ohhh, but I do mind," he said in an even cold voice, stepping in front of her mouse and taking the reins.

He gave a hand signal, and the next thing she knew she was off her mouse, and sleeping Zoe was resting gently in one of his helper's arms.

"Here are my terms. You get the packet of papers from Carl's tent. You bring them here by day after tomorrow, and you get your friend back."

Luna glared at his stony face, which was uncomfortably close to her own. "I will never help you," she said angrily.

"Oh, I think you will. I know how much you care about... what's her name? Ahhh, yes, Zoe. I'm grateful to you for saving our spy. And that's the only reason you're not in an Icelair prison right now, but gratefulness only goes so far."

"I've noticed," she whispered defiantly.

And with that, they released her and rode off into the breaking dawn. Luna was now alone and with few options. She needed time to carefully think through all that had happened before making a decision of whether or not to betray her loyalties.

31

Stephen

Stephen looked incredulously at Carl.

"What do you mean she's been expelled?" he asked, still not catching the full meaning of the story he had just heard.

"I mean, if you are caught talking to her on any other topic other than personal matters, you will also be banished from the resistance. Is that clear?" Carl's sharp reply surprised Stephen.

"Where is she now?" he asked, almost afraid that Carl would refuse to answer.

"We're not sure. She left early in the morning after she was banished." Carl sighed sadly and looked at the floor. "This has been a painful business. I'm sorry, Stephen. We will have to hope that she will be okay.

"Now, I want you to carry out the plans of warning the population of Icelair to be ready for their new ruler. Mostly, they need to be ready to protect him. Forget about Luna for now. She is no longer your partner. Actually, you have a new one."

"A new partner?" he asked the question out loud, although he didn't meant to.

"Yes, and I expect you to treat her with the same equality as you did Luna."

The person who walked into the room at Carl's bidding caught Stephen completely off guard.

"J-Janet?" he questioned disbelievingly, half-standing from his chair.

"Hi."

He noticed her immediate loss of confidence but did not welcome her readily. He couldn't imagine that she could have changed.

"Well, I'll let you two discuss the plans for the mission. I have work to finish," Carl announced briskly before leaving the cabin.

Stephen resumed his sitting position and watched Janet cautiously as she walked over to the table uncertainly and took a seat across him.

"I haven't seen you for a...while," he said with hesitation.

She was unresponsive, and he went into his plan for warning the people. "I think we should split up, both take different sections of the city during the dark hours. The work will go—"

"Stephen."

Her voice was so quiet, he wasn't sure if she really had said anything or not. He stopped and looked up at the girl across him once more. He saw her head was bent low over the table, and her hand was nervously playing with a scrap of wood coming loose from the table.

"Yes?" he asked, slightly impatiently, but also curious about her change in manners. It wasn't like Janet to seem so...well, so mild.

"I-I'm sorry, for the way...for the way I acted last time we met...for all the stuff I did to Luna. I wanted to apologize to her too, but I couldn't find her after she disappeared."

Here, she stopped and glanced up for a second at him. Guilt touched his heart as he saw tears in her eyes. "It's never too late to change," he said softly.

"I'll never be able to do anything as noble as she did."

Stephen was truly surprised by this statement. "What are you talking about? The story I heard could never be described as noble."

"Well, you must have heard wrong. She gave up her status to save his life." Janet was now looking at him in a sort of wonder.

"To save whose life? What are you talking about?"

Carl had told him that they had banished Luna for collaborating with the spy. There had been no details.

"To save Daniel's life. The council told her if she turned in the spy, they would not execute him. But she overheard them talking before she trapped him. When she heard that they were really planning on executing him anyway, she let him go. She traded cloaks with him and allowed him to escape. She was banished for aiding the enemy. She never told them who he was."

"And you knew too?"

"Yes, I did know…but I didn't have the courage that Luna had."

Stephen looked at Janet with new respect. Maybe there was hope for her after all.

"Uhm, Janet, thanks for telling me. I have something I need to do. But we'll meet first thing tomorrow morning to discuss the rest of the plan. See you later."

And with these words, he didn't as much as glance back as he headed full speed out the door.

It had been hours since Stephen had set out, and so far, he had not seen any clue as to where Luna had gone. He now sat in the dark ring of grasses right outside of the main resistance camp. Dusk had fallen, and a whole day without success had taken its toll on Stephen's spirits. He sat there thinking of all those times he had enjoyed with Luna. Why hadn't Carl told him the details of her banishment? Was it because he thought his friendship with Daniel would somehow create disloyalty? The whole thing puzzled him.

A noise in the nearby grasses caused his hand to go automatically to the bow at his side. The camp was unguarded besides the few sentries posted on the outskirts. Everyone had gone to an important meeting about the reinstatement of the young king.

A shadow passed across the moonlight-filled path. Immediately, Stephen was on his feet, creeping quietly in the direction where he had seen the shadow disappear. His bow was drawn back, ready with an arrow. Protection of the camp was the only thought in his mind. Slowly, he placed one foot in front of the other, trying to hold his breath as he came closer to the figure he had seen.

A noise behind him set him on his guard. Turning to face it, he demanded, "Put down your weapon!"

Before him, he saw a bow and a small collection of arrows fall to the ground. The response was a complete surprise. "Stephen?"

The dark shape removed the hood that covered her head.

"Luna!" He walked quickly over to her. "I missed you so much."

"And I missed you too," she said softly as he gave her a tight hug.

"I'm glad you are here," he whispered against the rough material of the black cloak she wore. Then he held her at an arm's length, looking her over. "You look about the same, just a bit... hmmm...not wiser...taller. Yup, I think that's it."

He laughed with her at his joke, realizing just how much he had missed the humor they shared.

"What are you doing here?" Her question was curious but glad.

"Looking for you," he answered, serious once more. "And what brings you to the resistance camp when you've been...banished?"

"I see news travels fast," she answered, looking away.

"Hey, what's wrong?" he asked, turning her toward him once more.

"Nothing. I-I forgot something when I left."

Stephen noticed her sudden inability to look him in the eyes. She had always been truthful and had no problem looking straight back at any approach. "I know you better than that. You're lying about something. Black has never been your color, and I'm not just talking about the cloak."

"It was Daniel's, when we traded. Well, it would be a shame to let a good cloak go to waste."

"Luna, what is really going on here?" he asked her, his hands on her arms, demanding a truthful answer.

"I'm here to steal."

Stephen stared at his friend disbelievingly. He had never imagined he would ever hear words even close to those coming from her lips.

Luna

Luna felt shame redden her cheeks. Why could she never hide anything from Stephen? His firm grip made her uncomfortable; she knew if she didn't give in, he wouldn't either. When she had stated her simple purpose of being there, he had backed away, as if burned.

"You're here to *steal*? Tell me I didn't hear that right!" he now asked her, his voice incredulous and somewhat angry.

"You heard right. It's the only way!" she retorted.

"It's the only way for what? You...you're so...good...so right, even when it's hard. What is so bad that it's pushed you this far? You can't do this. You know it isn't right. Have you joined with Daniel in his evil deeds?"

Stephen's tirade brought up all the battles she had fought with her conscience the entire day.

"Look, the rebels...have Zoe. And they won't give her back if I don't get them what they want."

"No one can ever satisfy what they need, much less what they want." Stephen replied emphatically. "If you try, they will only ask for more. You need to stop this before it goes too far."

Though she was afraid for Zoe's safety, she knew what he said was true. Isn't that how Daniel had become a spy? To save his sister? And how long would he have to do wrong for her safety? Would they ever let him go? But how would she get Zoe back? They were impossible to beat.

"How?" she asked, trying to hold back tears.

"I don't know how. But you need to have faith in the Lord of the Book, like you always have. Don't give up now. There is nothing you can do to help her. Only the Lord of the Book can." He reached over once more, squeezing her shoulder in comfort.

Luna sank to the ground, holding her head in her hands, and she cried. How would she ever get the little girl back? Was she really to do nothing?

Stephen

Stephen watched in despair at his friend's sadness. But there was nothing he could do. He could not allow her to steal. There must be some other way. But what if he had advised her to do the wrong thing? What if she did do nothing, and in consequence, Zoe was gone forever? Maybe if they went to Carl, he could help somehow. He wondered if he would choose to help her even though she was banished. While he struggled with these many thoughts, he was unaware of the lurking shadow.

Janet

Janet drew back from her post, terrible fear in her mind. She knew what she must do. Stephen and Luna would never fully trust her if she never proved herself to them, and after what she had done, it was the least she could do. Pulling her cloak tighter around her shoulders, she slipped into the now dark forest in search of the one whom most resistance members dreaded and hated: Daniel.

Stephen

The inability to sleep due to the occurrences of the night before caused Stephen to wake much later than his usual hour. As he dressed, he couldn't help but replay the events as they had unfolded. Still no idea came to him to solve Luna's dilemma. Stepping outside of his tent, he almost tripped over a bundle. Drawing off the sack of this concealed package, he gasped in surprise. There lay Zoe, tied and gagged, waiting for him to discover her. She cried as he freed her and threw her pudgy arms around his neck.

After a five-minute mouse ride, he reached Luna's camp in the woods. She was already up, leaning against an unopened pinecone, which, even on its side, reached above her head. She was reading her small copy of the book.

"Luna!" he called.

As soon as she saw Zoe standing there, she was across the small clearing in less than a second. After hugging the bewildered little girl, she stood to show her thanks.

"How did you...?" she asked.

"I don't know. She showed up at my tent door this morning."

"Thank you...for stopping me last night. I've realized that, well, that you were right."

As Stephen watched her, he realized she was slightly embarrassed with her own thank-you.

"Any time your conscience stops working, you just let me know, and I'll share mine," he said, trying to lighten the mood.

She smiled back at him, and the gratefulness in her eyes warmed his heart.

32

Luna

Luna adjusted the bow once more before letting the arrow fly straight to its mark. Even though she was pretty good with her archery, she still liked to keep in practice.

"Luna!"

The call stopped her in her tracks.

"Uncle Matthias?" she asked in surprise as she left her weapon and turned to fill his waiting arms. "I'm so glad you're back!" she whispered into his strong shoulder.

"Me too, and this time, I'm planning to stay," he said softly.

After a few more seconds of enjoying the safe feeling of the fatherly embrace, she pushed him away and turned to peer behind him. "Where's Nio?"

"Aghhh." Her uncle paused, running one of his big hands through his hair.

"Is he at the cabin?" she asked. It had nearly been seven months since she had seen her little friend, and she was eager to greet him.

"I left him in a safe orphanage in Talenia. He's waiting for us there."

Luna couldn't help but show her disappointment or her worry. "You're sure he's safe?"

"Yes, very safe," he assured her with a chuckle. "And you'll be happy to know that I've talked with the resistance leaders there about your banishment. Although you are still officially banished, they did agree to have a hearing in a few weeks."

"Oh, thank you!" she cried, flinging herself once more into his arms.

"I have some things to discuss with the strategy engineer, but I assure you I wouldn't miss seeing you later for anything."

Luna smiled. It sure was good to see Uncle Matthias again.

Carl

"How is she?" Carl asked Linda after she had finally come out of the queen's room. The strategy engineer's wife had sent the urgent message to Carl an hour earlier.

"I'm afraid she's not doing well. She's been slipping in and out of delirium," Linda replied, very concerned.

He glanced out the window at Elihu and his friend, who sat together leaning against a large acorn. The two had been inseparable ever since they had come to the resistance. Carl hoped Elihu would realize that when he became the ruler of Icelair, he would no longer have much time for such activities. In fact, he had been relying on the fact that the queen would assist him in his new position, but it seemed she would not recover in time for the uprising, which was due in two days' time.

"Do what you can for her," he said distractedly to Linda. "I will send Matthias to help you."

Then he hurried toward his tent; he needed time to think. Soon things would start to happen. They needed the full cooperation of the young heir, but if the queen recovered too slowly, or even worse, if she did not recover at all, their plans might be in vain.

Stephen

Stephen stepped quietly up to the next door. He was almost done with his part of the job, just two more houses then back to the rendezvous point he and Luna had agreed on. He thought back once more to who his intended partner would have been. Still, he worried about Janet. She never showed up at the meeting they had planned. And no one had seen her since. Pulling his mind back to his present task, he knocked loudly and clearly on the smooth door in front of him. It did not take long for the residents to answer.

"Hullo?" the man asked suspiciously as he held his door open a crack, just enough to see Stephen in the darkening evening.

"Hello, I won't bother you long, just enough to deliver you a message. Soon there will be an uprising. The true heir will reign once again. Be prepared to stand up for the rightful ruler, or there will be consequences for us all."

Not before he had finished saying the last word, the door slammed in his face. It was the reaction he had received at almost all the houses. Most people were so afraid of the king's soldiers, they didn't even dare talk to strange people, much less those with a message as his own. The next house passed in much of the same manner.

Finally, cold and tired, he met back with Luna, and they started their ride home. Hopefully, the efforts of their mission would prove fruitful when the time came to take back the kingdom of Icelair and once more put it in the hands of Prince Elihu and the Lord of the Book.

Luna

"Yes, I'm serious! It looks great!" Stephen laughed.

"Not true! It's all crooked and messed up," Luna exclaimed once more, looking at her failed carving. Stephen had to laugh once more at her attempt at a pouting face, which turned into a giggle. Suddenly their laughter stopped.

A shrill horn ripped through the still forest air. He didn't have to tell Luna its meaning, for before he had turned around, she had already dashed across the clearing and caught Zoe in her arms. He hurriedly helped her equip herself with her belt and bow and arrows.

"Eneva's is closest," she called to him over the blasting noise.

They took off riding full speed toward Eneva's house. It was only a five-minute ride, but it seemed like an eternity to the two youth. Quickly dismounting, they entered the open cabin. Eneva was there preparing herself as well.

Luna began giving Zoe instructions. "Get under the bed! Do not come out for any reason till I come back. Do you understand?"

The little girl nodded, her eyes round with fright. She quickly scooted into her hiding spot. Luna pushed a blanket behind her. "Maybe she would take a nap. We'll try to be back quickly."

Not waiting for confirmation, she rejoined Stephen, and the three of them rushed out the door. Mounting, they rode the fastest speed possible to the boundary line. The horn was a signal of attack, calling all resistance workers to assemble and protect the people they were currently responsible for: in this case, the queen and the rightful heir to the throne.

33

Luna

Luna forgot her fears as she and Stephen worked together to trap the enemy soldiers who seemed thicker than the underbrush so common in the forest. They both threw themselves once more behind the protection barrier, which they had left momentarily to set a net. Luna stood without thinking; as she turned, she was met face-to-face with an enemy soldier, his bow drawn. He only hesitated a second before letting loose the deadly weapon.

Stephen

Stephen came only to his knees after they reached the protection barrier. He examined briefly the cut below his elbow. Then he stood almost to his full height, cautious to keep his head under protection. As he looked up at his companion, he saw her freeze. Following her gaze, he realized what was about to happen and knew he had only a second to act.

Standing quickly, he hurled himself at Luna, pulling her down hard on the ground, just as the arrow whizzed by above them. He helped her to safety back behind the barrier.

"What were you thinking? You were almost killed!" He couldn't help yelling at her. How could she have been so careless?

"I'm sorry," she mumbled, nearly in tears and barely audible above the yelling and noise of chaos around them.

Stephen wondered how much longer they could bear the fighting. He breathed a prayer of thanks that she had not been killed.

———∘∘⊙∘∘———

The Castle of Icelair

"We're done here!" The king stared mercilessly at the trembling figure below him.

"I-I don't understand." The young man stared up at him in a sort of disbelieving stupor.

"You don't understand? Well, let me explain it to you. The resistance representatives are alive and well. Pyramidis is crumbling around its residents, and the resistance is stronger than ever! What is there not to understand? You failed! If I remember correctly, we had an agreement."

The king's driving eyes never left Daniel's now pale face. "In exchange for you ridding me of the pathetic resistance force, I was to spare your dear sister's life. However, in my mind, when a job is not done to the satisfaction of the employer, no payment is necessary. Don't ever expect to see your sister again...alive, that is. My soldiers are now taking care of things the right way. After tonight, the resistance will be a pile of ashes."

The king paused a second to watch the reaction of his listener. A sneer appeared on his wicked face as Daniel's countenance carried the response the king had been hoping for, and Daniel took a faltering step backward.

"Now get out of my castle!"

With only a glance of recognition toward Mikol, who stood sadly in the passageway, the betrayed servant fled into the dark cold night. He despaired for his sister. Fear came to haunt him as he thought of what he would find at the resistance. He was now turned away from every place he had known. But maybe, just maybe, he could repay a debt. First, however, he needed to make one thing right. He couldn't leave Janet in danger for his mistakes. Drawing his sword, he headed to the place he knew all too well: the castle dungeon.

Luna

Luna was unable to forget the moment when Stephen had saved her from certain death. Every now and then, she would glance at him as if trying to relive the scene. Luna and Stephen were out of arrows, but their portion of the boundary line was secure with two nets and several smaller traps, which would, and had, entangled several soldiers.

Luna looked toward her uncle. He and his partner still had possession of a good supply of arrows and were using them with precision and skill. She noticed that all of their arrows hit his victims in the lower calf. They fell and were incapacitated due to the sleeping medicine her uncle had previously dipped the arrows in. Luna remembered Uncle Matthias explaining the reason for leaving their enemy unharmed. He had explained that many were only loyal to the evil Elsiper because of fear for their lives or the lives of their families. When all of this was over and the kingdom was restored, they would sort out who was really loyal to the kingdom of Elihu. Whether they won or lost, the soldiers whose lives they had spared were sure to be grateful in some way.

Luna thought about how when this was over they would be able to talk about everything that had happened. And after the heir was returned to his proper place, they could go get Nio and once more be a family. But this time, she would no longer have to hide. She smiled at this thought, thinking of all the good times they would once again have. Suddenly, her joy turned to horror as her uncle clutched his chest in pain and desperation.

"No!" she screamed.

Stephen grabbed her arm tightly. "Stop!" he commanded, holding her back.

"I can help him!" she tried to explain.

"It's too dangerous! You could be killed!" he yelled back, trying to make his voice audible above the din of the fighting, which raged around them.

"Let me go!" she screamed desperately, trying to free herself from his iron grip.

"I'm sorry. I need to protect you."

Tears of anguish and despair engulfed her as she watched Uncle Matthias fall to the ground—and now lay as still as a stone.

"Please, Stephen, let me go. He...he's dying...," she said, the last words in a broken whisper as reality came to her.

Everything became a blur around her as she let herself go to the overwhelming grief and utter hopelessness she felt.

Stephen

Stephen wished more than anything to let go of Luna, to let her help her uncle; for if anyone could, it was her. But her life was at stake, and as little as he knew Mr. Matthias, he knew his niece's safety was one of the most important things to him. Her plea for release made his eyes well up with tears of his own, but he knew he couldn't. They sat there for another twenty minutes: he, trying his best not to go to Matthias himself, and she, not even aware of her surroundings any longer. Finally, the remaining soldiers retreated. There were few left uninjured.

Stephen helped Luna to her feet. "It's over," he whispered softly around the lump in his throat.

He gasped at the devastation that lay around him. Fighters from both sides lay injured, and some dead, making the once beautiful clearing a shattered picture of destruction. He and Luna were at Matthias's side. He held his breath in anxiousness as he watched Luna place her first two fingers against his neck. The words she spoke made him feel terrible. "He's gone."

His mind went to the lives that had been lost on their side; he thought back to the day he had joined the resistance and everything he had ever lost in sacrifice to this cause. And although he felt his friend's pain, he knew he would do it all again if it meant he could somehow give gratitude to the Lord of the Book for all he had made possible for himself. He prayed that the Lord of the Book would in some way comfort Luna in her losses because if anyone knew the pain of losing someone to cold, hurtful people, it was He, who had sacrificed his son for all of them.

34

Carl

Carl watched the scene of grief with building guilt. How had he done this? He knew deep in his heart he was responsible for this. If he had not kept the secret for so long from Luna, he could have protected her from this war. And most of all, he could comfort her now. But he could not leave the protection of the dark grasses he hid in. Would she ever forgive him? His brother, Matthias, was dead, and this was almost too much to bear, another terrible loss. And worst of all, would he ever forgive himself? With this last thought, he took one more forlorn look at the horrifying scene before him and then melted into the dark grass and bushes.

Daniel

As Daniel came to the edge of the forest, he was shocked at what he saw. How could he have ever helped such an ugly cause? He could change. Though most would never believe in him, he knew he could count on the girl who had said the kindest words anyone had ever said to him. He would find her. A wave of remorse passed over him as he thought of how he had treated Luna and how he had caused Janet's misery in prison. He had rescued her, but it hardly counted as much since it had been his fault to begin with. He knew now if he could change back time, he would never have treated Luna as he had.

How could he have done Elsiper's bidding, believing all along that Elsiper would free his sister? It was obvious to him now that he had been a fool to believe that anything good could ever come from the evil he had done. After looking once more at the destruction, he slipped back into the forest. He would find Luna and convince her he had changed, if it was the last thing he did. And maybe she and Stephen could help him find his sister, if she was still alive.

Luna

Luna adjusted the little prince's shirt one more time. The twelve-year-old was anything but ready for ruling, but they had no choice. A tear rolled down her cheek as she once more thought of the burial, which had taken place under the cover of darkness of the night before.

"Be strong, child, for the Lord of the Book is always with you."

She trembled slightly as she almost heard her uncle say these familiar words he had said so many times before. Even though the enemy of the book had worked so hard against them, he would lose, she was sure of that now. Neither her uncle's death nor the deaths of the other eighteen men who had given their lives the night before would be in vain. It was a noble cause—protecting the rightful rulers who revered the Great Book and who would set right the two lands that had so far lived in turmoil. They would fight for the rights of the resistance, as well as for their rights to be allowed to follow the book, which was meant for all. She and the resistance would make sure of that. They would start that fight today by putting the rightful heir in his place, on the throne.

"Are you okay?" Stephens's concerned voice broke into her thoughts.

"I'm doing okay." She nodded bravely back.

"Let's do this," Stephen whispered in assurance as he squeezed her hand.

With one more look toward Stephen for support, she took her place at the right side of the prince, and the three of them walked toward the crowd of people in the center of town. It was now that their destiny would change. It was now that the Lord of the Book would help them start their fight for good over evil.

The returned prince Elihu

Stephen

Stephen smiled at his friend once more. He now realized how much he cared about her and how glad he was it was she who was his partner in so many missions. They would succeed in this step toward the freeing of their people and restoring the standards they held. He was sure of it. As they walked into the crowd, he called out the words that would change their entire way of life.

"Long live King Elihu, servant of the Lord of the Book!"

Encouragement raced through him as the cry was picked up through the crowd. As they neared the castle, the cry changed to "Down with Elsiper!" As more people realized what was happening, the crowd grew larger, and their fear of the evil king was replaced with anger. The crowd raced toward the castle to remove the wicked king who had hurt so many. Stephen and Luna beamed at each other as the remaining crowd fought to touch the golden head of their new king. They had prevailed.

Castle Prison

"This is treason!" the angry king yelled at his guards while stomping around the cold, damp cell in a rage. "You'll never get away with this!" he screamed at their retreating backs while, in fury, he shook the bars.

"We just did. You are no longer in charge of us."

The reply struck the king hard. He realized his ruling days were now over. He sat back against the wall in despair and then drew out his one remaining possession. As he looked at it, a new determination filled his being and a sly smile began to spread across his face. The royal jewel sparkled up at him, its promise gleaming into his wicked soul.

EPILOGUE

Three months later

Luna

"We are gathered here today to thank the resistance for their never-ending efforts to restore the rightful heir to his throne and to restore the lost rights of mixlings."

Luna looked at the speaker, the high leader of the resistance. They were gathered in the castle of Icelair; Icelairians, Sandarians, and mixlings gathered as one to celebrate victory.

"I want to thank the group of youth who helped in a significant way to make this impossible dream become reality. Stephen, Johan, Thomas, Luna, and Madai, would you come up here please."

Luna stood with her four friends, and they made their way through the parting crowd. As she began the walk up the ramp, she paused a moment and looked over the roaring crowd. Her eyes blurred, and her mind went to all that had happened. Some would say she should be angry, bitter at her losses, but all she found in her heart was sadness at the price they had paid and gratefulness that it was over. There would always be a part of her that was sad about the people she had lost, but she trusted the

Lord of the Book. There was none other who could make her life better. Because of the trust she held in Him, she knew the events in her journey were as good as they were meant to be.

When she reached the top and stood on the platform with the high council behind her and her friends beside her, she felt a rush of excitement and a fulfillment knowing they had prevailed with the Lord of the Book on their side. Below the platform, near the front of the crowd, she saw the face that took her off guard but brought back another rush of memories.

"Janet!" she called out and helped the now changed girl up the nearby steps.

She hugged her tight and whispered in her ear, "I'm so glad you're here and that we're friends now. Stephen told me what you did for Zoe."

Her response gave Luna a rush of relief. "I'm so sorry for… everything. I hope I can be as good a friend as you were to me even though I didn't deserve it."

As they separated, they shared a warm smile and turned to the crowd.

"Hurray for the resistance!"

Luna saw Stephen raise his hand for silence, and as the crowd hushed, her smile grew wider at what he said: "Hurray for the Lord of the Book!"

ESCAPED

The battered and injured man crawled to the shelter he had fought so hard to reach. Most of the grand city of Pyramidis had been destroyed, but there were still houses standing in some sections. A few people continued to live in the city despite the disintegration of the order.

The man tried to quiet his fears as he knocked on the door. As he waited, he hoped the people here hadn't heard of the tragedies he had caused so far away in Icelair. He decided he would have to go by his middle name. The new king had already made his first mistake. If he would have killed him, there would be no chance of his escape. Well, it had been fortunate when part of the prison in Pyramidis had been destroyed. No one had thought to check the lower cells for prisoners since the new king had released everyone else.

Anger had pushed him every step of the way. He clenched his teeth in impatience. Anyone who didn't help him now, in his hard times—he could promise they would be executed when he was again ruler.

The door opened confidently, and a young mixling man stared down at him, a friendly smile on his face. "Come in out of the cold, sir. You look like you have had a rough day. My name is Nea'n. What's yours?"

The man accepted the outstretched hand and accepted the offer with relief. After giving his profuse thanks, he answered the question with only a small pause of indecision. "My name is… Jolson."

As Nea'n went about fixing a meal for him, the man opened his clasped hand; in it lay the hope that once again the throne would become his: the royal jewel of the kingdom.